Calvin

To our good friends,
Robin and Tom
Thanks for your support

Bill Lutenjor

Calvin

A Novel

WILLIAM LITTLEJOHN

Washington Writers' Publishing House
Washington, DC

COVER DESIGN by Gabrielle Bordwin

BOOK DESIGN AND TYPESETTING by Barbara Shaw

LIBRARY OF CONGRESS CATALOGUING-IN-PUBLICATION DATA

Littlejohn, William, 1931-
  Calvin : a novel / William Littlejohn.
    p. cm.
  ISBN 978-0-931846-92-2 (pbk. : alk. paper) —
  ISBN 978-0-931846-93-9 (alk. paper)
  1. Boys—Fiction. 2. African American men—Fiction.
  3. Southern States—Fiction. I. Title.
  PS3612.I8825C36 2009
  813'.6—dc22

                                                    2009020187

Printed in the United States of America

WASHINGTON WRITERS' PUBLISHING HOUSE
P. O. Box 15271
Washington, D.C. 20003

For
Marcia

1

A dream-sound.

Not real, not like any sound he'd ever heard before. A dull hollow thump followed by strange night noises, none natural, all sharp, with jagged edges, nothing that sounded like anything that belonged in this world—yet he came awake knowing right away what it was.

But he didn't move. He lay, waiting. After a time he sat up on the edge of the bed. A big man, he and the iron framed double bed seemed to fill what space there was in the small room. A chipped white porcelain chamber pot sat in the corner a few feet away. The room's only window etched a dark rectangular shadow on the water-stained and faded wallpaper where once, long ago, pink cherubs had danced among white clouds in a blue sky.

An alarm clock on the floor next to the bed ticked loudly. Every now and then the bell shivered, the muted tingling sound impatient, waiting for its time.

He got up once to piss in the chamber pot, then sat back down to wait. With eyes closed he could have been asleep, except every few minutes he lifted his heavy head, cocking it to one side or the other, listening, as if the pre-dawn silence were full of sounds.

At last a faint gray light crept into line around the drawn window shade. His closed eyes opened, called to account somehow by this shadowy penumbra. He looked around, wide-eyed, as if seeing the room for the first time. With a shake he made ready for whatever was to come.

He stood and walked to the kitchen at the rear of the house. With a few powerful strokes he pumped water at the sink. It rose quickly through exhausted air, then ran rocking and seeking through the aqueduct of the old-fashioned spout to splash heavy and hard against the metal sink below. As the flow of the cold well water eased he caught a glass full and drank it thirstily.

Under a plain wall mirror Calvin Lemoyne checked his kit, a carrying case from his years on the railroad. Except for his cash money, most of the things he owned of any value were in it. He took out a pearl-handled straight razor, opened it and stropped it several times against a wall strop with big, almost careless strokes before returning it to the case. Only then did he raise his head to look at himself in the dim, poorly lit mirror.

A large Negro, flat-faced and heavy browed, stared back.

His dark brown, near black eyes—half eclipsed by heavy brooding lids—were grim, threatening looking. For a moment he didn't move. Then he smiled, a small smile, but the face in the mirror stayed the same, just a faint golden grimace in the early morning gloom.

From his kit he took out a pair of round, metal-rimmed store-bought glasses and put them on, hooking each ear piece carefully into place, only to find they were broken. One lens was smashed into a cobweb pattern, a honeycombed scallop of jiggling glass. He searched for a narrow box at the back of the shelf below. When he found it he removed glasses identical to the broken pair. He put them on. They were a little stiff at the hinges.

When he'd finished dressing he went outside to the front of the house, where he'd parked the car on the street. A rusty tire iron lay amid broken glass on the front seat. He picked it up, felt its weight, then used it to knock out the jagged glass still lodged in the window. He cleaned off the front seat, picking up as much glass as he could see in the half light. As he worked the shards of glass nipped at his callused hands, like pecking chicks. But he was careful to see that no blood got on the new automobile's seats. Then, as he closed the car door he saw the metal license plate ('1940 South Carolina') bent in half, dented and battered looking, lying in the street half under the door. He put the tire iron and license plate on the back floor board. Then he started the engine.

While the car idled he went back inside, got his kit, then drove up to Calhoun Street. He followed Calhoun until it merged with State Road. He took State Road to Helene Street. He drove by the Five Points intersection and the pharmacy there. At that hour on Sunday morning no one was around, but he still drove slowly, as if no license plate and the missing window were invisible brakes. At Tigerville Road he sped up a little.

Beyond what was called the Forest View section of Athena, just outside the city limits, he slowed, then turned and drove across a shallow place in the ditch that ran parallel to Tigerville Road. With the car's lights on he bumped ahead slowly, pulling deep into a heavy stand of soldier pines, stopping only when the car was well out of sight from the road. The pines stood in dim military rows, seeded according to some long-forgotten battle plan.

The ancient forest began just beyond. There, the trees' canopy, interlaced with vines growing up from the open space next to the road, crowded out most of the sky even at midday, leaving the dark forest floor below bare, covered only by a thick brown blanket of dead pine needles.

He turned off his lights and waited in the idling car until his eyes grew accustomed to the dark. A sharp smell of pine tar flowed through the window. Then he shut off the motor and climbed out, taking a rough measure of the missing glass.

He struck off straight into the woods. Lower down he came to Water Moccasin Creek. On mornings after a good rain he sometimes had to walk north up the creek to find a dry crossing, but this time of year the creek was low and easy to cross. Even the snakes, the moccasins and the harmless green and garter snakes, were asleep at this hour; later, on his way home, he would heed the vipers.

On the opposite side of the creek he squatted beside the water, drank, then checked his traps. All were empty except one. A two or three month old jack lay panting, paralyzed by fear. It was game, a nice young rabbit, good for making a tender stew. He was about to kill it—the rock was raised, poised to deliver the death blow—when he saw the rock and his raised hand reflected in the unseeing, staring button eye. The jack had accepted its death, but something—he couldn't have said what—made him hesitate.

The rabbit's little heart thudded like a jackhammer in his hand. His fingers searched soft fur; it seemed he was holding the wildly beating heart itself.

He put the terrified animal down in the trampled grass. It didn't move. He nudged it, but it still wouldn't move. He spoke, not words so much as sounds of exasperation, meant more for himself than the jack. The gruff sound startled it. It shuddered. Shaking, one leg splayed fearfully outwards, and useless, it finally began to move. It hopped slowly and unsteadily away from the stream until at last it disappeared in the tall grass.

TEN MINUTES LATER Calvin reached the north edge of the forest. He stopped in the last shadow of the wood at Aiken Road and, as was his habit, he took stock of the house and its surroundings. Aiken Road wound upwards gradually to the right to dead end at the wash which lined the easterly edge of the Bacon property. To the left, a half mile to the west, where the road veered north to eventually join Ashville Road, were Raleigh Bacon's nearest neighbors, the Norrises. Beyond them, and lower down the road, other large homes had been built during the building boom of the late twenties.

Across Aiken road the Bacon house sat astride a broad hill. Facing southeast, it had been designed to catch the low winter sun. Without half trying it was the most important house in Athena. The surrounding porch, screened for comfort on the west and east, made the big white house appear larger than it was. Even the nearby forest, separated from the house by a wide, terraced lawn, seemed in service to its proud height.

By the time he reached the back steps of the house the big grandfather clock in the front hall was still ringing out the hour. On the stroke of six a brilliant shaft of sunlight broke through the trees below and flashed up the rise, leaving a sparkling blanket on the dewy grass. Blinded for a moment he waited for his eyes to recover.

As if on cue the new dog, Black Jim, began to bark. The other dogs in the kennel were quiet, but this new one had heard him somehow, knew that he was standing sun-blinded over by the house and would listen to a new dog. The hopeful, excited sound, like the sleek black animal itself, trembled and shook with joy. He listened for a few more seconds, then let himself into the house.

In the big house he followed a routine, a set round of tasks which he seldom varied, from first, firing the furnace to the hot water boiler to, last, making his grocery lists. In between he started breakfast and dinner, got biscuits into the oven, tended his vegetable garden in season, fed the dogs, and did anything else that needed doing, but always in the certain order. He didn't hurry, yet there were no pauses, no wasted motion.

As he worked he began to hum. The sound, at first hesitant, nearly inaudible, slowly began to close its own gaps until, finally, it was continuous, a presence. No song, it was toneless yet pure and as clean as the air. Like the silent wings of a hummingbird it vibrated, floated motionless about him, closer to touch than sound.

With the grocery list done he took off his glasses, then the black tie and white shirt. He scrubbed his hands and face in the kitchen sink, leaving a thin film of soap suds clinging to the stubble on his face. From his kit he took out the straight razor.

He took a deep breath, then closed his eyes. The whispering-humming sound grew, throbbing, until it was sometimes possible to hear—as he took a breath—when it began and when it paused, before streaming on. Soon the sound carried with it a sense of urgency. Yet the large black man was strangely apart, as calm as the sound was expectant.

He raised the razor. But didn't. Because it appeared to float, as if on its own, as if it were not connected to the hand that held it. Then, suddenly, everything changed. Its movement was faster now, more precise. The sharp edge of the steel blade flashed, and flashed again, moving quickly, almost heedlessly. Then, abruptly, after what felt like an impossibly short time, the floating razor and hand just stopped.

And the vibrating croon also stopped. Now the only sound in the kitchen was his breathing. He opened his eyes. For a moment or two he seemed dazed. Like the rabbit.

Calvin looked down at his V'd left arm, raised to a fist; dark red blood streamed from a straight fine cut, flowing down his arm several inches to his elbow where it arced over to fall into the sink. With a strange calm he caught his own blood in a chipped old white coffee mug, holding it rock steady until the flow trickled to a stop.

Afterward he cleaned up, carefully putting the razor away in the kit.

In Pineville, North Carolina the boy lay in his bed, listening. The old house was quiet. No people or animal sounds. Not even the house's mysterious groans and creaks that sometimes scared him in the dark. He turned to look out the window. Outside it was more dark than light, the air still and heavy. He waited, a little breathless, a little scared, listening now with the house, sensing that something was different.

A catbird called from the tree break at the edge of the yard. A second answered, its mewing sound mocking the house cats coming home from a night of hunting in the fields beyond. In the dark of his imagination all the cats carried mice and each, as he had seen once, was writhing in a mute struggle to escape as it was being shaken and smothered to death.

He shivered and ducked under the covers.

So Billy Smithson didn't hear Saypaugh's milk wagon or the songbirds or the first cut of the logger's ax echoing from down the county road. He didn't hear Mr. Perry's Model A cough to life and chuff past as he headed for his job as Stationmaster over in Bethel. Or the night freight's engine deadheading west to nowhere.

All Billy could hear now was his own breathing. It seemed to roar in his ears, like the waves of the ocean at Kill Devil Hill. He listened more closely. Waves, one after the other, pounding, pounding, pushing, shoving forever. Sonny had said the waves never stopped. Never in his lifetime.

A fortune teller at school—really Mrs. Timmons from fourth grade dressed as a fortune teller—had read his palm and told him that he would live to be seventy-five. "Seventy-five years old!" she'd said. Like she'd just given him a present. And what did he think about that? Up until then he had never even thought about how long he would live, and he wasn't sure he had wanted to know because after he knew he didn't think it sounded like enough.

His heartbeat was strong and regular but a little fast. His breathing, while loud, seemed normal enough. But what was normal?… Kill Devil Hill with its long rolling waves crashing on a near deserted beach in bright hot sunshine. That time he'd gotten so sunburned Sonny had worried he might die. Sonny had yelled at her and she had yelled at Sonny. They both said the other one was to blame.

But he didn't die then because kids don't just *die*. You got to do something to deserve it.

Now he felt smothered. He struggled free of the covers to find the sun was up. Like magic, it had wiped out the ground fog and was shining brightly through the leaves of the pecan tree just outside his screened window. With the sun he forgot he was ever scared. With its warmth he remembered that Sonny would be home from the hospital on Thursday.

Sonny had been in the hospital this time for almost a month. Gerry, his step-mother, didn't like to say what Sonny's ailment was, although everybody, including Billy, knew it wasn't for a broken arm or a busted appendix. It was for one of those mysterious sicknesses that nobody would ever talk about. It was a secret illness. Lately he had started listening at doors and reading papers with writings that had been left lying about. So far, though, he hadn't found out a thing.

Whenever Sonny came home from his hospital stays everything was always real good the first day or so. Sonny was his old self, joking and playful, especially with him and his friends. With their cook, Kallie, too. She was sure to cry some, and Sonny would laugh. Sonny always laughed when Kallie began to cry. When Sonny went back to the hospital that's what Billy always thought about: Kallie's tears and Sonny's laughter. The trouble was the more times Sonny had to go back into the hospital the more mixed up he got about who was happy and who was sad. Lately, if somebody had asked him he wouldn't have been able to say.

Thursday. Just thinking about it was exciting. Thursday was the big day. He and Kallie were planning a homecoming party. Even Gerry, who was kind of lazy, wanted to help.

Thoughts of the coming party made him restless to get out of bed. But he was supposed to wait until six-thirty, the time Kallie came to work. And Kallie, whose actual name was Sallie, didn't like him to get up until she had started breakfast. Sometimes lately, as he lay in bed, waiting for the sound of her slow, unhurried steps to signal the start of his day, he thought that she might be getting too old; maybe they should get a new cook. He might say something to Sonny. Sonny hated to wait even more than he did.

Some days he slept right through Kallie coming to work, not waking until the back screen door swung open a second time, the moment when Kallie opened the porch door to let the cat into the house. Then Zero would run to his room to jump up on the bed. Once after Venice day at school, the time with the fortune teller, and another night when he had been carried to bed by Sonny after a movie, Zero had caught him asleep. Each time he'd woke up with Zero parading impatiently back and forth across his chest, urging him with furry, tickling swipes of her tail to get up.

At last the back door squeaked open. Not able to wait any longer he slipped out of bed. He took his pajamas off and put on a shirt and a pair of clean but well-worn blue shorts. He noticed the ground-in dirt on his toughened bare feet. He'd washed them in the kitchen sink before going to bed. But in the morning light they didn't look so clean. He worried that Kallie wouldn't believe him and would send him out to wash them in the ice cold water of the outside pump. So at first he didn't miss Zero; he didn't notice that for the first time since they lived there she hadn't come down the hall to get him.

Zero was in the house, though, sitting on the threshold of the back door, grooming herself. When he came into the kitchen he saw her there: a brand new cat. She went right ahead grooming herself, ignoring him. He ignored her back.

"Morning, Kallie," he said.

Kallie didn't answer. She nodded, smiling crookedly around a bulge in her lower lip. She had just taken some snuff. It would take a minute or two to settle enough for talk. That was a little different, too, earlier than most days. While he was sure that Kallie didn't care if he watched her pinch some snuff from the red and silver can and put it between her lip and gum, she was kind of secretive about most anybody else seeing her do it. She almost always took her morning snuff after everybody had finished breakfast and always made sure that nobody—not even him—ever saw her spit.

It was already warm in the kitchen, the best room in the old house. And this was his favorite time, the time when the whole day, brimming with discovery and adventure, lay ahead. It was when the three of them, Billy, Kallie and Zero, talked about all the exciting things to come. He did most of the talking, because after all it was his day they were talking about. But Kallie liked to talk about it too. Even Zero, using special cat language that only he knew, was not shy about saying what she thought they should do. He peeked at Zero now, licking herself there in the doorway, aloof. What had got into her, he wondered.

Kallie put a box of Rice Krispies on the table.

"Now as soon as you eat, honey, I wants you to go out to play."

He had forgotten it was Sunday until he saw the cereal. He usually got what the family would eat later for breakfast, things like sausage and eggs and grits. But the Rice Krispies for breakfast meant it was Sunday, a different kind of day in the Smithson house, one when everybody but Billy slept late, and he got cereal. Sonny joked once that if God ever took a vacation he could find plenty of rooms to rent in Pineville. Ever since Billy had imagined God coming down to breakfast at Mrs. Speed's rooming house and ordering cereal.

As he ate he kept glancing over to where Zero was grooming herself. She hadn't stopped since he came into the kitchen.

Hadn't she already done her belly? He remembered reading that cats were feral, meaning they were wild. His teacher, Miss Harding, said we shouldn't own cats, that it was against the law of nature. Of course Miss Harding wouldn't have said that if she had had a cat herself. Because the way he figured it you didn't ever own a cat. The way you did a dog. With a cat you had to be more equal. With cats you had to negotiate. And sometimes you lost. That's what made them more interesting than dogs.

He wet his hand with milk from the cereal bowl, then let his arm drop toward the floor. Right away he felt Zero's small rough tongue methodically and fastidiously licking the milk off his hand.

"Kallie?" he said.

"Yes, honey?"

"Do you like Zero?"

"I don't like no cats, specially that Zero," Kallie said.

"She likes you."

"If she ain't careful we's gonna put her in a sack and throw her in the crick."

He laughed at the old joke and ran to the back door. Zero followed. He threw open the kitchen door and was pushing open the door on the porch when Kallie gave a muffled cry, "You, Billy!" and caught the first door before it slammed shut. Remembering he was supposed to be quiet he opened the second door with exaggerated care and closed it just as carefully, praising himself by tiptoeing down the back steps to where Zero waited.

THROUGH THE kitchen window Kallie watched the boy and cat leave, their movements like the cat's tail—starting and stopping, switching—running from side to side, they jerked to and fro, stooping here, squatting there, the cat mimicking the boy, to examine something interesting lying on the nearly bare surface of the heavily shaded back yard. Finally, with Billy leading, the cat following with raised, full-masted tail, they ran at top speed around the corner of the brown-shingled house. Kallie knew that the boy and the cat would both stop running just as soon as they were out of sight.

Billy's a good child, she thought, not much different from her Jefferson. The two or three times she had brought her second son with her to work the two boys had played together like old friends. Billy was a little bossy, but he bossed his white playmates too, making up all the games and settling all the trouble, like a judge. So it was natural for him to boss Jefferson. And Jefferson just loved to come to the Smithson house to play with Billy.

She wondered if Billy would notice the Ford station wagon parked in front of the house. Should she have said something? Warned the boy? With that thought she stopped. Stock still she listened to the silent house for a minute before turning back to slicing the large, just-picked vine tomatoes she'd brought from her own garden. As she worked she half-listened for sounds that would realize her fear. And then she may have heard them: bed slats creaking against side rails. The sound came from somewhere upstairs. But, superstitious about asking for trouble, she quickly denied her own thought. Could be just the fool, turning over in her sleep.

With this thought of Geraldine Smithson, Billy's stepmother, Kallie began to grumble, a kind of back-talk patois that was muttered so far under the breath that no one who heard it could understand anything she said, and, because of that, paid no attention. But sometimes it was her only weapon, this half-complaint, half-lament. She used it when unhappy, or secretly worried, as she was now. So for the next twenty minutes or so she talked to herself. She grumbled her vague, half-secret, half-defiant complaints, complaints about how hard she had to work, about missing church on Sundays, about white women, especially them two, the lazy fool and the other one. She'd never understood that one and, because of that, was a little afraid of her.

But Mister Sonny had always treated her good, giving her some extra now and then when like everybody else in the depression he hardly had enough for his own family. Poor Mister Sonny. Maybe the doctors has fixed him for good this time. She sure hoped so. Billy's daddy was sorely needed at home right now.

In her trance-like reverie Kallie didn't hear the two women come into the kitchen. Suddenly her worst fears were standing in the room: the fool and Elizabeth Webb, Billy's mother.

Startled, she almost dropped her knife. But she kept on working, careful to show nothing, pretending that having Sonny Smithson's two wives, past and present, in her kitchen at half past seven on a Sunday morning was a regular thing.

"Well, I suppose I surprised you some," Elizabeth said to her.

"No'm," Kallie said. "I seen your car."

"That's a different car, Kallie, my daddy's car, so you were surprised."

"No'm, I knowed it was you."

Who else could it be? Who else would come to visit with Mister Sonny gone, without warning in the middle of the night, put everybody out, make trouble. Only the woman that put Mister Sonny in the hospital in the first place.

"Where's Billy, Kallie? Does he know I'm here?"

Kallie's mouth began to work silently.

"Answer me, woman!"

"Mister Billy's out playing."

Elizabeth Webb and Kallie were both twenty-nine years old, a fact Kallie thought of from time to time with a kind of bewildered amazement. To start with Kallie wasn't exactly sure just how old she really was because at the time she married she was told that she was fourteen and a half when up to that point she had always thought she was thirteen. So she could be even younger than Elizabeth. The idea that she, a tired old colored woman—she'd thought of herself as old at twenty—could be even the same age as that...that child! It won't possible! Why, Kallie's Lucinda was nearly fifteen and begging to marry Armand Washington's boy. To Kallie Elizabeth had seemed even younger than Lucinda. But that was before Elizabeth left her child and her husband to run off with that man from Tarboro, that tobacco auction man.

Kallie opened the door to the cold cellar. She took a coffee can down from its hiding place. She spat loudly into the can.

"That's disgusting, Kallie," Gerry Smithson cried.

"Perfectly disgusting. You must never, never do that again."

Elizabeth lit a cigarette and stared through the smoke at her former servant.

BILLY AND ZERO waited for Cotton and the others near the big elm at the front of the house. A thick root from the tree grew to the middle of the dirt driveway where it curved and then grew straight down into the ground. Cars had to go slowly over that one-sided wooden bump to avoid a whack on the undercarriage. They usually left their car, a blue Buick four- door sedan, parked in front of the house. It was parked there now, along with a wood-sided station wagon, right behind. He scarcely glanced at the strange car, losing interest as soon as he made sure they could still use their driveway for marbles.

The streets were dirt, too. They could have played marbles in front of either Aaron's or Buddy's house, but not Cotton's. Cotton lived on the railroad tracks, not right on the tracks, of course, but so close that Cotton said the shaking from the night freight heading for Tarboro often rolled his baby brother right out of his mama's bed onto the floor.

Just then Cotton turned the corner a couple of blocks away, his jerky, hitching trot familiar to anyone who knew him. He walked down the center of the street, like he was trying to keep the greatest distance he could between himself and the houses on either side. He was like an intruder, moving guiltily, glancing right and left, as if at any moment he expected to be told to leave that part of town.

Sonny said that Cotton's family was dirt poor. But the way Sonny said that and the way Billy took what Sonny said made Cotton seem even more special, like dirt poor had no worries, no rules and nobody always in the hospital.

With the Smithson family's return from shopping in Tarboro on Saturday mornings they would bump back over the railroad tracks in the Buick past where Cotton had been waiting, waiting for how long he never knew, but Cotton was always there after they became friends. He would press a comic book, *Superman* or *Batman and Robin*, maybe, against the back window of the car and Cotton would run along behind the car all the way to their house. They would read the comic book together in the cool place under the grape arbor, arguing about who it would be best to be.

He liked the idea of Batman and Robin. After all Robin was

not that much older than he was. But Cotton liked Superman, probably because Cotton needed a bigger miracle.

ELIZABETH LIT her second cigarette. Gerry, as she had all morning, copied Elizabeth, lighting her own, as if this might mollify Elizabeth. Kallie muttered to herself in disgust. She escaped to the far end of the kitchen to work and to watch.

Elizabeth, just out of bed, waved, damp-looking hair clinging to her head, was beautiful in a careless, spendthrift way. Her eyes were still slightly puffy from sleep. But rather than marring her beauty, they enhanced it, giving her unlined, untroubled almost perfect face the look of a wounded child. One look at her made men want to protect her. It was a face still unmarked by two marriages and motherhood. The only sign of age was an air of bored resignation, as if she had been there before and now insisted on something new.

Elizabeth blew smoke at the ceiling.

"Daddy is so boring about these things," she said. "He acts like I'm one of his mill hands. He's almost sure to say I didn't use good sense in marrying Lawton. He'll lecture me. But I don't care. Eighteen months is enough. That's all I know. I gave it eighteen whole months.... At least I didn't get pregnant again."

Suddenly, Elizabeth turned to Kallie and asked, "Where's Billy, Kallie?"

Kallie grumbled an answer.

"Speak up, Kallie. I can't hear you."

"I done told you, Miz Elizabeth. Mister Billy's out in the yard, playing."

"Well go get him, I want to talk to him."

"Oh!" Gerry said. "I don't think you should do this, Elizabeth. Sonny's not going to like it at all, not at all."

"I don't care what Sonny likes. Billy's my son, my only child—"

"But you agreed Sonny could keep him this summer. You even said he could stay the fourth grade."

"That was before I knew Sonny was back in the hospital. I won't leave my son in this dreadful house."

Gerry didn't answer. She blinked back tears. From the far end of the room Kallie saw Billy's step-mother's shoulders sag and imagined the sigh.

Lazy fool woman, Kallie mumbled.

"Are you still here," Elizabeth said. "I told you to get the boy."

When Kallie didn't move, Elizabeth got to her feet.

"You're to pack Billy's bag. Put all his things in it. Anything left over you can put in mine."

"You're going to do it then?" Gerry cried. "You're going to take him after all?"

"I just decided," Elizabeth said.

"Make sure Billy is clean," she said to Kallie. "Especially his feet. I can't take him home to Athena looking like some share-cropper's boy dragged off the farm."

Kallie stopped grumbling. She stared at Elizabeth.

"What are you looking at?" Elizabeth said. "Don't stare at me like that. Didn't you hear what I told you to do?"

"No ma'am, I don't think I rightly did."

"I said to pack Mister Billy's clothes. He is leaving this house. I am taking him home. It's what I should've done long ago."

"Leaving, Miz Elizabeth? You mean…leaving with the boy?"

"That's what I said."

"But you don't mean *leaving*. You don't mean for good?"

Elizabeth turned away. She lit another cigarette.

"Don't question me, Kallie," she said. "I won't have it. I'm doing what I've got to do."

"But what about this here chicken I just cooked for dinner? And...and...and Mister Sonny. This is gonna try him sorely."

"We'll have to leave Zero here," Elizabeth said. "You'll have to take her, Kallie. I don't want to upset Billy, but Dot Jessop hates cats. Anyway, Zero would just smell up the car during the trip. So, it's best that nothing be said about the cat until right before we leave. Then I'll handle it. Do you understand?"

The twenty-nine-year old colored woman stared at the twenty-nine-year old white woman.

"Do you understand?" Elizabeth repeated.

Kallie wouldn't answer. She waited in silence for as long as she could. Finally, she slammed the knife down on the wooden counter with a loud bang and left the kitchen under the intense glare of Elizabeth's gaze.

COTTON SAT within the dirt circle on his right leg, his left leg raised akimbo, that leg's bare foot carefully placed so as not to disturb the marbles when he shot. He leaned forward, resting on his right forearm as he sighted down his arm at the mottled smoky green-and-white glass marble about twelve inches away. That marble, a stray deflected off to the side after his first shot, the breaking shot, was one of Billy's, one of the five he had anted into the circle to start the game.

Cotton's thumb flicked. The shooter, quicker than the eye, traveled the short distance and struck the marble, but at an angle and itself caromed out of the circle, leaving the spared marble behind. Cotton had barely moaned and flopped down in disgust with his miss when Aaron Parker was at the line with his black shooter. Just as quickly, and without apparent aim he shot and the recently reprieved marble flew out of the circle to come to rest against Cotton's sprawled leg.

Just then, right before Billy got his chance to shoot to finally prove he was better than Aaron Parker, Kallie's shadow slid across the circle. She slowly bent and picked up Zero.

"You gots to come into the house now, honey," she said quietly. "Your mama's here and she's got something she wants to tell you."

BENEATH HIM the steady thump-thump of the car's tires striking the tarred joints of the concrete highway grew louder with every mile. Billy listened, hoping for sounds of car trouble, but only discovered a rhythm, a thump-thump, thump-thump, thump-thump...and on and on, so that despite everything he was having trouble staying awake. Fighting sleep he sat up and looked out the open window.

In the bright hot sunshine the car droned on, moving steadily ahead on the flat straight road. No other cars passed for long stretches of the highway. Most people were busy some place else or just too smart to be out on a North Carolina highway in the midday heat. He thought about what those folks were doing at that very moment: probably eating cold fried chicken and potato salad, and drinking lots of iced tea. Except at Cotton's house where they never had iced tea. Just cold buttermilk, sometimes iced coffee, but usually buttermilk. Whenever he had been at Cotton's house they had always apologized when they didn't have iced tea for him.

His eyes burned. He spent the next few miles trying not to

cry, trying the best he could not to make a fool of himself. When he finally got himself under control he was embarrassed. He tried to console himself by thinking that in his place almost anyone would've felt the same way. Sonny might've cried if anyone had ever stole Lindy from him. Once when Lindy didn't hold his point old Parnell's boy had kicked Lindy. And then Sonny had kicked old Parnell's boy. Sonny would understand about Zero.

He couldn't think about Zero anymore or he might really begin to bawl. He glanced over at his mother, wondering if he should say what he'd been thinking from the moment they left Pineville. But her profile stood in his way. There was only a hint of the Bacon family's determined jaw, but he knew that if he said anything else her lips would harden, her mouth would turn under at the corners and she would scream at him again.

The first time had been when he had refused to get into the car unless Zero could come too. A blind man could have seen that there was something wrong, what with the way he was whisked into the house and out to the car. You don't just "visit" Papa Bacon in Athena with everything you own packed in suitcases. And when he'd asked about Sonny and did he know she'd screamed even louder. So to keep her from yelling any more he'd climbed into the car. That had been a big mistake.

He glanced over at her again. She must have caught the movement of his head out of the corner of her eye. Because she turned toward him with a smile, the same kind she used with Gerry.

"What is it, darling?"

"I was wondering how far we've come?"

"Oh, I don't know. About fifty or sixty miles? Why?"

He tried to figure out how to say it.

"Mama…I've been thinking…."

"Yes?"

"Well, you see, I don't think I can go with you to visit Papa Bacon after all. I can't go without Zero. We shouldn't have left her behind. She's a funny little cat. She and me are… well… we're real good friends. And she might not eat. She could run away even. You know, looking for me?"

She didn't have much of a reaction, just looked at him and raised her eyebrows.

He waited a little, then said, "So I'd be obliged if we could go back to get her…. If it wouldn't be too much trouble."

Now she smiled, as if what he'd just said was a big joke.

"It's real important…or I wouldn't ask." he said. "I've thought about it a lot. I have to go back. It's real important."

She smiled again, a maddening smile that said that whatever he wanted wasn't important at all.

"Mama—"

"Don't be silly," she said. "If we turned around now it would add three or four hours to the trip. Zero will be just fine."

"Well, then, I'll have to ask you to please stop the car. Because I ain't going to Athena without Zero."

Mocking him she said, "So you 'ain't going to Athena without Zero.' So…in other words…you want me to put you out so you can walk back to Pineville. Is that what you're saying, that you want to walk back?"

"If you won't take me."

She lifted her head, rolled her eyes, tried not to smile. But she couldn't stop a little smirk from crawling out of pressed lips. Then she lit a cigarette. She was putting the lighter back into the dash when he pulled up on the door handle. He pushed against the door. But it was glued shut by the wind.

She yelled for him to stop. She reached out blindly, grabbing at air. He ducked under her flailing hand, kept pushing. At that moment the car swerved off to the left. The door flew open with him only half aboard. It swung all the way to the front, then bounced back. It happened so fast he couldn't think; all he could do was hold on for dear life. He rode the door like a bronc rider. The car veered right then left again. He could feel his shoes bounce off the hot pavement, and one ankle turned painfully. She caught hold of him then, grabbing his flapping shirt and holding on. Somehow she brought the car to a stop. Tilted half over in a waste ditch, it bucked twice and died.

Still clutching fast to his shirt, he could hear her breathing fast behind him. He tested his sore ankle, wiggling his foot carefully back and forth. He was careful not to let her see he'd hurt it.

"Are you crazy!" she finally yelled at the back of his head. "You almost killed us!"

He turned to face her, "I ain't going."

"You're my son. You don't have any say in this. You have to do what I tell you."

"No I don't. Because you're kidnapping me. That's against the law. So I don't have to go with you. I could probably have you arrested if I wanted to."

Elizabeth loosened her grip.

"Look honey, this is just for a visit. I promise. You can see Sonny any time you want. He's your daddy. You don't think I would steal you from your own daddy do you?"

He peered at her suspiciously. For the moment at least he had the upper hand. The trouble was he had no plan beyond jumping out of the car and heading for Pineville. And now he'd twisted his ankle. Besides, there was at least one good reason to think she might be telling the truth: Kallie.

Kallie didn't say nothing after she came to get him from where he was playing marbles. Even when he and Elizabeth were leaving she didn't say a word. Just stood there holding Zero. That's why it could be true. Kallie would never let him go for good without saying good-bye. So he wavered a little.

"You might," he said. "Try to steal me I mean."

"No, no. I'll prove it. We'll stop to see Sonny on the way. The hospital is over in Rocky Mount. That's not too far out of the way. Won't that prove it? Won't that prove what I say is true."

He was still skeptical.

"What about Zero?"

"Honeee! This is just a visit."

LATER that same morning Calvin went back to the car. He carefully picked up pieces of glass he'd missed earlier and threw them into the woods. Afterward he screwed the straightened license plate back on and then he fashioned a temporary cover for the window from one of the two cardboard boxes he'd brought from the house. When he'd finished he patted the cardboard into place to see if it fit. Satisfied that it did, he took it off and stored it in the trunk. He looked skyward, through the narrow opening of vine and trees and saw there was a little more than an hour before he had to start fixing Sunday dinner. That was time enough. He started the car, backed it around and headed for town.

RALEIGH BACON walked slowly up the limestone block side-walk that edged through the cool along Little Beaver Creek and then up the hill in sunshine to where his sister, Victoria, lived. Or as she liked to say, to where she perched. It was hot and he took his time. The house itself, built in the plain style of the middle thirties, wasn't much to look at, certainly not after Market Street, but the setting, with the creek below and the terraced gardens above, was beautiful. He stopped for a moment to enjoy it, wondering as he did why she spent so much on the gardens, especially since she almost never left the house to enjoy them.

Unmarried, Victoria had lived most of her life in the Bacon house on Market Street. But on their father's death in 1929 the house was left to their oldest brother, Sam. She had waited—she had since told everyone who would listen—for some consideration, for evidence that she would not be turned out of the only home she had ever known. But she had waited in vain, and later Sam and Sam's wife, Lloyd, had used the excuse of painting the house to move her out for good.

Victoria had made it plain to Raleigh that she had no regrets about not marrying. She had always been more than willing to trade the so-called joys of family—forgoing messy and fearful childbirth—for the cool order of her maiden name and what that name meant in Athena. But with her choice of spinsterhood came a steady self-indulgence that left the once slim woman misshapened with fat. It had crept up between her shoulder blades and down her arms, leaving them heavy and capey. Her stomach protruded and her thighs had grown to where none of her dresses fit properly. Corseted and wrapped, instead of dressed, she sat, hour after hour, barrel-like, ordering the servants.

And waiting. Waiting especially for his visits.

RALEIGH LOOKED at his sister across the dim, closed room. He was tired. It had been a long meeting of the Woodside Mill's Board the afternoon before in Greenville, and he'd had to stay over. At total waste of time. That he'd been out of town didn't matter. It was Sunday and he was expected here.

"You're my church, Leigh, darling," she was fond of saying.

This morning he was tempted to complain about her over-dependence on him; Sam and Danny, their brothers, never came to see her—unless they wanted something. Particularly Danny who always had his hand out. But Raleigh's annoyance evaporated—as it always did—when he remembered why he paid her this homage. He was repaying a profound debt.

It was a debt incurred thirty-six years earlier, the day she announced that he, then only fourteen, would be the one—not Sam, not Danny—to head the family, to carry on the pride of the Bacon name. Since then he had treated her with the kind of respect he had paid few people in his life. His father. Mary, for awhile. And one or two others.

He hadn't recognized his own destiny until that day. He'd sensed it but he'd had only a vague, fragmented idea of who he was. Victoria's prediction had frightened him at the time. But that shadow was quickly replaced by a rushing excitement that seemed to make all things possible. Whatever that soul-like thing was it didn't permit doubts—or abide failure. And now, at fifty, true to her prediction, he was more successful than he had ever dared dream.

For him it had started that day when he was fourteen, but for most Athenians it began fifteen years later when he took over the operation of Bacon Mills from his father. Within a few

years his habit of working harder and longer hours than anyone at the mill, combined with a searching, innovative no-non-
sense business mind, made the people of Athena come to
respect him. They were willing to forget he was a Bacon; at
least, it was said, he didn't act like one.

The two Bacon mills employed over half the people in
Athena. The family controlled the largest bank in the northwest part of South Carolina. And those who read the Bacon
newspaper, *The Athena News*, were reminded almost daily of
how much Raleigh's decisions affected almost everybody in
town. He didn't often try to influence matters—especially at
the paper—not having to do with the mill, but then what in
Athena didn't have to do with Bacon Mills in one way or
another? In public he could be stiff to where even he was aware
of his formality, to where he became uncomfortable with himself. He put this reticence down to his hatred of cant, to any
kind of public display, certainly not hubris. Any pride he felt
was for the family name—and therefore excusable. Still, with
Victoria he could be an earlier, less sure version of himself. This
was the Raleigh Bacon they both liked best.

With the shades in the parlor already drawn against the
early afternoon heat, Victoria slowly rocked back and forth in
the upholstered chair, her exertion the least needed to keep it in
motion. A stately movement, it produced a slight breeze which
fought a losing battle against the fine film of perspiration
which seemed to lodge permanently on her upper lip. From
time to time she would blot the excess with a scented handker-
chief which she held wrapped over the index finger of her left
hand, unrolling it little by little as needed. A sherry glass,
recently filled in honor of his visit, rested in the other.

Victoria was fastidious in her over-mannered eating and

drinking habits. She appeared to nibble her food and to mere-
ly sip her iced tea, or in this case, her sherry, but, invariably, her
plate was the earliest cleaned. And her glass, the first emptied,
was always full. This trick, this illusion of moderation had not
fooled him. Until today he had never mentioned it.

"You ought to give up the liquor, Vickie," he said now. "It's
not good for you."

"Doctor John prescribed it, my dear," she said. "As you well
know a little alcohol for someone my age is medicinal."

Now, wishing he'd kept quiet, he said nothing. The body
powder she used—sweet, a little cloying—mixed with the faint
oily odor of the sherry. It made him a little queasy.

Victoria dabbed at her upper lip.

"And how are the children?" she asked. "How is that darling
Emily?"

"Emily's fine, just fine."

"Is she walking yet?"

"Not yet, but she will soon," he said. "It's just a matter of
time, Vickie. You remember Danny was slow that way. It runs
in the family."

She didn't answer. She sipped her sherry, then resumed the
rocking motion.

With that what little patience he had left vanished.

"Nothing's wrong with that child," he said, "and I wish to
God you would stop insinuating there is. Every time I drop by
here it's the same thing. You could ask about Dot or TJ but you
never do. It's always Emily.

"And what about Dot, Vickie? Why won't you ever invite
her over? I don't think it would hurt too much to have her to
one of your teas."

This was the closest he had ever come to complaining

about Athena's ostracism of his second wife. In ten years of marriage he had never acknowledged its existence, pretending indifference to the petty cruelties and slights by family and friends.

Family and friends. In one sense he had no family anymore. Except for Victoria there were only Dot's brothers, Eddie King and Ben Jessop, with whom he sometimes hunted. As for former friends like Blaine Stewart, Cobb Carington and the rest, he had only contempt. It so happened that most if not all of them had needed the bank's support in one way or another over the last decade. In a few selected, painful cases the bank didn't choose to accept his former so-called friends as customers. He'd made sure that all of Athena was reminded that it didn't pay to take public issue with Raleigh Bacon and that insults were always repaid, often with unpleasant interest.

"My, we're in a state today, aren't we?" Victoria said.

"Damn it, Vickie—"

"All right, Leigh, dear. All right. First, let me apologize if I gave any offense. But, I assure you that I am only interested in little Emily's welfare. I don't see how it can hurt to have the child examined. As you so rightly observed there may be some perfectly simple explanation for her slow development. But, God forbid, if something is, well, not right, you should know it as soon as possible. Then you can do whatever is necessary. I only want to put your mind to rest."

He sighed, "Miss Harp says that the youngest child is always the slowest to walk."

"And speak?"

"And to speak, too. According to Miss Harp, we spoil them. She told Dot that they want to stay babies longer. She says Emily is fine."

"Miss Harp," Victoria said with undisguised contempt.

He hurried to head off Victoria's complaint about Emily's colored nurse, "Let's not start that."

Victoria was about to complain that Miss Harp was a charlatan, to complain once again that Miss Harp was taking advantage of Dot. Victoria didn't understand. Dot depended on that colored woman. And, to some degree, so did he. When he had to think about Emily—as now—he found Miss Harp's folk remedies and ideas strangely comforting, if not explainable.

He looked at his watch. "I have to go now. Elizabeth called a little while ago and spoke to Calvin. She's driving down from Pineville. She should be at the house in less than an hour."

"Elizabeth's coming?" Victoria said. "And from Pineville? Why Leigh, I thought Elizabeth had left Sonny Smithson."

"She did. But she must have gone back. I guess she's taken the boy. She's bringing him with her."

"Taken? Taken? Why, has she stolen the boy away from Sonny?"

"Now don't jump to conclusions. She's coming with the boy. That's all I know."

He stood up to leave. The glass in Victoria's hand was full, as if it hadn't been touched. She didn't stir from the rocker. She sipped the sherry. With her tongue she saved a drop that ran down the side of the glass.

"I've never cared that much for Smithson," she said. "I expect the boy will grow up to be like his father, nothing but trouble."

At the door he turned and nodded goodbye.

"Tell Elizabeth I expect her to come to see me soon," she said.

"I will," he said.

"She shouldn't wait too long," she said.

"She won't. I'll see to it."

EXCEPT FOR Billy and Elizabeth, plus a man who snored softly off in one corner, the visitors' waiting room near the hospital entrance was empty. Back of where they sat the main corridor was almost deserted, too. It stretched right and left until it disappeared, finally, into dim nothingness at opposite ends of the building. It was a gloomy place, dark and old, with a peculiar sharp, antiseptic smell that made him want to hold his breath. If it hadn't been for Sonny he would have left right away.

He tried to imagine what it would be like to have to stay in this place. Even the people who worked here would need to go home every once in a while just to get rid of the strange, other-worldly feeling that must come with working in a hospital like this. He imagined the doctors and nurses leaving here and going off to church. He bet they sang the hymns louder than anybody.

And where were all the patients? So far he hadn't seen a single one. Was Sunday the day off for crazy people, too?

He hadn't wanted to believe it. He could barely make himself step through the entrance door. Walking into this asylum made it more real: that Sonny was a crazy lunatic who dribbled food from his mouth and had to wear a straitjacket to keep him from hurting himself and others.

But Sonny wasn't really crazy. This was all just a terrible mistake. He was glad they had stopped. They could tell the people who ran this place what a big mistake they'd made.

So far though they couldn't even get in to see Sonny. Elizabeth was trying hard to change that. She had argued, first, with a male nurse who said he was just holding down the reception desk until the receptionist returned, then with the receptionist, another man in a white suit and, finally, with a man in a business suit who came out of one of the offices up the hall. With him her argument had been the loudest of all. She demanded to see whoever was in charge. And now they were waiting for someone to come "down" from somewhere higher up so they could finally get in to see Sonny. They were waiting to tell the higher-up what a mistake he'd made.

The man in the business suit had glanced over at him curiously just as Elizabeth had begun her speech. She ignored whatever the business-suited man was hinting at, then plunged into her story about how this was an emergency and about how she and Mr. Smithson's son must be allowed in to see him, rules or no rules. She claimed that she had given the advance notice required for Sunday morning visits. That was a lie of course. But the man, ignoring the difference between her arguing it was an emergency and at the same time saying they gave notice, didn't show that he knew she was lying. All he did was smile at her unlined prettiness and say "I'm sorry, ma'am", over and over.

Billy lied sometimes, usually when someone—Aaron or sometimes Cotton—pushed him into a corner, asking him about why he didn't call Gerry 'mother' or why his last name was different from his real mother's. Only then did he feel the need to make something up. What came out then came out all on its own. Like someone else had said it. He felt that way right now. Like that other him—not Elizabeth—was telling these lies to get them in to see Sonny. He wanted to see Sonny bad, but what they were doing was making him feel sick.

He looked sideways at Elizabeth. She seemed even more nervous than him. She was smoking cigarette after cigarette directly beneath a red-lettered No Smoking sign. Since there were no ashtrays she had littered the squeaky, but polished, wooden floor with her cigarette stubs, grinding them out one after the other in little black semi-circles. With several she had waited too long and the burning cigarette had scorched the floor, something no one would discover until the floor was cleaned....

And then he knew what that peculiar smell was. Bleach. A ton of bleach.

"HELLO," a woman said. "My name is Rindhurst, Miss Rindhurst. May I help you?"

"I'm waiting for the Assistant Supervisor," Elizabeth said, standing.

"I am the Assistant Supervisor," Miss Rindhurst said. "How may I help you?"

Elizabeth explained again why they were there.

"When was that?" Miss Rindhurst asked. "When was the notice given?"

"Last Wednesday," Elizabeth said. "I mailed it last Wednesday. I really don't understand why it isn't here."

"The mail delivery in this part of the state is a disgrace, my dear," the Assistant Supervisor said.

And then for the first time he noticed a change in Elizabeth. With all the men she had acted one way, but now, with this Miss Rindhurst, she was just the opposite. She was now a Bacon, acting the way she acted with Kallie and the other coloreds. And her voice sounded just like she was talking to him. That is, like she didn't care how she sounded. At the same time the square-looking woman—even her hair was cut into bangs in front—sounded like his mother did with most men, a little flirtatious. Miss Rindhurst wanted to please Elizabeth. But, Elizabeth. But Elizabeth—

"You see the reason we need just a little notice for Sunday mornings, my dear," Miss Rindhurst continued, "is so we can arrange the staff's time. The rules of the hospital require that all visits on campus must have supervisory personnel present. And, of course, today is Sunday. But, under the circumstances I'm sure an exception—"

He didn't hear what Miss Rindhurst said next. Something about how they at the hospital recognized the patients' need to see their families. He didn't hear because he saw that Elizabeth had also stopped listening to the fawning, mannish woman. She seemed distracted; she was looking all around, as if she was looking to escape, as if....

Escape!

Yes, for sure. But why when they were so close to seeing Sonny would she want to leave? It didn't make any....

It came to him then, all at once, with the certainty and clarity of something that could only be called the truth.

It was a lie.

Elizabeth had trapped herself. It had all been one gigantic lie. Not only about giving notice but everything she'd said to him too.

This Miss Rindhurst was still talking, repeating herself like someone does when a person is not listening. She didn't know, or probably care, that she'd been lied to. All of his mother's lies had worked like a charm. The lie she had told him about how she would get them in to see Sonny when she must have known that they had to give notice to see him on Sunday morning.

And all the lies she'd told here. All those lies had suddenly turned on her. And were about to give her the last thing she wanted. To see Sonny. Well, for Sonny's sake he had to stop all the lies.

"—I'm sure an exception—" Miss Rindhurst continued.

"I bet I know what to do," he said in a voice loud enough that they were forced to pay attention.

"And this is—?"

"Yes," Elizabeth said, "his son."

"Give your notice now," he said.

Both women stared at him.

"So on our way back from our trip to Athena we can come in to see Sonny then."

Neither Elizabeth nor Miss Rindhurst said anything for a few seconds. Then Elizabeth with jerky, defiant movements lit a cigarette and flung the match on the floor.

"Forget it," she said to the astonished Miss Rindhurst. "Can't break your precious rules."

But she was staring at him.

WHEN HE CAME OUT she was waiting in the car. And very mad. A quick glance told him that. He got in. They sat not speaking in the oven-like heat of the car. After maybe a minute—it seemed a lot longer—she ground at the starter on the floor-board. The engine roared to life and the car leapt away from the curb. It careened around the flowered circle set in the middle of the driveway. The sudden start and swerve threw him to his left, toward her, but he grabbed the door handle and held on. They screeched down the winding drive to the highway below where, without slowing, she turned back toward Pineville.

His heart leapt with hope. In his imagination he saw Cotton running in welcome behind the car and a streaking Zero, tail raised, heading toward him from across the yard. But before the imaginary Zero reached him the car slid to a stop on the gravel shoulder of the highway. She turned to him. He wouldn't look at her.

"Why did you do that?" she said. "I thought you wanted to see him."

"Not that way," he said.

He turned away to look out the window.

For a few seconds he couldn't see anything past the aching pain in his throat. But in a little while the gloomy building at the top of the hill slowly swam into view. It looked like...like a prison. Massive, it was five stories of dirty quarry stone piled one on top of the other. All windows, except those on the fifth floor, were barred. A spiked wrought-iron fence, seven or eight feet high, wound around the foot of the hill.

"Don't turn your back on me," Elizabeth said.

Her voice was scratchy, as if she'd smoked too many cigarettes, or she was about to cry. Either one, he didn't care. She couldn't feel much worse than him.

"Did you hear me?" she said.

She didn't wait for an answer. She grabbed his head from behind with both hands and in a rough, crude way pulled him around so he was half facing her.

He tried to pull out of her hold. With that she awkwardly slapped at him, hitting him with a downward, glancing blow. He was surprised, and yet not surprised at all. He didn't actually feel anything. It wasn't until later, later that night, at a time when he was fingering the scab where one of her nails had scratched the side of his nose, that he really understood what had happened.

But now her face was swollen in rage. "You're just like him," she said. "Exactly like him. Stubborn, you're a stubborn, crazy know-it-all."

"Sonny isn't crazy!" he yelled. "You're the only crazy person in this family."

She started the car, looked at him.

"No one will ever make me stay," he said.

Then she backed around and headed south.

THE FIRST THING Dot Jessop thought when she woke up late that morning was that she wanted a grilled pimento cheese sandwich from Five Points Pharmacy. She felt the hot cheese—soft, a little runny—in her mouth, and it tasted good. Or would taste good if she could have one right now with a cherry Coke. Especially a Coke with lots and lots of ice. Her mouth was dry, caked dry. She ran her tongue over parched lips. Only after she licked them several more times did they start to get moist.

She swallowed and then suddenly gagged. Something awful, foul smelling was at the back of her throat. She remembered. Oh, God! Oh, God! she whimpered again. No more. No more liquor, ever! She swallowed again, slowly, then a third time, very careful to take only shallow breaths. When nothing bad happened she turned gingerly half way onto her right side, slowly stretching out her legs, one after the other.

Her feet found the junction of silk and footboard and she slid down a little so they rested flat against the padded wood.

Feet braced, she relaxed her buttocks, then carefully let her belly go. With each shallow breath the nausea stepped down. After a while the sense of panic that she would vomit in bed and ruin the silk sheets faded. But she still couldn't move.

She needed a drink. But she mustn't think that way. Never, never again.

She dozed, dreaming of swimming pools filled with Coca-Cola and pimento cheese and Four Roses, of being thrown into one after the other and not being able to swim. But when she woke again, sweating like a nigger, she felt a little better.

After a while she decided to try to get up. She slid to the side of the bed nearest the door to the bathroom where she pushed the sheet aside and stood shakily beside the bed. Her mind was blank, a monitor ready to record the first signs of trouble. Across from the bed she saw herself naked in the pier mirror behind the picture table, but at first glance even her own reflection wasn't enough to distract her.

Dot Jessop liked being female, and she took it for granted.

She knew that men liked her. They liked the soft roundness of her body. Her breasts were still good, even after nursing TJ and Emily. The only thing different from when she was first married was her belly hadn't come all the way back after Emily; it stuck out a little more than she would like. Her little pot.

That's what Leigh called it.

Do you see my little pot, Daddy? Do you like my little pot, Daddy?

She looked in the mirror again. When Leigh was away was the only time she got to sleep in the nude. She had never worn anything to bed when she lived at home. But he liked to take her nightgown off, so she had to wear one when he was here.

These thoughts of sex helped to distract her from her shaky

self. She felt a little better. It's like a job she told herself, and then sighed. I just had a night off. I think I'm going to ask for a five-day week. She giggled at her own joke, noticing now the reflection of thick pubic hair and the convex shape of her belly in the mirror opposite. She reshaped her belly with her soft hands and it protested.

"Oh," she said. "Uh-oh."

She tried to take her mind off men and women things, especially men's things. As she did she grimaced and adopted what she assumed was a look of distaste. But, in fact Dot Jessop had never refused Raleigh his rights in her bed because it would never have occurred to her that a woman did anything else. Lying under a man was being a woman. It was true there were times when she would rather be doing something else. But not often and almost never after they get started. Once they were going at it she liked it as much as he did. Sometimes more.

But men only thought about one thing. Sometimes it seemed like that was all she thought about, too. But, that was because men were always circling her, waiting until her guard was down. She never got to do anything or to go anywhere, to the show, to the drug store, without some man coming after her. It was all the watching, sometimes wary, sometimes not so wary, that made her think about it all the time.

Leigh had been a pleasant surprise. He was considerate, but not too considerate. And he was willing to take the time she needed. That was in the beginning. Now when he came upstairs, he didn't always want to make love. Sometimes he just wanted to sleep, and more and more often lately she had to be the aggressor. Dot Jessop didn't like being forward like that. It wasn't ladylike.

That was one of the troubles of being married to a man as old as Leigh. In fact, Leigh was three years older than her own daddy would be if he'd lived. He'd died when she was twelve. After that she had been raised by her mama and by her two brothers.

Raised? That was a good one. Raised meant that someone took care of you when she was the one who ended up taking care of all of them. She'd done it herself. All on her own. But, now that she was raised (and had two children of her own to raise) they didn't appreciate it at all. They took what she sent them for granted, like it was their due. Like any one of them could have married Raleigh Bacon.

Sometimes she still had trouble believing that she was Mrs. Raleigh Bacon. And the rest of Athena acted like they didn't believe it, either. From the beginning practically no one would call her Mrs. Bacon. Just Dot Jessop. She had changed to Belk's when the people at McMahon's kept on calling her Dot Jessop even after she'd asked to be called by her married name. The month after the change she charged over six hundred dollars at Belk's figuring that McMahon's would hear what they had missed.

Even the servants wouldn't call her 'Mrs. Bacon,' doing what the nigger did, copycatting his 'Missus Dot.' And that was when he called her anything at all. Usually it was nothing. He ignored her, pretending that she wasn't the mistress of Raleigh Bacon's house. It didn't bother her most of the time. She didn't like to fool with planning meals and things like that. No, it was his attitude; something about the way he looked at her, or wouldn't look her in the eye. "Most niggers won't look you in the eye," she said to herself, but somehow this one was different. Like he was afraid *for you* instead of the other way around.

Whenever she thought of the nigger it was always of how to get rid of him. But she was afraid to complain about Calvin to Leigh. She didn't know for sure what would happen if she made a big thing of it; it could be that he wouldn't do anything. Where would she be then? And, although she sometimes felt that her marriage to Leigh was like taking a long, all-expenses-paid trip with a stranger, the thought of going back to what she was before scared her.

SHE PADDED into the narrow bathroom where she sat down on the lowered toilet seat. She played with the paper roll, rolling it out and back. Every few seconds she straightened her back, at the same time pulling in and letting out her belly.

Then when things felt right she slipped to her knees on the cool tile floor, raised the seat and vomited into the bowl. She waited, then with her finger tickled the back of her throat with a manicured nail and vomited a second time. By now she felt as good as new; as she gargled with Listerine and brushed her teeth she was thinking what there was to do on a Sunday. And then with a little whimper she remembered that Emily and Harpie were staying over at her brothers' house. She missed them already.

She came out of the bathroom and went over to their room and peered in. Bright and spacious the room seemed much larger than it was because all the furniture had been lined up against the walls. On one side were Emily's crib and next to it the changing table, piled high with diapers. An unused training toilet sat forgotten under the table. On the opposite wall were Miss Harp's bed and dresser. They were white, like the nurses' uniforms she wore. She was tempted to go through the drawers of the dresser, to see if Harpie was hiding anything. But was it worth it? If she did Harpie might find out somehow. And then—what if she left?

She shuddered.

She could get sick again, just at the thought of it.

Why should Harpie want to leave? She was well paid, almost as much as the nigger. The only thing she had to do was take care of a darling three-year-old girl. No, nearer three and a half. But really a darling child. So sweet and no real trouble. No real trouble at all.

But the surge of affection she felt for her daughter was immediately conflicted by guilt, the same guilt she always felt whenever she thought of Emily, then always made worse by trying to put Emily out of her mind. But what was she to do? It wasn't her fault. Why should she feel guilty? It was old sperm that did it.

Miss Harp must never leave. That was the important thing now. Harpie must never leave.

She walked back over to beside the canopied bed where she picked the black telephone receiver out of its cradle.

She gave the number to the operator.

At six rings she began to count. At twenty she stopped counting. She stared fiercely at the telephone mouthpiece, tensely waiting.

At last the telephone was picked up at the Jessop house over in Alta Vista.

"Goddammit to hell!" she screamed into the receiver. "Why won't you answer the damn telephone? I'm not going to put up with this one more minute. I'm sick to death of the way you act. Do you hear me, goddammit?"

She glared at the silent telephone.

"Answer me, goddammit!" she said, her voice cracking in frustration.

The curved hard rubber lip of the telephone's black mouthpiece seemed to stare back. She wondered, without caring, if the operator had listened.

Finally a familiar low voice said, "Best you take it easy, little sister."

"I knew it was you, Eddie King," Dot Jessop said. "I knew it was you not answering. You better—"

"Don't you try that lady fingers business on me, miss," the calm voice said. "This is Eddie King, remember. Don't forget that I can still kick your hot little ass. And I sure as hell will."

"I bought the phone," Dot Jessop said in the same unrestrained yet intimate tone of voice. "I bought the goddamn telephone so I could call my family. But, if you won't answer what good is it?

"Yesterday," she continued, "I called a hundred times but no one answered. And, I know you were all there, that's why I called. But you wouldn't answer. That's what I mean. I pay for the phone—it don't cost you a cent—yet you won't answer it. What good is it if you won't answer?"

She thought she could see her brother shrug.

"What good is it? Answer me, Eddie King!"

"What do you want?" he said.

"What do you mean what do I want?" she said. "I want to talk to my child, of course. Please put Miss Harp on the telephone, Eddie King."

"They ain't here," Eddie King said.

"Where'd they go?"

"Ben and them went out to the airport."

A Sunday afternoon recreation for many Athenians was to go over to the Greenville airport to watch the planes take off and land. There was one flight from Charlotte that came in about two-fifteen. It terminated in Greenville, so often the crew was willing to chat with the hero worshipers that hung over the chain link fence outside the terminal. And the two stewardesses were always very pretty and smartly elegant in their boxy hats, wings, and patent leather high-heeled shoes. Ben Jessop never tired of acting like a fool around those unattainable women.

"Oh, Eddie King," Dot Jessop said, now conspiratorial, "Emily's way too young for that kind of talk. You shouldn't have let him take her."

"Oh, it's fine," Eddie King said. "Gonna be fine. And besides, Harpie's with them. She'll stop up Emily's ears if Ben goes on too much."

"I guess so," Dot Jessop said, bored now. "Have Miss Harp call me when they get back. And I'll come and pick them up."

"Make sure you do. Don't send that nigger over here like last time."

"I couldn't help it, you know that."

"Maybe. Just don't send him again."

"All right," she said.

But then she remembered who owed who.

"Then you better bring them home," she said.

OUTSIDE the Alta Vista house Eddie King Jessop looked at Ben's car. His brother had taken the good car, the Plymouth, to the airport. He was faced with the choice of walking or trying to start Ben's junker. Wertheimer's was only seven blocks but he quickly decided it was too hot to walk.

He got the beat-up old car rolling down the slight incline and jumped in, but the motor wouldn't start. On the next try he was sweating so much he wished to God he'd never started. But then the engine caught and sputtered to life. He nursed the car down to the corner.

Eddie King had never had a driver's license. Despite that he was, in most ways, a good driver. If anything, he was too careful when he drove. Part of that came from not having a license. Didn't want to get caught driving. But he never intended to apply for a driver's license. Once the government knew about you those people liked to dig into whatever you had ever done. Or not done. Like he had never paid a dime in income taxes. But that wasn't what worried him most. No, what kept him up at night was buried next to the railroad bridge over the Saluda River. When it flooded there in the spring he always drove out to see. On the way there, like now, he never drove over twenty miles an hour. He just couldn't seem to make himself go any faster.

When he got to Wertheimer's he parked on the street and went in the back door of the old red brick building. To get to the front part of the store he had to pass through a dim high-ceilinged room filled with new tires. The tires, mummy-wrapped in dusty reinforced six-inch-wide strips of paper, were haphazardly stacked, blocking the way. He didn't pause, walking familiarly into this rubber labyrinth and winding his way through to the heavy sliding door opposite.

He came to a smaller inner room, also filled with tires, some on display, others fresh from the recap vulcanizer. This room smelled of rubber, but it also had another, stronger smell of tobacco smoke and old sweat.

When Eddie King walked into the room, seven other men were already there. No one spoke, although several nodded.

Except for one wooden chair, which was placed in front of the sales counter, there were no chairs as such. Two of the men sat up on the recap counter. Three others leaned against or sat on waist-high piles of new tires. The sixth man, bald with a brown, recently barbered fringe of hair, leaned against the sales counter. The bald man lit a cigarette and glanced up at a tall thin man who had just come into the room from the front. Wertheimer, the owner of the tire store.

Eddie King Jessop walked straight to the chair and sat down. He said, "Lord, Wertheimer, you need fans in weather like this." Then he turned to the bald man. "Alright, shithead, what was so important that couldn't wait until tomorrow?"

The man pointed, half nodded, to a narrow, two-foot long package sitting on the recap counter behind Eddie King.

"What the fuck is it?" Eddie King said as he leaned around to look at what was in the box. "A tire iron? Why the fuck is it painted red?"

He touched it.

"Oh shit," he said.

"Yeah," Wertheimer said. "'Oh shit' is right. That's not paint. It happens to be blood."

IN ATHENA Elizabeth turned the station wagon onto the cinder service drive leading to the back of her father's house. Billy hardly noticed where they were. Hunched down on the seat he was vaguely aware of the car moving slowly past trimmed pines, the hardened ooze of healing resins glinting dully, like fireflies at dusk....

He imagined Zero jumping, trying to catch them when she knew she couldn't, just to make him laugh.

"Where are we?" he said, not that he cared where they were, but it gave him a chance to taunt her into not answering him again, and it let him think about something other than Pineville.

"Huh? Can you tell me where we are, please?"

At that moment though Elizabeth was turning the station wagon into a driveway. It eased down a fairly steep incline to a large parking area in front of a big three-car garage. A bur-gundy-colored Buick and a green Packard coupe were parked in the garage. Elizabeth climbed out of the car, slammed the door and walked off without a word. He watched as she walked down through the woods toward a big white house. It sat in a level clearing on a broad band of undulating land that descended to a road below. He tried to picture the inside of the house. He'd been here before, as a little kid, but he couldn't remember anything about it now. He watched until Elizabeth's figure, small, not so threatening at this distance, disappeared inside.

He climbed out of the car and walked about testing his ankle; it was painful but he could walk a ways on it if he had to. But one thing he hadn't been smart about at all. And that was not to have paid attention to the way into Athena; you needed to know the way in to get out.

For the time being though he had to make the best of it.

He got back into the car to wait. Very tired, he stretched out on the seat and was soon asleep.

A SCRAPING SOUND on the running board woke him.

"There he is, right there," a voice said. He knew he was being pointed at.

The pointer was TJ, Thurston John Bacon IV, his mother's

half-brother. Almost a year younger than he was, TJ had always
seemed like a little kid. But here TJ was now, as big if not bigger than him, smiling broadly. TJ's eyes were laughing, full of
mischief, waiting for something exciting to happen.

"Want me to open the door?" TJ said.

"In a minute, TJ," a rumbling deep voice said, "In just one
little minute."

A second face swam into view then, framed by the window.
At first he wondered if he was dreaming. This had to be Calvin.
He knew of Calvin of course; he knew about Calvin the same
way he knew about all the colored servants who worked for his
friends' parents. They were there, sometimes to be noticed,
sometimes not, depending. But here was the meanest looking
nigra he'd ever seen. A nigra that could squash you like a fly,
without a second thought, the kind of nigra all people in the
South were scared to death of. Was this mean-looking man
really Papa Bacon's Calvin?

"Billy, we was wondering if you'd like to come into the
house for some supper?" Calvin said, peering down at him.

He didn't answer.

"You must be hungry, boy."

"No, not really."

"You mean to sleep in this here car all night?"

He shrugged.

"You look hot," the black man said. "It must be a tight fit in
this here car. It's gonna be hard to sleep, too. You could sleep on
the ground, I suppose. But I'd be careful if I was you. Maybe
you better stay in the car."

"How come?"

"They's a family of bobcats that lives around here. But you
don't have to worry too much. Just listen to the dogs. They'll

start carrying on when they smell them critters. Then you just get back into this here car."

Billy laughed.

Calvin didn't smile. That made him nervous. And he'd really like something to eat. He also had to pee. Something awful.

"TJ," Calvin said, "I think it's time to open this here door."

TJ opened the door. TJ stood, holding it, peering around from its edge. TJ was excited, not only smiling to beat the band, but as red as a beet from all the excitement. TJ's honest pleasure made Billy feel like a dope. Then he sort of gave out. He didn't really surrender; he just decided to quit fighting for a while.

He stepped out of the station wagon.

"Hey, Billy" TJ said, smiling. "I reckon I'm your uncle."

"Come on boy," Calvin said. "We want to show you something."

"What?"

"The dogs. Best you let them smell you."

He limped along behind as TJ and Calvin went around to the other side of the garage.

There, five or six dogs barked and leaped about excitedly. They threw themselves against the wire fence as the three of them came close.

TJ proudly named each one.

"That's Caesar. And that's Ruthie. She just had a litter. Six puppies. We didn't keep none. We don't have the room and we don't have the time to train them. And that pointer there is Ruthie's husband, Falstaff. We call him Folly 'cause he's the silliest of all the dogs. Bet you didn't know a dog can be silly, just like a person."

"Sure I do," Billy said. "A cat's different, though. They ain't never silly."

"And that's Blueplate," TJ said. "He's the best pointer we got."

"What's that one?" Billy asked, pointing at a black dog lying apart in the far corner.

"That's Black Jim," TJ said. "He's new. Papa just got him a couple of weeks ago. Calvin is training him now."

"Is he sick? How come he ain't acting like the other dogs?"

"I don't know," TJ said. "Maybe he is sick."

"No, he ain't sick," Calvin said. "He's just homesick. Like you, Billy."

"Mister?"

"You can call me Calvin."

"Calvin?"

"What is it, boy?"

"Can I use your bathroom? I got to pee something awful."

And he did pee, with TJ watching. He peed for a long time. So long that when he was finished TJ said he had never seen anybody pee that long.

LONG AFTER TJ had gone to sleep that night Billy stared out the bedroom window, tracing the clouds as they covered the moon, listening for any familiar sound. A stray dog barked, then passed by without any answering cry from the kennel; and, once, a gobble of wild turkeys erupted from somewhere down the hill. Then, as he listened the sounds changed, grew strange, then stranger still. He imagined bobcats tearing into an opossum. And he was glad to be sleeping inside.

He looked over at TJ. The face collapsed in sleep still smiled. TJ wouldn't mind being shook awake to answer his questions. TJ was anxious to tell him everything he knew. It didn't take long to find out that TJ never held back on anything. He had been a gusher of information, spewing out so many stories and tales of this place and the people here that he was still trying to sort them all out.

It looked like he was going to have to live here for a while. TJ was the first to tell him that Elizabeth was going to someplace in Minnesota to take courses to become a Laboratory Technician. And by God if TJ didn't turn out to be right! He didn't know whether to be happy or sad when Papa Bacon told him she was going to leave him here in Athena.

Now, he tried to get to sleep. But he couldn't. He couldn't get that fellow, Calvin, out of his mind.

Right after visiting the dogs in the kennel, TJ had said, "Calvin's a wizard."

"He's your cook," he said, thinking of Kallie.

TJ had given him his hick from North Carolina look.

"A real wizard. He can do anything. Cooking is only one little thing. Like sewing. Like keeping the yard. He built that summer house there all by himself. Everything. Except cleaning. He don't clean nothing but his kitchen.

"What I mean," TJ continued, "is stuff nobody else does, or even heard of.... Like...."

"Like what!"

"Like eating frogs. He eats 'em whole. And raw. The same with steaks; he don't bother to cook 'em at all. And he makes things happen that ain't supposed to happen."

"Like what?"

"I don't know if I should say."

"Oh, come on!"

"Well, Miss Harp says Calvin uses voodoo."

"Voodoo. I never heard of it."

"Voodoo can make you disappear."

"You're crazy."

"Disappear off the face of the earth."

"I don't believe you."

"Wait and see."

"He's a magician you mean?"

"That too."

But one of the strangest things about Calvin had happened just after Papa Bacon had told him he would be living here for a while.

Papa Bacon had said, "Now we'll have to speak to Calvin."

And Papa Bacon's wife, Dot Jessop, had said, "It doesn't matter what he thinks. We've decided."

"No, Dot," Papa Bacon said. "This is Calvin's house to run and we should speak to him. I'm sure he'll have no objection, but it is his house."

"It's my house, Leigh," Dot Jessop said.

"Of course it is Dot, dear. You know what I mean."

It turned out that Billy's staying at Papa Bacon's was just fine with Calvin.

That was all well and good for them. But there was just one little thing. It wasn't "just fine" with him.

He was heading for Pineville.

The turkeys gobbled again.

But he only heard them in his dreams. He was finally asleep.

2

UNTIL he was fifteen years old Calvin lived in the country outside of Athena with his mother, two brothers and five sisters. His daddy, some man from down Louisiana way, left before memory started. His mother's name was Big Judy. One of his first memories of Big Judy was her glaring down at him from the wagon seat to where he lay on the ground. He couldn't exactly remember why she had knocked him out of the wagon. For him and his brothers, Willy and Leander, she didn't need reasons. Just being close was enough. She would push or poke or slap. Every now and then she punched one of them, but that had to be when she was real mad. During regular times she didn't really want to hurt them. The three boys had to be well enough to work Mr. Penrose's place.

They all lived together in one of Mr. Penrose's little rental houses. But they didn't rent it. The house was given to them—along with some food—in swap for work in the fields. And Big Judy washed for the Penrose family up at the big house. Every Monday Big Judy would climb up the hill and spend all day washing and drying and ironing a mountain of clothes and sheets for the Penrose family. More often than not she'd take him along to paddle the kettle and to keep the fire going. He grew up standing by that kettle, the smell of bleach and wood smoke as regular as anything in his life. On wash days he didn't have to work in the field; and sometimes he got to play with the older Penrose boys.

When Calvin was around ten he started going to school with the Penrose children. Not a real school it was a home school, Missus Penrose's school for her and her neighbor's children. Only him and Willy and Leander got asked to go. Missus Penrose wouldn't take any of the girls because they were too "dirty."

Then Willy and Leander stopped going, leaving only him at the school. He went to her school for almost two years, but never learned to read or get his numbers. One reason was because Missus Penrose taught them to read using only stories, mostly stories about animals with human names. And they never even opened the arithmetic book. Still, the Penrose children seemed to learn all right. It was just him that didn't. The big reason he didn't was Mr. Penrose.

One day early on in the first year Mr. Penrose walked into the parlor where the school was held and asked a lot of questions. And he answered them all. He didn't learn until later that that was the wrong thing to do. He shouldn't have answered the questions about Hannibal and the elephants and about the Book of Deuteronomy and the rest. But he had thought it was a game. He had believed that he was allowed to play along with the Penrose children, and so he had answered all the questions. Later that day Mr. Penrose whipped Dorcus and Remington, the two oldest Penrose boys. Nobody said nothing but everybody knew why they were whipped. He stayed in Missus Penrose's school for one more year. But he made sure he never learned nothing from then on.

As soon as he was big enough he quit the Penrose house, even refusing to go up there with Big Judy on wash days. She slapped him around some but he still wouldn't go. He went back to the fields.

By then he was almost fifteen. Up to that time he had never stopped to think if things would ever be different. Despite the hard work, despite Big Judy's bad temper, he accepted the way things were until the year his sister Gracie died.

Gracie, the second oldest girl, ate dirt. No one knew when it started, only that she stopped eating what the rest of them ate at supper. Nothing anybody said or did could get her to change. Big Judy slapped her whenever she caught her at it. Toward the end she had to tie Gracie to the bed.

He tried a different way. He got Gracie to show him the kind of dirt that could be eaten. That dirt came mostly from yards, or from around sheds, the pulverized brown silt found near the edges of porches or along the sides of barns where the splashing rain water had deposited the dirt off to the side in wavy mounding veins, veins that would pick free of pebbles and cinders, veins of dirt that made the kind of mud that fools the stomach for a while.

Show me he said, and they ate the dirt together. Afterward he had a little cornbread and sucked an egg, saying she would like them, too.

But she wouldn't eat, even for him. And then her teeth started to come out. Three months later she died, a bony, vacant-eyed thirteen-year-old crone. Mr. Penrose wouldn't let them bury Gracie on his land, so they had to find a colored burying place in Athena. As they walked the six miles home after the funeral Calvin spied out every family tombstone, every headstone he could find, guessing, pretending to read the names and dates.

At Mr. Lancaster's place he climbed up a wooded hill to the family's cemetery plot, a pretty, well-kept burying place where the white stones marked over three generations of Lancasters.

Big Judy and the rest of the family watched from the road as he wandered about calling out the names of dead folks he knew from hearing about over the years.

"And here's Nelson," he cried. "And Crawford. Mister Crawford lived for better'n eighty years. It says so right here."

By this time he was sobbing. He couldn't see nothing. But he kept pretending. He yelled out names. He made dates up out of his head. He wandered blindly about bumping into smooth white stones, and with each his sobs became wails of anguish.

Now Big Judy was yelling. She screamed up at him from down on the road. The rest of them, too. They were scared. What would happen if the Lancasters or Mr. Penrose saw what he was doing?

"Why did Mister Crawford get to live eighty whole years," he shouted. "How come he got to live so much longer than poor Gracie!"

By now Big Judy was beside herself. They were all yelling at him, together making enough noise to wake the whole county. Big Judy started up the hill toward him once but quit after only going a few feet. Because when he saw her coming he ran over to the edge of the cemetery, and kicked two or three of the headstones to the ground. When Big Judy saw that she ran for home. They all ran, even Willy, who hung back long enough to yell that he was a damn nigger fool who sure as hell had got them in awful trouble.

Calvin didn't care if he got caught. Sort of wanted to. He even sat down on one of the fallen headstones so the Lancasters would know who done it. He waited a long time. But nothing happened. After so much noise the cemetery now seemed awful quiet. He listened for birds, for the chirps and the rustles that always filled the country around there. But there didn't seem to be a creature to be heard anywhere. It was strange. As if he had scared all the living creatures off the face of the earth.

One by one he put the headstones back. He didn't hurry. He took extra care to make sure they were set solid. So some considerable time had passed by the time he was finished. The shadows of nearby trees had lengthened across most of the little cemetery. He looked up to find the sun; instead he saw mountains in the distance. They rested there, miles and miles away, mist covered, barely visible. And, for sure, had always been there, but he hadn't ever seen them. There! There was Caesar's Head! There was Hogback, all the really big mountains beginning at the foot of the Smokies. All his life they'd lain there, brooding. And he had never really seen them. Never in his fifteen years. Gracie had to die for him to see the mountains.

WHEN HE LEFT HOME later that year he said it was because of Big Judy. She was too mean, he said. Besides, there wasn't enough room for them all in the house. He said that about Big Judy without really meaning it. It wasn't anymore her doing than his. How could he blame some poor old nigger woman he hardly knew and would never see again? But he had to give Willy and the rest a reason for his leaving. He couldn't tell them what he knew for certain: he would die just like Gracie did if he had to stay on living in that place.

OUTSIDE OF picking a little cotton or running errands at tent markets there wasn't any work in 1908 for a loose Negro boy in that part of South Carolina. His world was made up of the narrow triangle of land connecting Greenville, Spartanburg and Athena, the smallest of the three. He roamed in and out of all three towns before settling for the last half of the summer in Greenville. That August and fall he picked cotton for a few cents a hundred pounds and, besides running errands, traded day-old vegetables and wilting flowers from the market for food, never stopping to ask himself why the colored cooks at the back doors of the big houses would want what he had to trade. In his mind it wasn't begging so long as he had something to offer in exchange. In the same way he did chores for meals. He chopped wood, dug gardens, cleaned hen houses and ran back-door errands, sometimes eating his cornbread or biscuit at a trot.

But by November the street market was closed. With nothing to trade and not enough chores he ate what rotten and wormy fruit he could find in the fields and orchards where he slept. He drank a lot of water. About that time he started to drift. Without any plan he wandered in an aimless circle, following one road, then another.

The days began to pass slowly, unnoticed, in a painful blur of hunger and cold. There wasn't a minute when his now gaunt frame wasn't crying out to be fed, when, even on warm days, he wasn't shivering, sometimes uncontrollably. And he had stopped thinking, he had stopped making even the simplest plans of where to go next and how to find food. His mind was shutting down as his big body wasted away.

And then one day, following some ancient instinct, he moved into the woods, into the vast anonymous forest that blanketed that part of the state. Every morning he woke without any idea of what he would do that day. He lay curled up on a bed of pine needles until hunger or the need to piss got him up. Then he would wander slowly down to the road and set off in a direction, any direction, anywhere that beckoned with the vague hope that that place might feed him that day. And on

some of those days he was lucky: he managed to catch a few
fish and frogs or was given cornbread or greens by kind folks
who didn't have to be begged. Some days he ate nothing. On
the bad days he filled his belly with water. Never dirt.

The weather turned colder. Now he spent half the day
searching for shelter at night. Hunger was still part of him, as
much as his arms and legs. But while he thought only of food
he had never been so cold. Often he had to make a blanket of
pine needles and earth. Then, shivering, half-waking, he
dreamed of Missus Penrose's school with its big pot-bellied
wood stove.

EARLY ONE EVENING before Thanksgiving he heard sounds
coming from the trees across the road. Weaving unsteadily, legs
shaking from the effort, he stumbled out his hiding place and
crept to the top of the hill across the highway. There, in the
middle of the trees, was a big open space. It was a railroad
repair yard. A pair of railroad tracks ran down the center of the
space parallel to the road behind him, and, like the road, disappeared into darkness in opposite directions. Right in front of
him were some low buildings scattered about in an opening the
size of three big barns strung end to end. A gray metal building
was off to one side, tall as a barn and half as wide. A section of
railroad track curved into it. A second spur curled out of sight
behind the other, bigger building. The sounds were coming
from there. Keeping in the shadow of the woods he skirted
around the opening to the opposite side. There, parked on the
siding next to the building, was a half-lit railroad dining car.
Farther down, toward the opposite end of the diner, was a
lighted service door. He crept toward the door, then stopped
when he could see through it.

Three men were inside, a white man and two Negroes. The two Negroes were washing dishes while the white man watched. He was wearing a dark blue coat trimmed in silver. From where he was at the edge of the woods he couldn't hear what was being said, just the murmur of voices, some laughter, the clink of dishes.

The white man was laughing, gesturing. Every now and then he pointed a finger at the older Negro. It jabbed at the older man, like a charmed snake.

The older Negro had protuberant eyes. The other one was young and thin.

The white man was restless, walking back and forth smoking a cigarette. The two colored men were also smoking. As they worked the long untended ash from the cigarettes in their mouths hung over the water, smoke curling up past nostrils and eyes.

Each time the white man moved both Negroes shifted their bodies slightly as they worked. The cigarette smoke shifted too, keeping a hazy blue curtain always between the two cocked black heads and the restless white man.

The white man said something, then left. The older man with the popping eyes spat his cigarette butt into the dishwater. He began to curse. His jaw jutted and worked. Suddenly he stopped talking. He plunged his hands into the water. The white man was back. He was followed by a gray-haired colored man wearing a waiter's uniform. The waiter carried a tray loaded with dirty dishes. He put it down next to the younger dishwasher.

The young dishwasher scraped all the plates onto one, then turned and walked to the open door where he again scraped the mounding plate of leftovers into a two-foot-tall slop bucket sitting in the opening of the door.

It took ten more minutes for the dishwashers to finish. They walked away then; just the murmur of their talk was left behind. And, at last, that was gone too.

Calvin ran over and pulled the large bucket to the doorway's edge. It teetered, then fell heavily to the ties below. Before he could right it, most of everything in it spilled onto the rocks of the railroad bed. Crying out he fell to his knees to save what he could. But the greasy, foul smelling liquid had already percolated downwards through the gravel and cinders. It disappeared in an instant. He wailed in angry frustration. As he cried out he pushed and shaped the rough pieces of gravel together, as if to stanch the hemorrhage of food. At the same time he licked the residue of flesh and vegetable from where it had lodged on the rough rocks.

Suddenly, from overhead, a voice, "Who's down there!"

He ran. But he hadn't gone more than a few steps when he stopped. Next thing he knew he was heading back for the bucket. Moving shadows suddenly filled up the lighted doorway. Whatever in him that meant to have that bucket held its ground for an agonizing second, then gave up. He really ran for it then. But it was too late. They caught him as he scrambled out from under the opposite side of the dining car.

They tied a rope tight around his left leg just above the ankle, then dragged him back through short brush toward the tall storage shed. At first he wasn't afraid. It was as if he were just a bystander. It seemed to be happening to somebody else. He was almost calm as he looked to see who the men were. But it was too dark to make out their faces.

Then they dragged him toward the light.

A flash, a hard glint of metal. In cold light the fear leaped back into his throat. No dream. This was no dream. A blind terror gripped him. He began to thrash about, flailing his arms wildly. Resisting heels ploughed the ground. Like a pig being dragged to a sticking. Somebody pulled at his tied leg. He tried to jerk it free. Then came a blinding scalding pain. He screamed. In agony he looked down to see a heavy boot riding his free foot. Twisted around that way he was split in two, facing both directions at once.

His wiry upper torso came erect, rearing up like a powerful spring. He swung around, grabbed the heavy leg standing on his foot and bit down hard just above the knee. Sharp white teeth sliced through thin cloth. Soft flesh give way under his maniacal bite. More screaming. But now it wasn't coming from him. A bright white flash and the pain stopped. He fell into a swirling bottomless black pool.

When he woke the first time the pain was so bad he couldn't see. A heavy sharp searing whiteness pounded and pounded. What happened? What happened he kept asking. Was there anybody to hear? He couldn't seem to get past the pain to care. Red hot pokers had been thrust through his eyes. They crossed then exploded out the back of his skull. In agony he tried to lift his hands to his face, but his arms wouldn't move.

The fierce burning sensation in his head grew worse. He blew air up his face to cool it. As he did he felt his lower lip slide into the spaces where his eye teeth used to be. He pushed to make sure and then felt the soreness and the pain coming from that part of his face.

He remembered: two teeth, bloody and broken, lying inches away from where his nose was kissing the ground.

As he had gazed at the first part of himself to die he heard a voice, a soft, patient voice, say, "You paid the Lord, brother. He took them. We were but his poor instruments."

Then he fell into another fitful sleep. He woke often, his heart racing wildly. One nightmare followed another until finally he couldn't tell when he was awake and when he was asleep. The same voice blew bubbles of words that floated over, just out of reach, like delicate dandelion pods. Then he was flying high in the air. Suddenly, his head flew in one direction and the rest of him in another. Blinding white blackness…blacker than….

WHEN HE WOKE finally from the long nightmare he was stiff with cold. Overhead, within his breath, an olive-brown metal sky pressed down and promised to smother him. He turned his head to escape. He saw him then. A white man sat next to where he lay.

The man smelled of fresh linen and lemon. He was dressed neatly in a long mid-blue blazer and white trousers. Hair tonic of some kind kept his thin brown hair close to his head. He wore rimless glasses. He was pale, a man not used to going outdoors much.

Cold. Cold. He shivered. His teeth chattered. A wet towel filled with ice was draped around his shoulders. It reached to the bottom of his jaw. A rivulet of water ran down the side of his face as he moved. He tried to reach it with his tongue.

"Well, brother," the white man said, "you almost died. It turned out that a tooth broke off when the Lord took them. It got infected, near killed you. Funny a little thing like that can almost kill a man.

"In a way you might say you rose, rose up from the dead. Doctor Leatham looked in for a meal and said to get the dentist. I hate dentists myself. Our Lord Jesus didn't have a dentist. But the fool dentist did have the right tools. Little Boss had to use the pliers. You can't expect to get at a broken root with pliers."

He lifted his hand and felt his mouth. No pain, just a soreness. There was a strange empty feeling where the teeth had been. He was careful to show nothing. But he couldn't stop his tongue. It secretly searched for the missing teeth.

"You stole our food, brother," the man said.

"No, suh," he said, shaking his head.

"God hates a thief. When He spies that scourge of the Earth He sends his angels with quivers full to unleash His fury. And He hates liars, too."

"No, suh," Calvin said, shaking his head.

"You are an accursed thief, brother. You are an accursed Hammite who stole the Lord's supper. And you were punished."

The white man leaned back, like he was finished. But he didn't stand up to leave. He sat very still, not moving for a long time.

"What is your name?" he said, finally. "What do they call you?"

"Nigger," Calvin said.

"What?"

"Nigger boy," he whispered.

"Don't use that 'nigger' word in the hearing of God, brother. The Lord Jesus taught us to love our neighbors. All men are our brothers. In the sight of God and his Son, who died for all of us, we are brothers.

"But you black Ethiopians are cursed. It is not your fault, brother. But, who are we to question the will of God? God himself made you our equals; he made you kings of Ethiopia and Pharaohs in Egypt, but he also made you the slaves of Shep and Cush."

As the man spoke his voice rose. His eyes rolled up almost out of sight. His excitement was crazy, frightening. Calvin flattened against the bed, trying to hide.

Then, abruptly, the dandelion voice was back, "Small wonder that accursed people such as you and the other boys here are driven to steal; but we can't let a thief go unpunished anymore than we can let murderers take our loved ones from us."

At last the man stopped talking, saying nothing more for a long time, maybe an hour. Or was it only minutes? Tired and battered, he had no way of rightly judging the passage of time.

"Now, what is your name, brother? Tell me your real name."

"Calvin, suh."

The man nodded.

"Where do you stay, Calvin?"

He shook his head.

"Where is your home?"

"Ain't got no home."

The dandelion man stared for a while, then smiled with the same inner excitement.

What? Calvin wondered.

"I want you to serve me, brother," the man said. "Serve me, brother. Serve Jesus. Serve us who love you and you will be saved."

Sounds came from the front of the diner. Cooks were preparing dinner. He thought of the forest. He thought of the trees and the hated pine needles. At the thought of the cold he shivered inside. But he still said nothing.

The man stared at him with wild eyes. But just as strange was the soft gentle voice.

"Yes, it is what our Lord wants. You are saved, brother. When the dentist pulled the last of your tooth the corruption, the poison of Satan flowed out. Sweeter than the sweetest candy the pus poured out of your body, cleansing it. And you were reborn. Yes, you were reborn, brother, to serve your destiny. I will say it, I will say it for Jesus. You have found your Master."

The white man dropped to his knees, "Praise the Lord!"

Praise the Lord? Calvin thought.

"Praise be to God!" the Steward of the dining car 'Azalea,' cried, tears flowing down his cheeks.

Calvin looked at the tear-stained, upraised face of this strange white man and whispered, "Yes, thank you sweet Jesus."

PERICLES SANDERS was Steward of the Flyer's second section dining car, the diner that was made up with the train in Atlanta, then was dropped off near Spartanburg, or, during the summer, at Greensboro, for the return run. To Sander's family in Baltimore he was Perry or Daddy, but to the eleven-man complement of waiters, chefs and kitchen crew of the Flyer's Saloon 'Azalea' diner he was Boss.

The man who ran the railroad.

Sanders was in charge of the Azalea for the railroad. Nothing else. But no one could tell his crew that. And it didn't take long for any skeptical newcomer to see what they were talking about. Unless Sanders allowed it no one passed through the front etched glass door of the Azalea. Coats and ties were required of the men. As for the women, Sanders standards were more subtle, going beyond the published requirement of dresses and stockings to exclude those women with small children or with too much make-up. Anything more than a small amount of lipstick could result in respectable women being sent, often in tears, back to their cars to wait for service. Sanders was not a forgiving man. He did not excuse mistakes. Any business run without mistakes, or nearly so, should operate at a high level of success. And the Azalea operated at the highest level, a level that most assumed was based on hard work and attention to the needs of the passengers. That was true. But only to a point. Fear was the overriding factor in the Azalea's success. A fear that each member of the dining crew felt of Sanders, a fear that went beyond losing their jobs, a fear that even seemed to be shared by the silent management of the railroad company whenever it was suggested that Sanders, the Steward, was presuming too much.

That fear, unnamed, existing only at some subconscious, visceral level, was the strange fear all men seem to have of religious zealots, those who are willing to kill *you* for their god.

"GODDAMN, Red Man," Calvin said to the waiter with the orange hair and freckles. "You are one smart nigger. How you know I ain't filled that straight?"

Red Man, a waiter on Washington and Southern's diner, smiled broadly. White teeth flashed, blooming from a mouth that seemed too small to hold their large square brightness. A winner of the last hand, but not on the evening, Red Man would be back tomorrow night. To get Red Man and his money to come back to the poker table Calvin had had to lose the last hand. He'd had to ignore the fact that a nine spot had already been played three times.

FIVE YEARS after coming to work on the Azalea Calvin was an assistant cook. In the beginning Boss had put him to work washing dishes. That, and doing anything else Boss and Little Boss, the Assistant Steward, wanted. The two white men had seemed the same to him then because they were about the same size and dressed pretty much alike. Except the piping on Boss's blue coat was gold instead of silver.

But then one day in Atlanta Little Boss sent him on an errand to deliver a package to the Steward of the Mobile Trace. The Trace's Steward, a man called Captain Johnny, sent back another package to Little Boss. This happened three or four times over several months, always while they were laying over in Atlanta. But after a while Captain Johnny stopped sending packages back to Little Boss. And Calvin knew then that Little Boss was stealing from the Azalea.

The Azalea was about the only dining car in the Atlanta yards where a little stealing wasn't part of the pay. It didn't take long for him to figure out that Little Boss was putting him in the way of blame. If Boss ever found out it would be Little Boss's word against his.

For a long time he pondered what to do, all the while making the trips across the Atlanta yard, each time carrying a wrapped package of whatever Little Boss had stolen and was selling to Captain Johnny. Finally, he made up his mind.

Two days later he delivered not one but two packages to the

Mobile Trace. All he could do then was wait. Fighting an urge
to run, he could hardly eat for two days. Then on the third
morning word flashed across Alabama to the Atlanta yards how
maggots had erupted out of a carcass found in old flour in the
Mobile Trace's kitchen, how the white wormy creatures had
exploded out onto the passage way at dinner time and how the
tender maggots were crushed underfoot to cause a disgusting-
ly slippery passageway into the elegant dining car.

In all the turmoil afterward, with Captain Johnny being
"retired," with all forty-two other dining cars, including the
Azalea, searching their lockers and bins, no one ever connected
Little Boss's packages or him to the maggots. Little Boss may
have looked at him in a funny way a few times but that was all.
He was never asked to make any more deliveries to any other
cars.

So, except for Little Boss he was happy with his work on the
Azalea. Dishwasher, then kitchen man, finally assistant cook.
Nearly twenty years old and almost a cook on the most famous
railroad diner in the country. About that time he began to strut
a little. Not only an assistant cook he had also learned to read
and to add and subtract his numbers.

Boss had given him the books and had taught him by
answering questions. But then one day three years after they
started Boss stopped the books and wouldn't answer any more
questions.

"You've had what learning is proper, brother Calvin," Boss
explained. "The children of Ham weren't meant to know more
than the brethren."

He wanted to know plenty more; but by then he did whatever Boss wanted. No questions. He was, he thought, no longer
a nigger; he was a Negro, a Negro with pride a mile high and

ten miles wide. No. He didn't complain when Boss took away his books. He knew better. Complaining never got you nothing. That was as true for Negroes as for niggers.

THE REGULAR poker players, the boys Calvin won money from night after night in Atlanta and Washington—Red Man and Gee Gee and the others—never stopped to wonder why he never complained about anything, not even losing at cards. To them the 'Ice Man' was the luckiest poker player alive. Some whispered the cheatingest. But what everyone could agree on was that the Ice Man didn't drink liquor or mess with the young nigger girls that liked to hang around the crew dormitories.

"Ice Man," Likker Dick said now after losing for the third straight night, "your 'ole daddy must've been a jackass for sure. Otherwise you be screwing that Poppy bitch now 'stead of taking my money."

Several of the players nodded, grinning.

Then Likker Dick, who should have known better, said, "Drop your drawers and give us a look-see. Bet there ain't nothing swinging there 'cept an ole candle without no wick."

The table fell silent. He let the silence grow, let it dig into them a little, then laughed. No one else did, not even Likker Dick who suddenly had a stricken look on his face.

"Let's play cards, Mr. Likker Dick," Calvin said. "You still got money sittin' in front of you, man. I mean to have it all."

He laughed again. Tonight he wouldn't have to lose to Likker Dick, or to any of them. The little New Orleans nigger's insult had given him the right to skin them all alive. For this night's game at least he wouldn't have to be careful to lose once in a while just to make it look good.

He remembered all the cards. Sometimes when he was trying to lose he could actually see the spots of the face down card. Hard, it was the hardest thing, knowing you had a winning hand, and then folding it. When that got too obvious he had to figure out another way to lose without it being plain to everybody. He began to overplay the hands, staying in the game until the next to last or last card and then betting the hand. Sometimes he won, but more often than not he lost. In that way he won steadily but not in a way that kept players away for too long. Sooner or later the money on the table would draw them back to lose the money in their pockets.

Somehow Boss heard, as he heard everything, that he was the Ice Man.

"Gambling is a sin, brother," Boss said.

"This ain't gambling, Boss," he said. "Now, if I was shootin' dice, that would be gambling. This here's just plain hard work."

After five years he thought he understood Boss pretty well. To his mind Boss was a hard but fair man. But no one in the crew, him included, could ever please the man. He cussed and yelled at everybody, especially him. And Boss always seemed to get the maddest at him around other people.

"Why do I let you cook," Boss complained. "You are too big for the galley. Your hands are too big. Look at how big your feet are. We all trip over your feet. I'd put you in the front if I could."

That was another of Boss's insults. Only the light-skinned colored worked out front. He was too black, or as Boss said, more black than the pitch tar that streaked the railroad ties below. Everybody knew he would never leave the galley of the Azalea.

"You are ungrateful for all I have done for you," Sanders

would say to him. "I have done everything for you. Tell me, brother, what have you ever done for me? Except eat my food and take my money, what have you ever done for me?"

"Nothin' Boss," he would say.

"Well, it's about time you started."

Usually there would be a pause, Sanders waiting for him to argue or to say something. But, in the half-dozen or so times that the scene was replayed for all in the galley to hear, he never answered.

Finally, Sanders would say, "You're getting too big for me to keep. I've got to get rid of you. Looks like I'll have to send you home. What do you say to that?"

"Yes suh, Mr. Bossman, suh," he would always say.

If Calvin smiled, as he always did, that would be the end of it until the next time.

YOU TRAIN a nigger, Little Boss liked to say, the same way you do a good bird dog. First, you kick the shit out of him to show him exactly who is boss, and then you kick the shit out of him again to make sure he remembers. That's the only way a dog learns to hunt birds good. The same is true for niggers; unless they are scared of what you might do to them they'll just lie around all day eating your food and sucking you dry. Niggers, he said, are a luxury you can't afford unless you are willing to beat the piss out of them.

That was what made it all so hard to understand. It was Little Boss they all hated. At one time or another almost every one of them had threatened to kill him. And one of them might have got the courage to do what they just whispered about if he ever had the chance. But no one ever did.

Because after what happened on the Azalea Little Boss left in the middle of the night without a word to anyone. And they never saw him again.

BEFORE the first call for dinner the routine on the Azalea was for Boss to come out of his small office at the rear of the car to inspect the tables and the waiters. That day, as was his custom, Boss passed the open galley door—which would be closed during dinner. He popped his head in to complain about something, then walked out into the dining area. Little Boss, whose place was in front or at the entrance of the Azalea whenever Boss was not there, walked to the center of the car to meet the Steward. To this point everyone agreed on what had happened.

But what followed next was so confused in their minds that Calvin never did find out for sure if Little Boss, or Boss, did something to cause it, or if it happened the way most of the stories said....

One of the waiters, Hector, a thirty-three-year old Negro from Newport News, suddenly and with no warning, hurled himself across the narrow car toward the two white men. Little Boss's back was to Hector so he couldn't see him coming. Boss, bored with the routine of serving just one of more than six thousand similar dinners, yawned. Eyes shut in the reflex of the yawn Boss didn't see Hector until he was right on top of him. But everyone who saw the fury of Hector's attack on Boss said it wouldn't have made any difference whether Boss's eyes were open or shut.

Hector flew past Little Boss without a glance. He threw himself on Boss with the fury and purpose of a madman. Hector, who had been one of the Azalea's most cheerful and popular waiters, knocked Boss to the floor and began to strangle him.

At first no one could move. Then two of the waiters ran over and tried to pull Hector off Boss. But they were ordinary men trying to stop a raging lunatic with the mad strength of ten men. When Benny and Claude, the two waiters, couldn't get Hector off Boss they began to wail and curse. These sounds and the scene in front of them, one of their own sitting on top of the man who controlled their lives, triggered some deep, violent response in the other waiters. Suddenly, like a school of piranha attracted by the smell of blood, the other waiters joined in what, in only a few seconds, became a frenzied wild attack. They attacked, but without any purpose. Cursing, they lashed out at anything within reach and fought among themselves.

In the galley the others heard loud voices and the sounds of fighting. They ran in. At the center of the dining car was a melee, twisted bodies thrashing about among the upended chairs. The anchored dining room tables stood bare. The linen and service, so carefully laid only minutes before, were now strewn about, scattered among decapitated flowers and broken glass.

No one could tell what was happening. Everybody seemed to have gone crazy at once. Like the others for a moment Calvin didn't know what to do. He stood watching, paralyzed with indecision. Out of the corner of his eye he saw Little Boss standing apart, up near the front. The Assistant Steward was looking away, in the opposite direction, as if embarrassed to have any passengers see the brawl.

No, Little Boss was looking to run.

Calvin took all this in in an instant. In that same instant he saw the flash of Boss's white trousers and smelled the sour odor of hate. The smell was so strong he didn't need to know anything else. Someone was dead, or about to be.

He jumped in among the writhing, wrestling waiters and with strong hands pulled arms and legs apart. Digging hard he ripped pants and shredded shirts. He aimed kicks for places he couldn't reach. In a short time he separated most of the fighters, then kept them apart with rough pokes and threats.

As quickly as it had started the wild fight was over.

Except for Hector. He was still clamped onto Boss's throat. He held tight with a two-handed, vise-like grip. He had to break Hector's fingers to make him let go. Hector screamed in pain, then, teeth bared, he dove at Calvin's legs like a wild animal. Calvin brought his heavy hand down hard against the side of Hector's head. The waiter fell unconscious to the floor. Blood oozed from one ear.

Sanders lay still on the floor. He was pale, he seemed close to death. His glasses were gone. There was a scarlet welt alongside and under his right ear. As Calvin looked at Boss he thought that Hector must be left-handed. He'd never noticed that before. And Boss's white pants were dirty. More than dirty. They were stained dark where the sleeve of his left arm lay on the trousers.

He saw it then. The knife. As he saw it Boss opened his eyes.

The crew gathered in a rough semi-circle near where Boss lay. They looked down at him. They stared at the knife. They shifted about nervously, hesitant to do anything without being told. No one was about to touch the white man. It was up to him to say, to tell them what to do.

Boss gazed at them, one by one, until, finally, he spoke to Calvin.

"You'll have to help me," he said in a faint voice. "You'll have to help me to my feet."

It was an ordinary dinner knife, a knife like those laid out at every place at every meal. It had been driven through the tough fabric of the mid-blue jacket, driven through the skin and muscle of Boss's left forearm just below the elbow before stopping somewhere on the inside of the coat sleeve. The blood was now trickling down in small rivulets from the hidden wound to a soggy slough of blood. As they watched it grew to a small red lake on the Steward's pants.

Braced, Calvin gently helped Boss to his feet, careful not to touch the knife. Boss leaned weakly against him. Calvin waited for instructions but none came. When he was sure there wouldn't be any he led the Steward toward the back of the car. After a few shuffling steps they stopped. With Boss held against falling, he turned back and looked at the others.

Little Boss had disappeared. The others, the once proud waiters of the Azalea, now ragged and torn, looked lost and frightened. They stared at him hopefully.

"Better you put the 'No Service' sign up Claude," he said. "And one of you—you, Henry, you not so tore up—has to go and make the call. You got to tell them passengers that the stove done broke down and there won't be no more cooking today on the Azalea."

He thought for a moment, "And tell them we are right sorry."

Then he turned and helped Boss to the back.

THE CREW spent the next two months in Atlanta waiting for Boss to recover. After the incident the men in New Orleans who ran the company pulled the Azalea in and dismantled her.

Then right before Boss got back, all the waiters were fired. Claude, who had been with Boss from the start, wandered for days like a lost child among the dormitory beds. All the others had been gone a week when two uniformed security officers came in and made Claude leave the company's property.

The security people had taken Hector off the train at Charlotte. Calvin had watched as two of his kitchen helpers had carried the stretcher with Hector on it into the shed next to the company office. Boss had watched, too, but said nothing.

THE NIGHT of the stabbing it had taken hospital surgeons two hours to remove the knife wedged in Boss's arm. Before he'd taken Boss to the hospital Calvin had had to clean the blood off. And as he'd gently raised the arm to cut off the coat Boss had screamed. Screamed in pain. And fear. And then Sanders had cursed him. Sobbing he had cursed him and all niggers. But Boss had just seen the dinner knife lodged in its terrible place. Somehow Calvin understood that Boss's cries of pain and his curses didn't have so much to do with the knife sticking in his arm as with what had put it there.

WHEN BOSS and Calvin came back to work it was on the dining car, 'Holcomb.' As on the Azalea the Steward was Pericles Sanders. Although Boss walked a little slower and, for the first time, seemed to be slightly hard of hearing, no one who didn't know him well would have noticed the difference. At first even he didn't see it.

Calvin had a new job. He was the head waiter. Boss couldn't make him Assistant Steward so he became head of the waiters.

There was so much for him to learn about waiting tables

and memorizing menus and passengers names that for many months Boss was just a bluish blur, his usual tyrannical presence. But then Calvin began to notice things. First, Boss never came out of his office, either to give orders in the kitchen or to supervise serving in the dining area, unless Calvin was present. At first he thought it just happened that way, but he soon saw that it wasn't just chance. Boss wouldn't move among the other Negroes without him. Then he discovered that Boss was living on the Holcomb. It didn't happen all at once; it was gradual. But by the end of their first year on the Holcomb, Boss was spending all of his time on the dining car. He realized then what Boss was doing.

He had moved onto the Holcomb to die.

FIVE YEARS LATER when Pericles Sanders lay dead in his oak coffin at Major Thomas's Funeral Home in Baltimore they made Calvin wait outside until the family and last visitors were gone. When at last he stood alone next to the coffin he gazed down at Boss's sunken, waxen face.

"Yes suh, Mr. Bossman, suh," he said, "I come to say goodbye. We're alone now just like always lately so there ain't nobody what's gonna hear us. You probably wondering what's gonna happen to the Holcomb boys. Well, there's talk they'll take the Holcomb to Atlanta and make her a yards car. Can't be too soon for me. Never did like the Holcomb. Course we was spoiled by the 'Z'. Us boys lucky enough to work on the 'Z' don't look so kindly on them trashy cars they's building these days."

He stopped talking. It was almost as if he were waiting for Sanders to answer.

Then Calvin said, "I supposed you wondered why I never

said nothing about being obliged for your helping me to learn my numbers…and to read. Course, you didn't help me none with learning to write, but it's the truth sure enough that I wouldn't have learned to write if you hadn't showed me how to read. Some might say I'm obliged. I ain't one of them. It's the truth that you took me in and fed me, but you know I worked hard for what you give me. Some might say though that learning me puts you ahead and me behind. Well, you and me know that that ain't true. When you take part of a man you can never pay it back. When you had Little Boss take my teeth with them pliers you got behind for good."

He raised his head in thought. After a few moments he sighed, then said, "That's all. That's all I come to say."

THE PACKAGE arrived over a year after Boss's death. Calvin had played poker that night. And lost. He hadn't been able to keep his mind on the cards. Something had made him uneasy. He'd folded a promising hand and left for the yards, arriving more than an hour before the second section was due to pull out for Atlanta at 11:00 P.M.

The package, addressed to him by name, was sitting on the top of his linen. His name on the package should have alerted him. But, he didn't notice. The Pullman Company, where he had worked as a porter since Boss died, often packaged special soaps and toiletries. Thinking it was that he put it aside to open after the departure.

It was after midnight when he finally opened it. About the size of a shoe box, it had been wrapped twice. As he unwrapped it, carefully unknotting the string that held the outer covering of brown wrapping paper, a note from Samantha Sanders, Boss's daughter, fluttered to the floor:

"Dear Calvin—

My father wanted you to have this box. It was in his will. I'm sorry that it's taken so long but I wasn't able to send it until Mama was gone. She died on the sixth of last month and my brothers and I have been trying to sort it all out.

"Hope you are well—

"Samantha

"P.S. You may not remember, but I rode the Azalea a lot between Baltimore and Washington when I was a little girl."

It was a shoe box. A box that had once contained a pair of Debutante Shoes ("Size 6 1/2"), one whose top had been glued with added paper where it had been torn at the corners through frequent use.

But in fact it was Boss's 'Treasure Box.' All the waiters had had to give Boss twenty-five cents of every dollar of their tip money. The waiters put Boss's share into the Treasure Box which always sat in the same place on the corner of Boss's small desk. You put the money in the box and—as Boss was famous for saying—no questions asked if you didn't try to cheat him.

He began to carefully remove the contents of the box.

First, a faded copy of an announcement that the Southern Railroad would be running the dining car, Azalea, Pericles Sanders-Steward, on the Flyer commencing August 24, 1901. Then Calvin found a large number of keys, keys to all the Azalea's and the Holcomb's doors, including the liquor chests and the meat lockers. On a separate chain was a plated silver wine steward's key with "Azalea" breasting the open ring as if some elderly silversmith had written it with a looping, spidery hand. And there were three paper sleeves each about one and one-half inches wide and three inches long. Something was in each of the sleeves wrapped in tissue paper.

For a moment or two he turned over the small green and white packages, trying to guess what was inside. Then he carefully lay each aside, unopened. At the bottom of the Treasure Box he found Boss's bible. Under its front cover was an envelope addressed to him.

The writing on the envelope was shaky and hesitant, but the hand that had written the letter inside started out strong:

"Brother Calvin!

"The Lord be with you.

"A railroad man doesn't need to write letters. He is there before the letter. My father used to say What's the use? Why write something that's already been told? I never wrote letters because there was no need.

"But what I want to say is better put in writing."

And then Boss's handwriting changed, almost imperceptibly. It was more exact, more carefully drawn, as if Boss had self-consciously begun to form each and every word. But nothing else was different. The same color ink picked up where it had left off on the same piece of the Holcomb's stationery. Yet Calvin read what followed and knew that months, maybe years, had passed with the letter incomplete:

"The love of God is our only reward. What one man does for another is always too little in our Lord's eyes. We are imperfect. We are sinners whose only hope is Jesus's love."

The letter broke off here again. There was a gap—like a long pause—on the paper, and where the letter resumed the change was startling. Shaky, crabbed words, some broken and others illegible from ink stains alternated, faint and bold, as if Boss were moving in and out of consciousness. It was as if death itself guided his hand.

> "My time has come. I tried to live as He wanted. I did not always succeed. God forgive me! 'Fear not says the Lord for He is with us.'
>
> "Calvin, my friend, I have no fear.
>
> "I have left you my Box."

It was signed "P. Sanders."

One by one Calvin opened the green and white sleeves. And then looked with confusion at what rested on the table in front of him. Then, slowly, a smile broke through his frown of concentration. Out of habit he sucked in cold air through the spaces of his teeth. Then the grin on his face turned into deep rumbling laughter.

On the table lay two perfectly formed but oversized gold eye teeth. And between them the fifty dollar gold piece for the dentist.

3

As RALEIGH BACON walked out of his bedroom he heard Robert wheeling his squeaky barrow past the front living room windows heading for the lowest terrace next to Aiken Road. A bank of the lawn was washed out there; a red clay gash had appeared after the last big rain. It needed to be fixed, smoothed out and the clay top-dressed.

To satisfy himself that's where Robert was heading Raleigh paused to look out the window. The gray-haired colored man had just maneuvered the barrow of black dirt down over the first rise. Now as he moved across the wide expanse of lawn to the middle terrace he gradually sank from sight until all you could see was his top half, his head rhythmically bobbing up and down in time with slow steps. Robert didn't have his tools, no shovels, no rake, nothing. If he was willing to wait long enough he would see the old man trudge all the way back up the hill to get them. A complete waste of time. He shook his head in annoyance, then went in to breakfast.

As he settled into his place at the head of the dining room table, its rich wood gleaming, reflecting the carefully arranged sterling and the crisp white linen of his place mat and napkin, Raleigh looked at his pocket watch, a gold Elgin. Ten minutes of seven. The watch had belonged to his father. Old TJ Bacon had given it to him the day Raleigh took over the mill. That was in 1929 and the watch still kept perfect time. He picked up *The Athena News.* He read for a few minutes. But he couldn't concentrate. He was re-reading sentences and entire paragraphs. Annoyed with this waste of time he put the paper aside.

Calvin came in from the kitchen. In silence he served the first part of Raleigh's breakfast: coffee, one three-minute egg, a patty of country sausage and a covered silver chafing dish that contained either grits or oatmeal. This morning it happened to be grits. A portion of game or fish, most often smoked mackerel, would be served next along with buttered toast. On some days berries, or other fruits in season, were the last serving, a kind of gentle surprise that often, but not always, elicited the first words spoken that particular day by either man.

"Mighty sweet," Raleigh said later as he finished the fruit. "Firm."

Calvin nodded, pleased that Mr. Faxon's first freestone Alberta peaches tasted as good as they looked.

"See that Robert finishes fixing that washout sometime today."

"Yessuh," Calvin said, smiling. "I'll take care that Robert finishes up."

"Sometimes I think we should get a new yardman."

"Oh, nosuh. Robert ain't the fastest yardman alive, but he's mighty steady."

With his napkin Raleigh dabbed the remnants of peach juice off his mouth, grunting noncommittally in response to Calvin's support of Robert. As expected. The truth was he counted on Calvin's nearly supernatural understanding of his moods, even, it sometimes seemed, knowing what he was thinking. Today for instance. Today he really was not himself. He hadn't known it at first. An active man, not given to monitoring his own moods, he hadn't realized that anything was different. But he was out of sorts. His critical reaction to Robert's familiar work habits should have told him something. It was only after eating a good breakfast without much pleasure that he finally understood what was happening.

The usual at the mill, and Elizabeth could be counted on to keep him awake nights, but the big worry today was the boy. In the last month—starting almost from the moment he arrived—Billy had tried to run away at least three times, the last time only the week before. The boy had been picked up on the Ashville road by a neighbor, Jefferson Poag, who lived down Aiken Road. When he brought Billy back to the house Poag had asked a lot of fool questions, about things that were none of his business. He'd had to be more rude to Poag than he liked.

Calvin was busy clearing his dishes from the table. The grandfather clock in the hall struck the quarter-hour, Raleigh's usual signal to get ready to drive over to the mill. He didn't move. Instead he picked up the newspaper again and glanced through it. He read that there had been a two-alarm fire in the train depot storage annex, and the German Army was about to overrun the Russians.

He looked up. Calvin was standing at the far end of the table, exactly where he expected to see him. The tray with the cleared dishes was sitting on the sideboard.

"Somebody has got to do something about this fellow Hitler," he said.

"Yessuh."

"The Bolsheviks are murderers, no question about that. But this fellow, Hitler, has to be stopped."

Calvin nodded.

He glanced through the paper for another few seconds before putting it aside.

"I'm considering sending Billy back to Elizabeth," he said.

Calvin waited silently. He seemed to know that Raleigh was only trying to sort out his thoughts

"He's been a lot more trouble than I expected," Raleigh said.

Raleigh knew that you don't just uproot a young boy and throw him together with people who, though family, are really little more than strangers without expecting some trouble. He'd known of course how different the boys were, but he hadn't understood how strong-minded and stubborn Billy could be. Worse yet the boy's defiance seemed to grow each time he tried to get back to Pineville. Billy was starting to affect everybody around him. He worried that TJ might get ideas, or worse, lose his self-confidence in Billy's shadow. And yet, in good conscience, he couldn't send Billy to live with Elizabeth any sooner than he had to. Because if Elizabeth got her selfish hands on him....

"Poag enjoyed telling me that we were handling Billy all wrong," Raleigh said. "The old fool. He should have to watch Billy all the time. He'd learn quick enough that you can't just lock the boy in his room."

A slow laugh rumbled up from Calvin's throat.

"Billy is awful smart," Calvin said. "You might even say he's slick. Just when I think I know where he's at he's half way to Charlotte."

"I don't think I can take the responsibility of him running out to the highway every week. Better to send him to Elizabeth."

Now *there* was the question.

Raleigh was used to waiting for Calvin's answer, for days if need be. He'd learned over the years that the big colored man couldn't be hurried. Nor was he predictable in what he might say or do. So this morning Raleigh, as he started to rise from the table, was a bit surprised to hear Calvin clear his throat, a hint that he had something to say now.

Raleigh settled back in his seat.

Calvin wiped his hands on his apron and spoke slowly, "Well, Mister Raleigh, I expect Billy's running days is over, leastways for a while. Why don't you give him to me for a few weeks. I think that I can pretty much make sure it don't happen again."

How could Calvin be so sure?

Raleigh probed, "I have noticed a little change since old man Poag brought him back last week. Seems quieter. Maybe he's decided to stop this foolishness?"

"Yessuh, I think that's right."

"I hope so. But tell me why you think so."

"Mister Sonny, he gone back into the hospital."

Sonny back in the hospital! Hadn't heard that. By rights he should be one of the first to know. But Calvin knowing about Sonny before he did wasn't that surprising. The nigras' lightning-fast privy "telegraph" almost always beat the pants off the real thing. The telephones in white parts of town were often used just to confirm what the nigras had already reported. Raleigh had always viewed the privy line with amusement since its information could be as wild as it was sometimes accurate. Somehow, though, he knew the news about Sonny was right. That could explain why Billy seemed a bit more tractable lately. Before, every time Billy had run off he'd been trying to get to where Sonny was. Somehow Billy had heard. Now with his daddy back in the hospital the boy didn't have any place to run to.

"Well," Raleigh said, rising from the table, "with things

being as they are this is the time to give him to you to set straight. So, take him. Take the boy. He's all yours, Calvin."

He smiled when he said this, as if it were one of their private jokes, but when he left the house it was with a big sense of relief.

"MY NAME is Bacon. Raleigh Bacon, from Athena," Raleigh had said to Calvin that time. Then he'd offered his hand. It wasn't the first time that one of them had spoken to the other, but it was the first time that made any difference.

It was the summer of 1929 on the Flyer, The Potomac Flyer, running between Atlanta and Washington, D.C. Raleigh had been riding the Flyer to Washington regularly on business since early in the year. More often than not he'd ended up in Calvin's car, an all-bedroom Pullman sleeper. To Calvin Raleigh was probably just another passenger. But by the end of that final trip to Washington Raleigh was resolved.

In Washington he'd put out his hand to say goodbye. To this day he remembered how Calvin's hand felt in his. It was limp, as if shaking hands with a white man had to be handled carefully, as if the act itself summed up the difference between a Pullman porter and a white passenger. It seemed to say that Negroes' hands were for hard work and not for dangerous, often misunderstood things such as shaking a white man's hand.

There was of course a line that respectable people, black or white, didn't cross. Yet there were permissible touchings. For instance, Pullman porters, like Calvin at that time, guided their passengers up and down vestibule steps with a light touch.

They delivered clean hand towels into groping hands. They made beds, shined shoes, cleaned compartments, supplied playing cards, occasional still liquor and sometimes tended to unwell passengers in spaces that were too small almost for one man alone.

But even in those ways Calvin was different. He never intruded, either physically or with unwanted conversation. Instead he always anticipated his passengers' needs; it was almost as if the big colored man didn't exist. Calvin did his job so well that many of the passengers wouldn't remember him at all.

Invisible, yes. But not obsequious. Calvin was curiously uninterested in the tips thrust into his hands—almost to the point of rudeness. Here was a remarkable looking colored man with his hand out, but not out, not really. Here was a correctly polite Negro who didn't give a fig.

Raleigh was intrigued.

When the train pulled into Washington that last time he had asked Calvin to come to work for him. Of course he'd sensed Calvin would be a good and loyal servant, or he wouldn't have wanted him in his home. He realized now—maybe for the first time—that his motive had been more complicated than that. It was the smoldering blackness and hard intelligent eyes that had really attracted him. Calvin was a throwback, a maverick, out of place in time. Now Raleigh understood that despite the obvious risks he'd felt obliged to know the man better.

Back then on the Flyer Calvin hadn't given his answer directly. Instead he answered with his eyes. He'd looked at Raleigh. He covered the unequal space between them with some of his own. With a nod and smile he returned the pressure of the handshake, then walked into Raleigh's compartment.

AT THE MILL Raleigh found his brother, Sam, waiting for him in his office. The sight of his brother sitting there made him wonder if this explained his waking up feeling sour. Had he sensed this trouble to come?

"Why, Sam, good morning."

"Good morning, brother," Sam said.

His brother, Seneca Marcellus Bacon, seldom got to work before ten, and he usually made a point of insisting that Raleigh come to see him, this despite the fact that Raleigh had been president of Bacon Mills now for over fifteen years.

As usual, or perhaps because he so seldom saw Sam, he was struck by what a fine looking man Sam was. He seemed the younger of the two of them. His unlined, apple-cheeked appearance radiated good health and bonhomie. But Raleigh had seen the same network of veins and capillaries bulging with anger too many times not to be wary of Sam's visits.

"How is Lloyd?" he asked politely.

"Why she's fine. Just fine. Working with the Garden Club as hard as when she was president."

"Well, give her my regards."

Purely out of habit he waited for the reciprocal courtesy. But Sam did not ask about Dot.

Instead he pulled his pipe from his coat pocket. He went through the motions of inspecting it. Next he struck two matches against the sole of his shoe and made a show of lighting the pipe. A thin disguise of rude behavior. And meant to be. Raleigh marveled at how expert nasty people were at their nastiness.

As with the sumac the internecine poison bred into the Bacons seemed to spring out of some natural, ever existing condition in the family, going back almost to the beginning.

Inevitable as nature itself. Raleigh had lately begun to worry about the poison spreading and infecting TJ. Would TJ have the stomach when the time came to do what was necessary to protect his mother and sister?

When Raleigh had come home from Harvard in 1911, Sam, whom their father, Thurston John Bacon III, had groomed for ten years to take over the mill, had just moved into the president's office. But by 1917 Sam had long since proved himself to be inept. Arrogant and indecisive—their sister, Vickie, said that Sam was the only man in Athena who could be arrogant about not making a decision—Sam failed to anticipate the upsurge of business the First World War would mean for the cotton mills of the South. Had it not been for Raleigh's insistence that his father review Sam's conservative business plan for Bacon Mills, the Bacon business would have been trampled to death by their competition in the rush to supply the cotton needs of the nation. Sam was thrust aside by old TJ, who resumed the presidency of Bacon Mills and who, with his help, guided Bacon Mills back to prosperity.

So Sam's and Danny's hatred of him was nothing new. There was little though that his brothers could do about it. Raleigh had the votes, his, Vickie's and most of the non-family shareholders, to run the mill for as long as he cared to.

Sam's visit was almost certainly about money. It usually was. And soon Sam proved him right. Sam demanded an increase in the dividend.

"It's time, brother," Sam said. "We been holding at five dollars for better than four years now.

Any other day Raleigh might have smoothed the way to the next time, but this morning he felt his patience snap.

"What is the matter with you, Sam? You know what the

Limestone Mill contract will cost. Besides, we discussed this last week."

"Discussed? We have never discussed anything to do with increasing the dividend. You told us there will be no increase, but we have never discussed anything. I'll have you know that I—we, Danfield and I—are most unhappy that you care so little about the needs of your family."

Raleigh scoffed, "You and Lloyd have plenty of money. Why keep bringing this up? You know we can't afford to raise the dividend now."

"How dare you tell me how to spend my money," Sam said. "How dare you put your nose in my business. Danny and me, we don't mean to put up with what's going on here one more minute—"

At that moment Miss Christopher, Raleigh's elderly secretary, came into the large office with the last month's sales figures. She looked startled to find Sam Bacon there. As soon as she handed Raleigh the report she turned to leave. He stopped her.

"Would you please wait one minute Miss Christopher. Mr. Sam has just decided to leave Bacon Mills. You will find old Mr. TJ's letter of resignation in the minute book. Please copy that for Mr. Sam's signature."

"Do you want to wait, Sam?" he asked politely. "Or Miss Christopher could bring it to your office when she's through?"

"OH, MY, Mr. Bacon," Miss Christopher said after Sam left.

"Yes," he sighed. "I know."

They both understood, as did Sam, that no resignation letter would be typed that day. And perhaps never, although he did toy with the idea of actually presenting it to Sam, put it in his seldom-used roll-top desk, like a day-old catfish. But he was almost fifty-one. He had to act his age.

He turned to the day's business.

"You said to remind you, today," Miss Christopher said smiling, "to call about the Virginia fishing license for the Homestead trip. I'm suppose to remind you, too, to get one for Calvin."

He and Calvin were due to leave for Hot Springs on the eighteenth. It would be the fifth or sixth such trip. Soon, next year perhaps, he should start to include TJ. Both boys if Billy was still at the house. They were the right age to start learning the fine points of fly fishing. But for this year, perhaps the last, it would be just the two of them.

B ILLY LAY in the bathtub, hidden from the people in the big house, out of sight of Dot Jessop and TJ. Especially from TJ, who, while a friend, could be a pest sometimes with his having to know everything and always wanting to do everything he did. This was where he came to get away. The bathroom, with this bathtub, was part of Papa Bacon's garage. Yet everybody seemed to have forgotten that it was still here. He came here sometimes to hide or sometimes just to feel closer to Pineville.

The bathroom was part of servants' quarters built into the back side of the garage. Two small rooms and a bath. Despite having its own bathroom this place looked like it had never been lived in. It was used for storage now. The two rooms were crammed full of things, window screens, old furniture, folded awnings, steamer trunks, even two old dress mannequins which leaned against each other like armless wrestlers. Everything was draped with sheets which were torn and gray with mold. It was a dirty place. He'd had to crawl through and under a maze of cobwebs and dumped stuff to find the bathroom. The bathroom was also filled with things long-ago forgotten. Like the mattress he lay on now. Like a broken high chair that flipped its wooden tin-lined tray up to let the child in and out. Someone had written *Lizzie* on the chair's backrest. But one thing, a 1935 calendar of a near naked woman, hadn't been in the bathroom before he got there. He'd found the calendar in an old chest of drawers. The lady on it leaned on a big tire with spread legs looking back at you over her shoulder. Her name was Miss Tireless. He had tacked her up on the wall.

The bunk mattress filled the tub and served as his headquarters. He'd stored everything he needed to get back to Pineville in different sized holes under the striped ticking, an old Esso map of North and South Carolina, a compass from the Pathfinder game, a flashlight which he'd taken from the front hall closet, and candy and apples and pieces of bread, all of which had to be replaced since the fruit rotted, the bread got stale and he ate the candy.

He'd eaten the candy because he'd given up running away for the time being. Not because they had caught him. He wouldn't have stopped trying to get home because of that. Sonny was back in the hospital. He'd surprised himself by taking the news of Sonny's new hospitalization pretty calmly. It had happened enough times before that he was pretty sure that Sonny would be home from the hospital within a month. All he had to do was wait a couple of more weeks.

Back of where he was, on the other side of the wall, the dogs snarled in a furious but short-lived fight. Billy hardly heard the high-pitched quarrel. The kennel had been built so that the doghouse itself was smack up against the wall just inches from where his head now rested. The chicken wire enclosing the run included his bathroom window. Dog sounds were so much a part of this place that he didn't hear them any more.

At that moment though a different sound was coming from the other side of the wall. It was a voice, a man's voice, almost too low for the words to be understood amid the dogs' frenzied barks and swooning howls of pleasure. The voice rumbled, like distant thunder, and he realized the man wasn't talking so much as laughing. After a bit the dogs quieted enough for him to actually hear who he'd already guessed was out there. Calvin.

"You're next Miss Ruthie. Hey, Miss Ruthie, darling. Let's see how sharp them little critters' teeths is…. Oh, that's fine, truly fine, darlin'. Hold still for just a minute so's I can….

He imagined Calvin working on Miss Ruthie, putting a little Vaseline on her sore teats. The sound of Calvin's voice faded in and out as he moved around the kennel, competing with crooning howls as each dog, in its turn, got his attention. After a while things quieted down and it was hard to tell what was happening. He put his ear to the wall, straining to hear.

Lately he'd developed a taste for other people's secrets, the kind of things made all the more interesting because somebody was trying to hide them. If a person was willing to go to a lot of trouble to keep you from finding out something about him it made it almost your duty to see that he didn't.

He knew now that Sonny's secret—a secret at least from him—was that Sonny was an addict of some kind, although if asked he wouldn't have been able to say what exactly an addict was, just that it wasn't good. And Papa Bacon's big secret was Grandmother Mary, a hidden secret because TJ had whispered and looked guilty when he said the name of Papa Bacon's first wife, and if TJ himself had no secrets he was the opposite of Emily whose very life was a mystery, a terrible secret. But the most mysterious person of all was Calvin. He had, according to TJ, so many secrets you couldn't even begin to count them, like nobody knew for certain where he lived and—

"What you doing in here boy?"

Billy, stunned, froze up against the wall. In the shock of being found out he was dimly aware that the little bathroom had gone dark. He wanted to run, but there was no place to run to. Calvin's looming figure completely filled the doorway. Behind metal-rimmed glasses black eyes traveled from secret to secret, from the stale bread to the shriveled apples to the Baby Ruth candy wrappers to, finally, Miss Tireless.

He didn't have any say after that. There wasn't any use in arguing with Calvin. You don't argue with any man, black or white, who says something in just the way Calvin had. So he'd had to do what Calvin said, he'd had to climb into the station wagon with Calvin and Black Jim and drive out to somewhere in the country.

They had started out on Tigerville Road. He knew that much. But he had no idea where they were now. Back of him Black Jim was leaning out the window of the car whimpering with excitement. Next to him Calvin tended to his driving; he hadn't bothered to say one word since Billy got in the car.

"How'd you find me, anyway?" Billy demanded, trying hard not to sound scared. "There must be a secret door in there somewhere. I know because I had to crawl through all that stuff, and right before I saw you I didn't hear nothing."

"You left me a trail."

"What do you mean, what kind of trail?"

"A trail as plain as that nose on your face."

After that Calvin wouldn't talk. He was busy looking for something, a road to turn onto or a place to stop. Farther on they did turn onto a dirt road. It ran straight back through some woods. Black Jim was whining and carrying on in the back. Before they even reached the woods he'd squeezed out through the back window and had began running alongside, barking, urging the car on.

They drove into the woods and followed a road for maybe a half mile. Finally they came out of the woods at the edge of a big open field and stopped. All this time Black Jim was running in mad circles around them and didn't stop even when the car did. But when Calvin got out of the car the dog skidded to a stop on his haunches, right at Calvin's feet. He sat there, the muscles of his legs quivering, his tail thrashing the tall grass. Panting furiously, his mouth open, it sure seemed like he was smiling. Then, with just a slight tilt of his head and a half-raised arm, Calvin released Black Jim. The dog lit out across the field. He seemed like a black bullet, speeding a thousand miles an hour, skipping along the top of the tall grass. When he got to a split-rail fence at the far end he zoomed over it like it wasn't there. But in seconds Black Jim was back and running from side to side and from one corner to the other without so much as a sign that he meant to quit running during the twentieth century. Then Calvin whistled through his fingers, a short shrill sound. Black Jim stopped in his tracks.

Calvin moved Black Jim around the field with whistles. He used his hands some, too, but mostly it was the whistles, a combination of long and short, of different tones, which moved Black Jim to where Calvin wanted him.

After about ten minutes Calvin let go with a kind of stutter whistle, a trilling sound, and the moment Black Jim heard it he began to circle, searching for something. He stopped, rooted at something, and then, suddenly, the dog was streaking right at them. When Black Jim was twenty or thirty yards away Billy could see that the dog was holding something in his mouth. It was a big stick, about two feet long.

Black Jim didn't slow down at all. Instead he speeded up, because when he was nine or ten feet away he launched himself into the air with a tremendous jump.

The picture of Black Jim in mid-air froze itself on his brain. The dog's neck and chest, black and glistening, seemed to strain forward. The stick in his mouth was wet with bubbling saliva, and he imagined he heard the first sounds come from the dog, the rasping gurgle of the air forced from his lungs, and the sound of the jump itself, a kind of final thuummp as Black Jim's paws all left the ground at once. And, then, in his imagination, the dog floated, weightless, timeless, and would have never come down if Calvin hadn't grabbed the stick.

Suddenly the stick with Black Jim still clamped onto it was in Calvin's hand. And the static frozen picture in Billy's head dissolved into a dark blur of swinging dog, swooping down to just above the ground, being thrown high into the air. There, at the top, the dog, facing skyward, still biting the stick, burned itself on his brain so strong that he seemed to go blind for a second or two. He couldn't be sure he actually saw Black Jim flip over to land, like Zero or any cat would've.

But he must have. Because the next thing Billy knew Black Jim was sitting at Calvin's feet, smiling, begging for more.

LATER, IN THE CAR, Calvin said to him, "Tell me, Billy Smithson, what do you do with a dog that breaks, that won't hold a line he's supposed to set on?"

"You talking about Black Jim?"

"That's right, I am."

"Not Black Jim. I've never seen a dog trained so good. Even Lindy, Sonny's dog, isn't as good as Black Jim."

"Yes, Black Jim. He's the best retriever I ever saw on the practice field. But with other dogs, with guns close by in a real hunt, he breaks, breaks off on his own before you can give him his commands."

"What makes him do that?"

"I don't rightly know. I'm trying to find out. It's like a hound that won't hunt the pack. A hound that won't hunt the pack is worse than useless. So what do you do with a dog like Black Jim, a dog that won't do what he's supposed to?"

"You could give him away?"

"Who'd take a dog that will only retrieve birds when he feels like it."

"You could let him go?"

"We could, we could do that. But what if he got lost and starved to death off in the woods someplace? Would that be our blame?"

Billy was silent for a few seconds.

"Black Jim is too smart to get lost in the woods."

He waited a few seconds before adding, "And too smart to leave any trail behind."

"You did."

"That's what *you* say."

"Sometimes a trail is no trail at all. Sometimes no tracks tells you the most."

"Huh? No tracks. That's crazy!"

"You didn't leave track one this time. Them other times you lit out for Carolina my kitchen was short of things like a half loaf of bread, maybe three sometimes four apples and them five-cent Baby Ruth candy bars that I bought at the store for my sweet tooth."

"I didn't know they was yours! I'll pay you back."

"Like I said," Calvin continued. "When you was missing all afternoon and there weren't no tracks in my kitchen, when no bread and no apples had been stole, I figured there was only one place other than the woods that a young boy could hide."

They drove on in silence for the next few miles. Black Jim, tired from all his running, was sleeping quietly on a blanket in the back. Billy was thinking about what had just happened, only half-watching the road. Calvin drove right by the turnoff to Aiken Road. About a quarter mile farther on the car slowed and Calvin drove across a shallow ditch toward a stand of pine trees. The car rolled right into the trees before stopping.

"See that?" Calvin said.

"See what?" he said, not knowing what was happening.

"Come with me," Calvin said.

They walked into the woods together. About twenty or twenty-five yards farther in, he saw it.

A car was parked, nestled among trunks of the pines. In the dim light it seemed like a huge animal, like a black rhino, or even an elephant, but as they moved toward it the brooding menace of its presence faded into its details. It was a Chevrolet car. Black, its windshield and door handles gleamed, like a car you might find in a rich man's garage.

They stood together, admiring the automobile.

"I wants to tell you something, Billy Smithson," Calvin said.

Billy nodded.

"This here is my automobile. I keep it here in these woods since it wouldn't be right for me to drive it up to the big house and then leave it sittin' there with all of Mister Bacon's automobiles, taking up space and maybe causing trouble."

"It's beautiful."

"It is right beautiful, ain't it?... Now both of us knows things about the other fellow. I know where you keep hid—in the back of the garage. I know where you'll be if I need to find you. And you know now where I keep my Chevrolet automobile. I don't reckon anybody knows for sure where I keep it but you and me."

On the way home Billy's head swam from trying to figure things out. Black Jim was up now; he had taken to licking Billy's ear. Distracted, confused, he petted the dog and stole looks at Calvin.

But like on the way out Calvin wasn't talking. Instead, he was just humming away.

A COOL TILE FLOOR and two ceiling fans were good reasons for stopping by the barber shop in hot weather. The near-silent fans whooshed in unison to shove moving air against their damp, sun-browned necks. And the black and white floor tiles, worn, cracked in places, seemed to always stay cool no matter how hot it was outside. The tiles were also easy to clean in case someone should miss one of the two brass spittoons. But nobody gathered in Frank's Mid-Town Hair Salon this day would be caught dead with a plug of tobacco in his mouth. Snuff or chewing tobacco meant you were country, like the rubes in from the farms on Saturday mornings, someone to laugh at.

They were all cigarette smokers.

The smoke from their cigarettes, Camels mostly, mingled with fumes of witch hazel and Vitalis and Wildroot Cream Oil. Pungent, sharp, these odors, mixed with their own sweat, lured them first to Frank's and only secondly to Wertheimer's where the heavy smell of rubber reminded them too much of work. These men, a ragged half-dozen, depending on whether Al Wertheimer and Ben Jessop were around, seemed to be always together, to never work and always in need of something to do.

At the moment it was watching Eddie King Jessop getting a shave.

The single barber's chair, raised to its greatest height, was laid as flat as it would go. Eddie King lolled on it under a blue striped sheet. He was talking, holding court. He waved a free arm about, smoking and gesticulating, seemingly paying no attention to Frank's problem of how to shave a face in motion. But about every half-minute he would pause long enough for Frank to wield his razor for a couple of strokes, little by little allowing Frank to earn the twenty-five cents Eddie King paid him every day except Sunday (Frank's was closed Sundays) for his shave.

Raised as it was the barber chair's lifting mechanism was exposed above a white porcelain base. Under the three globe lights hanging from the tin ceiling the chair seemed to them like an operating room table where just now the patient had awakened early, before the operation was over, to insist that only he was capable of performing the surgery.

"Christ almighty, Frank," said Eddie King, "you are slower than molasses. I got things to do, business to take care of, a pot full of things that only Eddie King Jessop can handle and I got to put up with a nigger shave. You'd think you was shaving a nigger. Give me that goddamn razor. I'll do it myself."

He swung his legs over the chair's arms, hopped down and took the straight razor out of Frank's hand. Frank, playing his part, pretended to be insulted, but quickly gave in and smiled. His eyes, though, were wary.

"You owe me ten cents, you robber," Eddie King said.

The others laughed. They all called Frank a robber. Nobody, they hooted, was safe in Frank's, not while Frank the robber had a razor in his hand.

Eddie King, the sheet dragging on the tile floor, made an elaborate show in the mirror of shaving, pulling his upper lip down tight over his teeth and talking like he thought Ronald Coleman was supposed to.

"Frank, Frank," he mimicked the actor. "Frank..." he started again, but couldn't seem to figure out how to bring it off.

He tossed his head in the general direction of the barber.

"How about it, Frank? You ever shave a nigger? You ever did? I mean you ever have to over at the jail? Or somewhere like that?"

That got everybody excited. They all wanted to know what it was like, was it like cutting wire? And how in the fucking world does a fucking nigger barber keep his fucking razor sharp. They all laughed hard enough that Frank didn't need to answer. But he did anyway, denying that he had ever cut a nigger's hair, at the jailhouse, or anywhere. Eddie King gave Frank the razor and climbed back on the chair. He lay still until the barber was finished, even then not bothering to get up.

He was silent, and so were the others. With some uneasiness they waited for Eddie King to break this rare moment of quiet.

Suddenly he sat up.

"We are at a moment of truth," he announced. "A moment of truth. And not one of you nitwits has any idea. You wouldn't know a moment of truth if it bit every one of you in the ass. I mean in the fucking ass!"

They all knew now that an Eddie King joke was coming. Elaborate, obscure, winding, digressive, but nevertheless, a joke. So they laughed and felt free to insult him back. He wouldn't know the truth from Tasmania, because he hadn't made its acquaintance since he was a five-year old squirt. And the only time he ever told the truth he got the clap.

Much laughter, joined in by Eddie King.

"Yessirrebob, a moment of truth," he said. "This here is your chance. The Gamecocks don't need any of you from shit. But you boys have me worried. I mean how could you be so dumb!"

More laughter, made louder than before from relief that the joke has been finally pinned down. Eddie King, a fervent South Carolina Gamecock fan, has been unhappy for most of the fall with the football team's performances. And this Saturday the Gamecocks were a ten-and-one-half point underdog to the Clemson Tigers.

"The Clemson team is just a bunch of pansies," he said. "They only play football so they can take showers together."

He laughed along with the rest, bringing himself almost to the brink of tears. As he laughed he was busy looking around the shop, taking note as to who might be brought over to his side. But no one would budge. They had almost a sure thing with the Tigers, and they weren't about to give it up.

Arms outstretched, head raised, Eddie King implored, "Ain't there no loyalty left in this here world?"

At that moment a dark Chevrolet sedan passed slowly by the front of the shop.

"Did you see what I just seen," one of them cried, pointing at the now empty street.

"What?" Eddie King demanded, always resentful when anyone knew anything before him.

"The nigger's car!"

"Which nigger's car you damn fool?"

"The Chevy. The black Chevy. He drove it right by, as sassy as you please."

Eddie King looked out at the empty street, "Bullshit. You didn't see nothing. The heat's got to you boy."

"Bullshit yourself, Eddie King. I seen the Chevy. I ain't blind, you know."

"You may not be blind, but you're the same asshole who was gonna bet on the fucking Tigers, ain't you? Ain't you!"

"Je-sus Christ! What's that got to do with anything?"

"What's that got to do with anything?" Eddie King mimicked. "Let me tell you, Mr. Smartass. Let me explain a few things. First off, the nigger works for my fucking brother-in-law, Raleigh Bacon. That's Ra-leigh Ba-con in case you don't hear so good. Raleigh Bacon, my fucking brother-in-law. Do you think a man like my brother-in-law allows his nigger to go tooling around in his own car at two o'clock on Thursday afternoons when he is supposed to be taking care of my fucking brother-in-law? Think about that…. Did you see the nigger driving?"

"Well, no. I—"

"You see. You see."

"But it was the car, Eddie King."

"Are you sure?"

"I told you. It was the fucking car!"

"You're sure?"

"Yes!"

"Was the window out? Did you see the fucking cardboard?"

"Well, no."

"You see what I mean."

"He could have got it fixed by now."

"Ain't nobody fixed no nigger's car in this town. You heard Wertheimer. He ought to know."

No point in anybody arguing any more. Eddie King wasn't going to admit the nigger had driven past. Just like he wouldn't admit the nigger was the one who had left the bloody tire iron, claiming that one of them or some other smart-ass sonofabitch had sent it as a joke. And they all knew why. It would mean that the nigger wasn't afraid to drive past the place Eddie King Jessop was known to be found that time of day. More than that it meant the nigger wasn't afraid of Eddie King at all. It would mean, too, that the Chevy had been fixed, and was just as much a kick in the ass as ever.

In the quiet of the shop Eddie King said, "A moment of truth. That's what this is."

The air from the fans took on a momentary chill. They all nodded, in agreement, even though some were not exactly sure what they were agreeing to. But not one of them would have dreamed of doing otherwise.

First of all, Eddie King was smart, smarter than almost any-body but Wertheimer, and even Wertheimer was only really smart about business things. More than that, they were all afraid not to go along with Eddie King. Especially at a time like this. They remembered Charley McDaniels who had disappeared seven years earlier. And they remembered what Eddie King said after Charley was known to be missing.

"Keep in mind Charley McDaniels," he would say vaguely. "Things can happen to a man."

THE RENT COLLECTOR for Blacktown was Sampson Thompson. Each Saturday afternoon Thompson, a small, wizened, leathery-faced man dressed in a dark meeting suit and stiff collar, climbed up and down the streets of Blacktown, collecting nickels and dimes and quarters from colored families who seemed to welcome his weekly visit as an important event in their lives, often offering Thompson food or drink as if he were the preacher come to call. It had something to do with them admiring people with money, or at least people—especially one of their own—who handled it. But mostly it was the mystery of this little man; sit him down, get him talking and maybe you could learn a thing or two.

Although Thompson had a small one-room office at the top of Pine Street, no one knew where he lived. He didn't live in Athena and no one had been able to find out where he did live, although many had tried. Another mystery was who Thompson collected the rents for. He wouldn't say. This led to rumors that Sampson Thompson owned Blacktown.

Blacktown lay west of Calhoun Street, the dividing line between the white and Negro sections of Athena. Calhoun Street itself ran south, past the turn off to Bacon Mills Road, then merged with South Carolina State Highway 14 for the run to Greenville. The streets of Blacktown, Clay, Pine, Sycamore, Stone and the rest, were paved for half a block west of Calhoun where they stopped abruptly, cut off like useless, amputated limbs. But they continued, recognizable as streets because, although dirt and rutted, they were clear and straight with unpainted wooden houses, little more than cabins, lining both sides. The houses ended, finally, a step above the streets' low end where the run-off and floods of Spring had silted a broad red clay moat.

Extending farther west were low vacant fields where nothing grew in the red clay except weeds and an occasional stunted mulberry bush. From the top of Pine Street the rotting quarter-section line fences and the straight walking paths, worn smooth and inhospitable to weeds by many thousands of feet over the years, seemed like the intelligent remains of some dead, ancient civilization. Far in the distance, just beyond the vacant fields at the top of the next rise was State Road, Athena's most industrial street.

The paved end of Sycamore Street crowned at its highest point between Pine and Stone Streets, making it necessary to use stilts to raise the houses there above the gullies on the north and south sides of the street. Most of those supporting stilts were made of brick, but some were wooden four by fours with a few two by fours which, in places, were warped and twisted from the weather. This made the gray unpainted houses above lean and sag toward one side or the other like weathered markers in an old graveyard. Beneath the houses paths ran from back stairs to the privies behind.

Calvin's house on Sycamore was the fifth down from Calhoun on the north side of the street. Like the others it had four rooms, a kind of parlor or front room as they were called, a kitchen and two bedrooms. He paid two dollars and fifty cents a week rent, and when he first came to Athena he had tried to buy it.

"Why waste your money?" Thompson said when Calvin had asked. "You ain't married. You should get 'ole Raleigh Bacon to fix you up someplace nice."

A small diamond pin flashed from the middle of a bloom on Thompson's broad flowered tie. Pearl cuff links fastened a shirt which stopped a couple inches short of covering Thompson's long arms. A thin pencil mustache grew on Thompson's upper lip. It looked like it had been pasted there. But it would have never occurred to Calvin to smile about Sampson Thompson. The clothes, the jewels, even the mustache were badges of power, props to help collect the rent. Thompson was not a fool. He was a man to take seriously.

When Calvin had persisted about buying the house, Thompson said, "Old man Raleigh got that place up against the back of the garage. Even got its own toilet. That not good enough for you?"

"I'll have my own place," Calvin said.

"Course, there is them new kennels up against that fancy shithouse. Can't you sing with the hounds, friend?"

The little old man laughed, a sort of cackle, and then jumped up and wandered restlessly about the room as if it were too small to contain him. Then he sat back down and took another drink from the liquor jar that Calvin kept for him.

"Instead of a house what you need is a woman," Thompson said. "Ain't healthy for a growed-up man to live alone like you is. House gets run down. Everything gets run down including your peter. Guess I'm gonna have to find you a woman so's I can be sure to collect my two fifty a week."

It went on that way for a long time. And turned into a kind of game, the kind of game which each played by a different set of rules. Thompson would never talk about selling Calvin the house and Calvin ignored Thompson's jokes about women.

Then one night Thompson asked, "How much you got, by the way?"

"Enough," Calvin said.

"How you know enough until we know what's needed?"

"Enough. I got enough money for a house. Why can't I buy one?"

"Because there ain't one for sale."

"Well, you must own some of these houses," Calvin said, "I'll just buy one off of you."

"Man alive," Thompson laughed. "Lord God almighty! Don't I wish it was true! But it ain't. I just collects the rent."

"Well," Calvin asked, "Who does own them? I expect I'll just buy one off of whoever owns them houses."

"I 'spect you won't," Thompson said, the smile gone now.

THEY ARGUED about the house again the next week.

"Suppose you bought a house," Sampson asked. "What would you do with it?"

"Live in it," Calvin said.

"After the livin', what?"

Calvin didn't answer.

"So when you done all your living in it, then what?" Thompson asked.

"I expect I'll be dead," Calvin said.

"No, no," Thompson said. "Before you're dead. What happens when you got to leave the house? Old Raleigh, he fire your ass. He say git you dumb nigger. Then what do you do with the house?"

When Calvin didn't answer, Thompson continued, "Instead, you rent from Meeting Real Estate for $10 a month. Collected by me, two dollars and fifty cents a week."

"I'll sell it," Calvin said. "Some other nigger will want it."

At this point there was an explosion of sound from Sampson, part cackle and part disdainful huffing.

"Or I could rent it, the same as Meeting," Calvin said.

"For nothing?" Thompson said.

"What you mean, for nothing?" Calvin said.

"Niggers don't rent to niggers." Thompson said. "A nigger renting to a nigger is like renting to hisself. And when did us niggers ever take care of our own property? A nigger will only pay his rent regular to a white man. He knows better not to."

Thompson's face was flushed, his eyes watery. He wiped his mouth in preparation for another drink from the jar.

Calvin knew now that Thompson would tell him the name of the owner. Not so he could buy it, but so he wouldn't try. Better off not to try, Thompson was saying.

Calvin brooded about that for weeks, but in the end he heeded Thompson's warning. He did not ask again to buy the house. About that time, though, he decided to buy himself a car, not a second-hand car like Mister Ohlinger's green Model A, with its neatly printed For Sale sign hanging like a necklace from its radiator cap, and not like the cars, the Buicks, the Cadillacs, the DeSotos, the Hudsons, lined up on Mister Porterfield's used car lot, but a new car, a brand new Chevy. He had his eye on the sedan, the four-door model, the Chevrolet people's most expensive car.

But he had to travel to Gaffney to buy it. The man at the new car agency in Athena had pretended to take his name, but then never had a car to sell him. The same thing happened in Greenville before he found a man in Gaffney who, after he saw Calvin's cash, took $714 for the car. That man had run after him to ask if he didn't need some insurance. But he'd come home and bought his insurance from the same folks that insured Bacon Mills. He'd had no trouble there; first, Mister Jones knew he worked for Mister Raleigh and knew that since he must have paid cash money for the car he would be good for the insurance. And he had been; he paid his insurance premium regular, stopping by every month to leave three dollars and eighty-six cents with Mister Jones's girl.

He kept the car as clean as his kitchen. It pleased him to wash it, to make sure the black finish was always shining and to see that not a speck of anything but car ever showed up inside.

Not too long after he bought the Chevy a new family, a woman with two little girls, moved into the house next door on Sycamore. The woman worked as a maid for Miss Helen Dillard over on East Buncombe Street. Thompson, with wild-eyed glee, told him how he broke one of his own rules renting the house to the woman, whose name was Virginia May. Her husband had left her after the second child was born. So now, said Thompson, she didn't have a husband. How long before she wouldn't be able to pay his two-fifty a week? How long before he would have to throw her ass out?

Calvin knew that, like him, this woman had to put up with the little man poking into her business. Because each week, after telling him that he had a "nice quiet little family who wanted to rent his place" Thompson would run next door and say the exact same thing to this Virginia May. He knew this because Thompson told him; he would drink his liquor, and, in that same almost demonic, gleeful tone, tell him exactly what he was doing, exactly what he had said to his new tenant. But Calvin never heard what she said, or how she felt about what the little man was up to. And the truth was that months passed without him even knowing what she looked like.

Then one Sunday evening he was washing the Chevrolet in front of the house when she walked by. She stopped to watch.

"Mighty fancy for these parts," she said.

He kept on working, like he hadn't heard. It was still warm. He had taken off his coat and Sunday shirt and put on an apron to cover his good suit pants. But, he was still sweating a lot. His heavy long-sleeved undershirt was already wet clean through. Suddenly it bothered him that he sweated so much.

"You keepin' it for somebody?" Virginia May asked.

Something about her, about her tone which was friendly without being too friendly, about the way she looked at him, sweat and all, straight on, made him hesitate in his work. He smiled slightly, non-committally, then went on working.

"Today's my youngest's birthday. Towhee. She's three."

He stopped then and for the first time looked square at her. She was one fine-looking woman for sure.

"How come you named her that?"

She shrugged, then said, "Like the bird. She named for the bird."

"Towhee?" he asked.

"And Phoebe, too," she said.

Later that week, he went into Raleigh Bacon's library and looked up the two birds in a book. He read about the Towhee and the Phoebe and then studied the plates.

THE COLORED of Athena held church twice on Sunday at the Second African Baptist Church, the second service for those who had to work during the regular morning hour. Many attended both.

Before church the men all gathered early off to one side and talked among themselves. The women did the same except some were getting the church ready for the service or busy herding excited children. The women in charge of decorating the church—mainly colored streamers of paper in the winter, flowers and greens the rest of year—also got the children's choir lined up ready to march in. They were Deaconesses and they all dressed in white.

Most of the men wore suits; some had on vests and a few wore hats which they would remove and hold during the service. All looked stiff and uncomfortable as if they were wearing garments of pine bark instead of cloth. And none seemed more stiff or less suited to Sunday clothes that particular evening than Calvin.

He stood a little off from the other men. His body seemed oversized and top heavy; muscles strained under heavy cloth. Occasionally, he smiled and said hello in response to a greeting but otherwise said nothing.

When the summons bell rang he followed as the others went inside the small brick church to take their usual seats. Sometimes when there was a newcomer the congregation held its breath to see whose seat he would sit in; there was always considerable giggling and poking of persons sitting close as the reaction set in. So, with bright eyes, they now watched excitedly as Calvin stood waiting at the back of the church. He might have stayed there for the entire service but the preacher, Reverend Train, took his arm and led him down to the front.

"Good to see you after all this time, Calvin," the preacher said. "You need a place where you can stretch out those legs and I need a man as big as you to start the basket."

So he ended up alone in the front pew. And when it came time for the offering he put his coin into an empty basket.

That Sunday Reverend Train's sermon was on Moses and the miracles found in the Book of Exodus. As the preacher told of the rod becoming a serpent, of the burning bush, of the Red Sea parting and the rest, the congregation began to chant. The transported calls of the women, the full-throated bass of the men, flowed around him from back up the church. The rich mixture of voices soon wove a sensual blanket of sound that seemed ready to carry him off. It felt like the congregation was calling to him alone. And then the hymns, beautiful, familiar hymns that he knew, some by heart, and one, now, not heard since Gracie's funeral.

"...Glory Alleluia, Glory Alleluia, My eyes have seen the Lord...."

Reverend Train, voice quivering, overflowing with the tumult of rich rhythms, eyes streaming with tears of honest wonder, turned to look down at him. The preacher nodded, smiling encouragement for him to sing. But he couldn't.

Reverend Train, distracted now, fell a full beat behind his congregation, his voice a ghostly echo of what it had been a minute before.

The preacher nodded again.

Calvin stared blankly back at the preacher through store bought glasses.

AFTER THE SERVICE he waited in line to pay his respects. Virginia May and her two girls stood apart, talking with another family. He caught Virginia May's eye. After meeting his gaze she looked at the ground. The girls pulled her toward home. His eyes followed them around the top of Pine Street. Suddenly, he found himself standing in front of the preacher.

He stared for a moment at Reverend Train. The preacher's smile was hopeful, yet a little unsure. He took the preacher's hand.

"Well, Reverend, it's the man who knows better who's the biggest fool of all. Ain't that right? You and me might just be the two biggest fools there is in this town."

But he was smiling as he vigorously shook Reverend Train's hand.

THERE WAS no school that particular day, it being a hot Saturday in early October. Billy and TJ sat rather disconsolately together at noontime at the small table in the butler's pantry just off the kitchen, picking at their plates. Not too long before Calvin had heaped those plates with food and ordered them to eat the midday dinner he'd just cooked, this practically right after breakfast and not one half-hour after each of them had snuck peach turnovers off the wax paper in the bread box.

Billy, bored, twirled his fork over his head, trying to weave it through his fingers like a cheerleader's baton. He missed and the fork fell and clanked against his plate and rattled to a stop on the table. He left it there.

He was still kind of a prisoner in Papa Bacon's house. But lately, for the last two or three weeks at least, he had more freedom. He was allowed to leave the house without asking permission, with fewer questions asked about where he'd been and what he'd been doing. And—he had to admit—despite everything he felt okay. Not happy, but okay. It was like he was a prison trusty here. While nothing had been said, he'd more or less given his word to Calvin that he wouldn't leave until Elizabeth or Sonny came to take him away.

To pass the time he pointed at his plate.

"Ugh!" he said with one eye on TJ.

"Yaauuggghhh!" TJ said.

And in fact what little solid food there was on their plates seemed to melt from the heat, turning soupy with the okra and the stewed tomatoes.

"What do you say?" he said.

"I will if you will," TJ said.

He and TJ had not really been apart since he first moved into TJ's room. Even Dot Jessop had got into the act of keeping them together. She had gone over to Stone Elementary School and got the Principal, Miss Davenport, to skip TJ into his class. Now, they were side by side in Miss O'Brien's fourth grade room.

He was lucky to have found TJ here at Papa Bacon's. But sometimes TJ could be too nice. TJ was usually willing to do pretty much whatever he wanted. When you're able to get somebody to do things as easy as he could with TJ it can get to be boring. Not much point in finagling somebody who wants to be finagled.

"Okay," he said now. "I'm gonna stuff half the okra in one pocket and all the squash in the other. That should do it."

"Ecchh. If I touch the okra I'll puke," TJ said, shivering. "I couldn't stand to do it."

"Well don't do it then. Sit here all day if that's what you want."

"What if Calvin catches us? He might tell Papa we're cheating."

And what would his grandfather do then? Like TJ he worried about that. He was a little afraid of Papa Bacon. So far his grandfather had barely spoken to him, and when he did it was with the formal speech that he'd only heard at school. "Good morning, sir." And "Hello, how are you today, young man." Things like that.

He really only saw Papa Bacon when he was coming or going, passing by you might say, so that neither of them had much of a chance to say a whole lot to the other. At most other times when not at the mill Papa Bacon was back in his rooms, reading. Or at the supper table, where he mostly always ate in silence.

Billy knew though that Papa Bacon was watching him. He wondered if his grandfather realized that he was being watched, too.

He saw a somber man who didn't smile a lot, but also a man who was protecting all of them, even him, sort of like an eagle sitting on its nest with its wings spread, willing to take him in and protect him along with the other nestlings. When Papa Bacon lost his temper, as he had once with TJ, he could be awful fierce. Like the eagle. But he wouldn't have any use for a sparrow of a grandfather.

In the last eight weeks he'd learned a lot about Papa Bacon. One important thing he knew was that Papa Bacon had married Mary Canning, his grandmother, a great lady from Spartanburg, and that she died before he was born. He also knew that Papa Bacon was about the most important man in Athena—this overheard in Five Points Pharmacy. When he'd heard that at the drug store he'd wanted to run around the counter to tell the man exactly who he was. And while he hadn't he'd gone around for hours afterwards, puffed up like a blue jay.

Even if Papa Bacon had stopped to talk what was there to say? It would be silly, for example, for him to ask his grandfather about the price of cotton. And would his grandfather ask him what he thought about Elizabeth kidnapping him, or whether he liked being here? Not likely! Better that they just pass by each other until they really had something to say.

TJ, he saw, had finished the stewed tomatoes on his plate. He hadn't touched his. Until it—and the squash—was at least half gone Calvin wouldn't allow him to leave the table. He poked at it with his finger to see if the gooey mass had cooled enough, was firm enough to put in his pocket. Agggh. No. He tapped the buttered squash with his fork. It left an inch long dent when it should have bounced. Too soft by a mile!

His stomach flip-flopped. He felt queasy. He was plotting desperate solutions when Miss Harp, wearing an old pair of Dot Jessop's dark glasses, came down from upstairs.

They didn't see much of Miss Harp. She spent most of her day upstairs, tending to Emily. She was carrying the little embroidered cloth carpet-bag where she kept Emily's diapers and food. Miss Harp was supposed to be weaning Emily from the bottle and baby food, but he had never seen Emily eat anything that didn't come right out of that bag. At odd times during the day Miss Harp would take a Gerber jar—usually fruit of some kind—and then spoon a mouthful into Emily's mouth. After Emily's mouth snapped shut on the food Miss Harp would jerk the spoon free and clean Emily's lips with it. It was done in one motion, like feeding an animal at the Zoo.

Miss Harp was wearing a white uniform, not too different from the dresses worn by Mattie and Cordelia, the housemaid and the laundress. But Miss Harp's was supposed to be a real nurse's uniform. Hers did have more starch than the other two.

And she wore white shoes and stockings, while Mattie and Cordelia didn't.

At the hospital nurses wore stiff caps. Miss Harp's hat was more like a white turban, pushed back so that it covered the back of her head and then looped under, cradling and hiding her hair underneath. She had applied a pomade to the front of her head so that her black hair, parted square in the middle, would lie flat and straight.

Miss Harp didn't just walk, she zipped. She reminded him of a small bird on the ground, its wary, head-cocking stillness separating abrupt, lightning-like bursts of movement. Miss Harp would stand in one place, at Emily's crib, for instance, and then, with a rushing sound, scoot to the other side of the room, her thin legs moving so fast as to be a near blur.

Now she whizzed right past him and TJ, then went on into the kitchen. This could be entertainment, so he and TJ—with nothing else to do—stopped making faces at each other so they could listen.

For maybe ten or fifteen seconds nothing happened.

Then Calvin's voice rumbled, "Something wrong with your eye, woman?"

Miss Harp's quick steps skittered somewhere but she didn't say nothing.

"Woman," the rich deep voice took on an edge of menace, "you blind and deaf?"

"None of your business," Miss Harp said, her voice as sharp edged as the rest of her.

"You got a sty in the eye, woman?" Calvin persisted.

"You know I ain't. I got sensitive eyes. You know that."

"Woman, don't you know you a nigger?"

Nigger! Only trashy white folks, the people who everybody

in the South blamed everything on, used that word. To hear it now, used this way, made the blood pop in his ears.

Miss Harp must not have heard what he heard in Calvin's voice.

Because then she said, "Least ways, I ain't no black African nigger. Least ways, I don't sweat like one."

Billy couldn't breathe.

Calvin, in a raspy baritone, his breath held against mounting rage, said, "I guess you needs fixin' Miss Sharp."

Now you could almost reach out and feel Miss Harp's terror.

"I'm gonna leave just as soon as I take care of this for Miss Dot."

"You fixing to leave all right."

"You don't scare me," she said. "I work for Miss Dot."

"You a nigger ain't you?" Calvin said. "All niggers in this house work for me."

Billy hunched down. TJ was doing the same. Wide-eyed, they stared unblinking at each other. Suddenly, there was a scraping sound from where the stove was.

"What you doing on my stove, woman," Calvin said.

"I'm boiling it," Miss Harp said.

"Not in my kitchen. You don't boil no needles on my stove."

With that Miss Harp burst into tears and ran out of the kitchen, past him and TJ. He could hear her quick steps climb the stairs and, with the sound of her wailing, cross overhead. Neither of them moved one inch. Any fool knew what would happen next. Sure enough, in what must have been only a minute or two, but what seemed like hours, Dot Jessop, barefoot, suddenly appeared at the door of the pantry.

Not only barefoot, she was nearly naked. She had on a nightgown, but in her anger she must have forgotten to put on a robe. Since the nightgown was the kind that you can see right through, she was really naked. He watched, open-mouthed, only glancing at her contorted face. He was transfixed by what was underneath the gown.

He had never seen a grown-up naked woman before. While he stared at what was forbidden he was aware, as if a picture of her had been printed large in his head, of all of her nakedness, the full breasts, alternately rising and falling with each step, the slightly protruding belly, sucked in now in determination, and the dark place between her legs which didn't look like much of anything but was the most interesting of all.

She hurried past. His last frozen image was of her hips and perfect buttocks, scooped, and rounded in the clinging material.

Dot Jessop's anger was awful. So intense that she seemed to have trouble getting her words out. At first all she could sputter was "How dare you!" and "This is my house!" over and over, forwards and backwards, as if these were the only two ladylike phrases she knew. Then she seemed to calm herself a bit. She said something about it being her house, that she could do whatever she wanted in it. To this point she was real angry, but in control. Then something must have happened. Or didn't happen.

"Stand up when I talk to you, you damn black son-ofabitch," she yelled, all pretense of being reasonable, of being a lady, forgotten. She waited, breathing heavily before screaming, screeching really, "Stand up, I said! Stand up! Stand up! Stand up you damn nigger! Stand up!...You better stand up!"

Silence. And then, once more, pleading now, "You should stand up when I talk to you."

She began to cry. At the same time the pan on the stove began to rattle as the water came to a boil.

Her crying grew louder.

"I'm sick," she sobbed. "The doctor said I should take vitamins every morning.... He said so, goddammit!"

All of a sudden she stopped crying. And Billy figured that she must have finally realized that she was half-naked. He strained but you couldn't tell what Calvin was doing; he couldn't tell if Calvin was looking at her the way he had.

The water boiled. The sauce pan continued to rattle on the burner. It was loud, insistent. It went on for what seemed like forever, a minute at least. Then that noise stopped. Water was poured into the sink, followed by the clatter of the syringe and needle in the empty pan. There were, he knew, without actually knowing exactly what, things that followed the cooling of needle and syringe. So he was startled to see Dot Jessop appear right away in the doorway. Her hands were empty. She padded right past TJ and him as if they didn't exist. She didn't hurry. She was calm, even a little proud, as if somebody else had had that screaming fit. Then she disappeared through the door.

He let his breath go. Across the table TJ sat staring down at his plate. TJ wouldn't look at him. Finally, TJ stood up with his almost full plate and went into the kitchen.

"Well now," Calvin said, "TJ, you didn't eat none of my okra. When are you boys gonna get to love okra like I do. My, it's good, sopped up with cornbread and all.... All right, boy, put your plate in the sink. And don't look so sad. Okra just ain't for some folks."

ARLENE'S PLACE was a diner, a former Washington, D.C. trolley, with a ramshackle kitchen added on. A scant half mile from the center of Bristol, Virginia, it perched on the side of the road where the foothills of the Appalachians began. The clearing where it sat was small and muddy and was only large enough for three or four carefully parked cars. But, the food was good, and every time that Raleigh and Calvin had stopped there for breakfast the cars and trucks were lined up and down the highway for more than a hundred feet.

Arlene's didn't serve coloreds but Arlene, an oversized, good-natured widow of about fifty, had at first let Calvin eat in the kitchen. On a later trip Calvin had been moved to a small table for two just inside the diner, next to the kitchen door.

"That buck of yours is just too big for my kitchen, Mr. Bacon," she'd said.

And, she still said in warning to every customer who came into the diner, "That there's this here Mr. Raleigh's buck."

On their way to Hot Springs he and Calvin always stopped for the night at Bristol. It was just over two hundred miles from there to the Cascades; from Bristol they would get an early start the next morning, driving around the hairpin turns of the Covington mountain road, well rested and in daylight. He liked to arrive in the early afternoon, have something to eat and still have two hours or so of daylight left for fishing at Two Holes.

He'd driven for most of the way on their first trip, but after watching how Calvin had handled the big car in the mountains he had let Calvin do all the driving since. His place now was in front, in the passenger's seat next to Calvin. Originally the idea had been to help Calvin during the trip over Covington mountain. But even after he was no longer needed he'd stayed. The views were lovely and he enjoyed Calvin's company. There was another reason though for where he'd chosen to sit: the rude, sometimes threatening stares they encountered at stoplights and stop signs in many of the small towns along the way. No one, by God, was going to dictate to him where he sat in his own car. People like him didn't give in to hillbillies. He would sit where he pleased.

Rude stares, however, were only a small part of the real inconvenience of traveling with a colored man.

His habit was to stay overnight at the Bristol Theatre Hotel, the only decent hotel in Bristol. But the hotel had balked at opening its dining room early for his breakfast. And there weren't any colored lodging places near the hotel, so Calvin had to find a room for himself in the colored section of town. For this he had to have the car. There was no way to get in touch with him if he were needed. After a couple of years of this kind of inconvenience he had just about decided to drive straight through when Calvin found Arlene's place. And now he couldn't imagine not stopping in Bristol.

SOMEONE PULLED OPEN the crowded diner's door and Arlene, without looking up from her work, sang out her usual, "That there's this here Mr. Raleigh's buck." But by that time no one really heard the words. They became lost in the bright morning sounds of too many people eating and talking loudly in too small a space. Yet, when this door opened the sound, especially the laughter, stepped down a little. Raleigh didn't notice, only registering that fact later. At the time he had been busy getting ready to leave. He'd nodded at Calvin, swiveled his stool around to get up. Behind him a customer, waiting impatiently for the empty seat, squeezed in before he'd left, bumping him slightly. It was only then that he noticed two police officers, dressed in the blue-and-gray uniform of the Virginia State Police, waiting for seats along with the other customers. He pushed through the waiting crowd, nodding and returning friendly greetings. The same with the two policemen.

"You have to be quick to get a seat in Arlene's, officer," he said to the first, smiling.

That trooper smiled back, touched his hat, then turned toward his partner. For a moment he thought he was about to be introduced.

But then the second officer said, "Are you the owner of the Buick?"

"Why, yes," he said.

"And is that your man?" the officer said, indicating Calvin, who was just passing through the door to the kitchen.

"Calvin?" he said. "Yes, he works for me. I'm heading for a little fishing up at the Cascades."

"Licensed?" the trooper asked.

Taken aback by the abrupt manner of the officer, he said, "Of course I'm licensed. Or I will be just as soon as I get there."

"I mean him," the trooper said, watching Calvin as he walked around the end of the diner toward the car.

"Oh," he said. "You mean Calvin. A driver's license. Yes, of course he's licensed. In fact, he's an excellent driver. We've been coming this way, stopping at Arlene's for years."

"So I've heard," the officer said. "Well, good-bye, sir."

He touched the wide brim of his hat and stepped aside. Very polite, if anything too polite. He was older than the other officer. Maybe that was why. Better manners in older men. Still, his eyes were flat, no depth at all. No humor there. Raleigh glanced again at the brown, almond shaped eyes. A no-non-sense lawman. A good thing that was, too. An officer of the law has to be serious about what he was doing.

THE HIGHWAY after Covington was worse than he remembered. Danger stretched alongside just a few feet away. The road over the crest changed from a twisting narrow ribbon of concrete to a poorly graded gravel road. The gravel had washed out in places along the side, leaving gaping holes between the outer edge of highway and the wooden barriers. He braced with each turn and congratulated himself that he had had the good sense to have the car and its brakes thoroughly checked before they left. Calvin guided the car easily around the twisting curves. They, Calvin and the car, seemed bred to narrow gravel roads and twisting hair-pin curves. He relaxed.

"One of the policemen thought I might be letting you drive without a driver's license."

Calvin smiled, but said nothing.

"I set him straight."

A few minutes later he said, "Calvin. Tell me. Does it ever bother you that you have to eat in Miss Arlene's kitchen?"

"Well, I reckon I don't eat in Miss Arlene's kitchen."

"You know what I mean," he said.

Calvin drove on, slowing to move around a washed-out cut that had eaten into the edge of the road.

"Don't bother me at all," Calvin said. "Besides there's nothing to do about it even if it did."

"That's probably true," he said. "I think it would bother me."

"You're a white man, Mr. Raleigh."

"I mean if I were colored."

"If you was colored then it wouldn't bother you none," Calvin said.

The car moved solidly ahead.

He thought about Calvin's answer. He should be comforted by it. It was just that he didn't want any pain to be visited on Calvin—or for that matter on any of his servants. But if Calvin didn't care if he was made to eat in Arlene's kitchen why should he make it his business? No reason to worry about something neither of them had any part in making or could do anything about.

The way things were. Wasn't that what Calvin was saying?

Without his even realizing it, they had come off the mountain; the last yellow highway caution sign slipped behind. The automobile, released from the shackle of the lower gears, rolled smoothly down the narrow highway. At a signal from him, Calvin, grinning, pushed the gas pedal near to the floorboard. In the deserted quiet of the rural Virginia countryside the maroon Buick hurtled forward, dividing the highway. It rocked back and forth over the center of the road, the stately movement like the pendulum of a large grandfather clock.

With the rhythmic, lulling movement of the car Raleigh's thoughts soon turned to Dot; she materialized as she always did—out of the mists of desire, accompanied by guilty longing. In this erotic daydream she was naked, spent from their love making the night before the trip. Used up, battered, still beautiful. And, as always lately, resentful.

"I hate you, Leigh," she'd said. "I hate your old trips."

She'd pouted, scratched a breast with long painted nails. Dot had no modesty. She liked to parade her nakedness. More natural she said; she was more comfortable with no clothes on.

She would like, she giggled, to just take off all her clothes and run stark naked right down the middle of Main Street.

He was embarrassed by his own lack of muscularity, in fact, painfully modest because of it. So Dot's ease in intimate situations both repelled and fascinated him.

She never closed any door and it was he who usually covered her after they made love. As she lay sprawled, asleep but offering, in moonlight, the dark splotch joining splayed legs, he would carefully arrange the bed covers against prying eyes. It was the kind of thing, covering the nakedness of a wife at two in the morning in a room that no one would dare enter, that some men might do without knowing why. But that wasn't true of him. He knew why he protected Dot. He was also clear-eyed about why he'd married her in the first place.

His first wife, Mary, was beautiful, more lovely than Dot, taller and more elegant. That was what had attracted him in the first place. Her elegance. She had a patrician air, enhanced by a preciseness of speech that, he learned later, was an affected trait of the entire Canning family. They were Anglophiles, with an overweening love of all things English. But, just home from Harvard at the time, he was blind to such things. It was only after their wedding that he discovered a wife more fearful than loving.

In those early months of marriage, deeply in love, he made excuses for her stiff reticence. She was shy; he was a boor. He must learn to curb his excesses. It was shameful that he mostly thought of her beautiful body and what it offered him. This emotional turmoil was relieved a little when Mary became pregnant with Elizabeth. But months after Elizabeth's birth Mary still claimed physical reasons to keep them apart. By that time he was nearly crazy with desire for her. He forced her to talk about what was then a forbidden subject, one no decent person ever mentioned. But he only succeeded in humiliating himself. Because Mary, with shrewd instinct, lashed out, accusing him of not being understanding, of not caring anything about her health.

It was true that there was a history among the Canning women of difficult child births, including the death of one of Mary's mother's sisters. To that had been added the hectoring that came from women members of the Canning family who believed that the relations between men and women were not only a fearful duty for the delicate Canning women but unspeakable in their vulgarity. Guilt ridden, ashamed of his animal need, he gave up.

Yet Mary never refused him completely. Legs together, arms crossed, she waited in bed as a trembling Aztec captive might have waited for sacrifice. And, like her sacrificial sister, she kept eyes tightly closed against the coming assault. As he mounted her, as he lifted and arranged unresisting but passive legs and arms he was always struck by how cold her body was. He knew she hated him. Or, if not him, certainly his lust. But even this was not enough to completely dampen his desire. To keep his sanity he adapted, coming to Mary only when what drove him became unbearable.

Adapted? Yes, they both adapted. For the next fourteen years he and Mary managed somehow to convince themselves that they were reasonably happy together. Mary lavished attention on Elizabeth. And he spent long hours at the mill establishing the work habits and developing his life long interest in the growth and improvement of Bacon Mills. It took time, but he did forget. He forgot the pain, that endless physical torture of love denied. In its place he substituted a less satisfying but more stable love of the business he was helping his father run.

Every few weeks he went to Mary's room and, without words, demanded his rights. Then one night, full of bourbon, caring only to rid himself of the tyrant if only for a few moments, he found her, as always, waiting in her usual defensive, tremulous state. That hated sacrificial posture suddenly made him very angry. He roughly jerked her into position on the bed and, then, without any preliminaries, took her. In his drunkenness he mistook her cries of anger as the pent up passion he'd longed for. No stopping him then. He may, as she claimed, have raped her. He was never sure. Rape or not, their marriage ended. She left him the next day, taking Elizabeth with her to London. They stayed in England for over a year.

After Mary left he raged. But, it was an impotent rage, directed inward, because no one in Athena could know. Soon he was sick, obsessed with the need to kill Mary or, better yet, himself. Then late one night he drove back from Ashville on a road not that different from the one that he and Calvin had just driven over from Covington—winding, with very sharp turns that could make any mistake fatal. He drove very fast, tempting fate. Twice, in anguish, he started to drive the Packard over the side of the mountain. But each time he thought: What if he didn't die? What if, instead, he was crippled, crippled for life? And each time the panicky, self-destructive mix of emotions stopped him. Then, without any sense that he'd willed it, he jerked the steering wheel toward the barrier and jammed the accelerator to the floor. With the sharp turn the heavy car skidded half way around, then righted itself in the opposite direction. The spinning right rear of the Packard struck the low barrier a glancing blow, which, like a catapult, threw the three-thousand pound car across the road. It struck the opposite bank heading forward, shot over the chest high bed of loose rocks on the shoulder and smashed into the huge rock outcropping the road had been built around. The car, pointed skyward, fell back. As it fell it turned slowly onto its side where its weight rolled it over half again. The left rear tire spun in furious, useless motion; then the Packard, like a great beast, shuddered, coughed and died. For several minutes he lay there, not moving, on his side in the silent, flipped car. Slowly, resigned now, he reached forward and turned the ignition key off.

Months later when Mary and Elizabeth came home from England he had withdrawn into himself. Elizabeth complained bitterly that he acted like he wasn't glad to see them. It wasn't that so much as the deflation of his resentment. It was gone. In its place was an indifference to Mary and their marriage. As Mary complained later, the first thing she noticed was that he was elusive and, while courteous, was not interested in the least in what she said or did. In her anger Mary also told him how she'd also sought the advice of the Spartanburg Aunts, who it turned out were not very interested. When pressed they told Mary to count her blessings that she didn't have to welcome the brute into her bed any longer.

In the end no one would listen to Mary when she complained that she was being treated as if she didn't exist.

Mary died three years later, age thirty-eight. A sudden, unexpected death. One day she arose in mid-morning, bathed, then asked to be driven to her parents' home in Spartanburg. She decided to stay overnight in her old room, where she was found dead in bed the next morning. No autopsy was performed, and death was listed simply as heart failure. Her family wanted Mary buried in the Canning family cemetery in

Spartanburg. He considered their suggestion because he thought Mary might have wanted it. But, in the end he brought her home to Athena for burial.

It was the only thing in all of the years of their marriage that he was sure he had done right.

After Mary was buried, he grieved. As he mourned for them, for himself and Mary and the lost years, he was dead inside. Had he bothered to monitor his emotional feelings during those months, which eventually stretched over nearly two years, he would have found an arid, numb wasteland where there was no hope of anything better.

ONE MORNING on his way to work many months later he happened to detour onto Hampton Boulevard and then he made the turn for the mill at McColloch Street. A girl was sitting on the concrete bench there waiting for the Alta Vista bus. He was waiting for the light to change, so he didn't notice her at first. But, something caught his attention and just as he pulled away he caught a glimpse of a young girl, olive skinned, with dark, almost black hair, staring at him. Or was it the automobile?

To find out he passed that way at the same time the next day but she wasn't there. And then he forgot about her. Another two or three months went by before he saw her again, and when he did he didn't realize at first that it was the same girl. The girl he saw the second time had reddish-blond hair and she was waiting for the Bacon Mill bus at a corner on Calhoun Street. But, as he drove slowly by, nodding in response to the smiling greetings of his employees, he looked up and met her eyes. The same eyes as before. And she wasn't looking at the large car. She was staring with undisguised interest at him.

The jolt of sexual desire was so swift and so strong he missed the turnoff to the mill. He had to turn around at High Street. For several days after that he timed his drive to the mill to pass the bus stop at the same hour and was rewarded several times by seeing her there. Whether she still looked in the same way at him he couldn't know because he was careful not to show any interest in anyone standing there.

For the next several days he didn't drive by that bus stop. Yet in his mind he drove by it constantly. From his earlier moribund state he had changed in only a week's time to where he now did nothing but fantasize about a young girl and her body. Finally, in near torment, he followed close after the mill bus the next Monday, and as if they were conspirators and had planned the whole thing, she did not get on the bus but let it go on without her.

The ride to the mill that morning could have been a ride on a roman candle. It was all he could do to hold on. He could have been seventeen and she forty. In fact, after he asked if she would like a ride, and then, her name, he didn't say anything more during the entire five-minute ride. On the other hand Dot chatted on as if they were old friends. She was pretty in a dark sulky way which she had apparently tried to change by dying her hair a miscolored blond. The effect was cheap, but, for him, it only made her more desirable. It was a call, a sexual call such as he had never known before. It shook him to his core. Nothing was said about meeting again but because of that it seemed to be assumed that he would pick her up the following day. And he did. And the day after. And the day after that, until he was giving her a ride to the mill every day.

Dot perched on the edge of the seat of his car, a studied coquette, facing in his direction with breasts (they were as full then as now) brought to attention as if she were a cadet of love and he her helpless commander. She even bit her lip in a suggestive way. It was ludicrous it was so obvious, but he couldn't resist it. And then after a few days, when he'd not yet even hinted at any personal interest, she had tried to slide over to sit close to him in the car. He'd had to gently push her away.

It wasn't a question of whether Dot was available. She may have been. But, no one would ever know for sure because by the end of the summer he was determined to have her. And that could only be at his home, in his bed. It was not possible for him to engage in groping and fondling in his car; he was not able to demean himself that way. For him marriage was the only choice.

Vickie warned him exactly what would happen. And it did. Athena sent its word anonymously over hidden, mean-spirited pathways; it was lightning fast and merciless in its universal condemnation. In fact, the approval of the town, if it ever existed for anything he had ever done before, was withdrawn. There was a small run on the First National Bank, and business at the mill dipped for a few months.

But the way Elizabeth acted surprised him the most. He expected her to be upset, even angry. But he was unprepared for her vehemence. And he certainly didn't expect her to throw her life away in the process. But when she realized that he really intended to marry Dot, that it wasn't all just a joke, out of pure spite she decided to marry Sonny Smithson. He turned out to be the worthless emotional cripple you would expect to find in any hospital for morphine addicts.

Each of Elizabeth's two marriages had been a disaster. The only good thing to come out of them was Billy. Raleigh wondered sometimes if Elizabeth's deplorable taste in men had anything to do with him. But, look at the last one, almost a door-to-door salesman. A cheap, good-for-nothing tobacco broker, with a line.

For the life of him he couldn't remember the broker's name. What was it?... No, nothing like him at all.

Elizabeth had called him an old goat. She hinted broadly that he should sleep with Dot, or as she put it, "do what is necessary, Daddy," until he got it out of his system. But, she didn't understand.

In Athena a respectable unmarried man of normal appetites had no sexual outlet. He could go to New Orleans or to New York, perhaps, but relief at those wells was foul tasting; it never slaked honest thirst. The loneliness of that temporary coupling was like death.

How do you explain to anyone—much less a daughter—what it means to have a woman of your own? It was not something he could explain. Yes, he'd paid a high price, but Dot hadn't disappointed him yet.

THE TOWN LIMITS of Hot Springs, Virginia, came into view.

Excited at the prospect of the fishing to come, he turned toward Calvin. But, he had nothing to say. Instead, he smiled at Calvin's questioning glance, then turned back to the front.

Remarkable. Truly remarkable. He felt closer to this colored man than almost anybody.

In that warm, happy moment he let it go at that.

CALVIN'S ROOM in the small white fishing cabin was the same as Raleigh Bacon's. It had a bed and a dresser, with a few wooden clothing pegs screwed onto the wall. Over the years he'd gotten used to staying in this plain room, so that now when they left, as they would the next morning, he was always sorry.

In the early evening, while Mr. Bacon napped before supper, he would lie on the narrow bed for nearly an hour so as not to make any noise in the little kitchen. At first, not used to lying about, he'd been uneasy doing nothing. But, after a while he'd come to look forward to this time, to this hour, which, with no conscious effort from him, would sometimes expand and flow forward or backward along paths that were both strange and familiar. Suspended in memory and imagination he often lost track of time, and sometimes, as now, where he was.

He had just had a vision, a premonition. As he shook himself back to the present he looked blindly around the Spartan room, aware only of bright cracks of light in the opposite wall marking the places where the boards didn't quite meet.

Where? On a railroad car, not the Azalea, not the Holcomb. And he was crying. No, not crying. No tears. He wasn't part of the car, as he always had been before. He was just visiting....

He squeezed his eyes shut. Now he could see. No beginning, no end, blinding in its instant, bright reality.

Mr. Bacon was not in the car; but then Mr. Bacon waved him away. And he had to leave the train....

Mr. Bacon always asked him to fish alongside. They brought a fly rod—one of Mr. Bacon's old ones—each year just for his fishing. *You pack the old rod?* Mr. Bacon always asked.

But it never left the cabin and would be stored after this trip for next year. The old fly rod, like everything else on these trips, was part of the tradition. Everything was the same, the time of year, the equipment, the route, Bristol, Arlene's Place, this cabin, Mr. Bacon's civilized snores, the fishing, the asking and the refusing—"I'd just scare all them trout away, Mister Raleigh." It was real comfortable. Each one knew what was expected of him. More than comfortable; any other way wouldn't be right.

—as he walked from the long train someone in a window was waving...not Mr. Bacon...but who? Who was waving goodbye....

Where was he? "Who's leaving, Mister Raleigh?"

At the sound of his own voice he opened his eyes, saw the cabin walls. It was just a dream. The fishing was over. They were going home to Athena tomorrow. Mr. Bacon hadn't left. He could hear the proof in careful snores coming through the cabin's wall.

Just a dream.

CALVIN SHIFTED the Buick into third gear as they came down the last stretch off Covington mountain. Soon they reached the outskirts of Bristol where he slowed the big car. The falling red needle arced slowly downwards past the '40' painted on the speedometer. He engaged the clutch, pulled back on the round knob of the gear shift. Under the car spinning gears meshed smoothly. He grunted in silent satisfaction. Humming, murmuring to himself in accompaniment to the music of the engine, he sang the big car through its paces. Raleigh Bacon didn't like the jerky halts and starts of a carelessly operated car. The same with him. In his mind he patted the big car, holding its speed constant for the next mile. A sign for Arlene's sailed by.

Raleigh Bacon said something just as he felt it.

A prickling chill just under the skin. The road was clear, front and back. Couldn't see no trouble. But it was there all right. He looked up. A police cruiser came into view in the rear view mirror.

They drove past Arlene's. The police car didn't turn in as he'd hoped, but continued to follow along behind. His brain raced ahead, sorting out what wasn't useful, noticing everything now. The clock on the dash gave the time at two minutes before noon. He calculated the distance to downtown Bristol. Raleigh Bacon said something again. He answered absently, automatically, without any idea of what he'd said.

The speedometer registered exactly thirty-five miles per hour. He eased off the gas pedal. The Buick slowed slightly. The squad fell back, keeping its distance.

In downtown Bristol Monday deliveries to the stores were at their peak. Delivery trucks were double-parked all up and down Euclid Street. He slowed to a crawl, carefully picked his way through. But a bread truck blocked the street. He waited for a moment, then pulled around.

When he looked back down the road the police car had disappeared.

"What is it?" Raleigh Bacon asked. "Why are you going so damn slow?"

He laughed, "Guess I'm just a vacation man, Mister Raleigh. Can't seem to get back up to working speed."

Relieved, he was still cautious. He practically crept out of Bristol—like a car thief hoping not to be noticed. With each stop, each turn, each signal he paused, looking up and down before going on. He drove as if the dark, blood-red color of the Bacon car itself was some kind of an affront to the town.

But he didn't see anything.

He started to hum again. But the sound was faint, a little thin, as if he really didn't believe.

And then, as he'd feared, there it was, the cruiser. It was parked, waiting at the far edge of town. As they passed it pulled out and followed. For several miles it stayed at a distance. Then, suddenly, it sped up, closing the gap.

"Mister Raleigh," he warned.

Out of the corner of his eye he could see the cruiser, a black-and-white, nineteen thirty-eight Ford, come abreast. Then they were motioned to pull over. He glided to a stop on the edge of the highway. The squad stopped a few yards behind. It sat there, its motor idling. But no one got out.

"What in the world is the matter with these people," Raleigh Bacon fumed. "You didn't do one blame thing that was wrong. Nothing I could see."

Raleigh Bacon started to get out of the car. But at that moment two policemen climbed out of the squad. "Well," Raleigh Bacon said, a tone of relief in his voice.

The two troopers walked up to the Buick, one on either side, boots scraping on the pavement. Calvin didn't move. He kept his eyes to the front, staring at the neutral expanse of road ahead.

The policeman on the driver's side stopped. He could feel the man looking him over, then lean into the car's window.

He turned, glanced at the officer. It was the same policeman they'd seen at Arlene's four days before.

"Yessuh?" he asked, trying to keep his voice regular.

Stitched above the policeman's left breast pocket in gold thread was his name.

'Holland'

The second policeman was one they hadn't seen before.

"Good morning officer," Raleigh Bacon said across him. "Is something wrong?"

"May I see your driver's license, sir," Holland said to Calvin.

For just a moment he didn't move.

"Don't you know who I am officer," Raleigh Bacon said, his voice rising. "I talked to you only a few days ago. I told you then that my driver is licensed. I don't understand this."

Holland pointed at Calvin, "You. Step out of the car. Slowly remove your license from your wallet. Then hand it to me. One hand."

Raleigh Bacon tried to open his door. The other policeman leaned against it.

"You better stay in the car, mister."

Holland stepped back, one, two, three deliberate steps, then stopped. As he moved the policeman's eyes didn't leave Calvin's face.

Calvin climbed out. One foot, his left, numb from sitting in the car, caused him to stumble a little before he caught himself. He fumbled in his pocket for his driver's license, then handed it over. Holland took a long time studying it.

"You're Calvin Lemoyne?"

"Yessuh."

"I never heard of Lemoyne."

"Yessuh."

"Mr. Lemoyne, *suh*, where'd you get a name like *Lemoyne*?"

Before he could answer Holland said, "Lemoyne? That your name, boy? Lemoyne? That your *real* name?"

"Yessuh."

Then Calvin added, "Same name that's on that there license."

Holland's eyes narrowed under the wide brim of his peaked hat.

After a moment he said, "Earl, lets us take this boy in."

By then Raleigh Bacon had slid across the seat and was outside the car.

"What do you think you're doing?" he said to Holland, trying to put himself between Calvin and the policeman.

Raleigh Bacon was using the same tone that said who he was at home. But Holland didn't bother to answer, didn't even look at him.

"This is my automobile, officer," Raleigh Bacon said, his voice shrill now. "You had better deal with me. I'm the one who can tell you anything you got to know. If you don't I can't be responsible what will happen to you. Do you hear? You let him go. You better. I can't be responsible— "

Holland roughly pushed Calvin ahead, toward the squad car.

And then took his revolver out.

The other one named Earl drew his pistol, too.

Raleigh Bacon stunned, looked at the guns. For a moment he didn't say anything. He followed silently behind as they marched Calvin over to the cruiser. But at the squad car he tried again to put himself between them.

"What are you doing?" he said. "How dare you arrest my driver."

And then, after a pause, he said, "Who's going to drive my car?"

"You people from Carolina sure are spoiled," Holland said.

"I'll tell you what. I'll send a tow truck. State law says you'll have to ride up front with the driver. He's a nigger too, but that shouldn't bother you none."

Out of the corner of his eye Calvin saw the other police-man suddenly flinch and raise his arm. At the same time Holland tried to duck out of the way, but not in time to avoid Raleigh Bacon's rush. He shoved both hands hard against Holland's chest. Caught off guard Holland fell back against the squad car. His large, wide-brimmed hat shook loose. It slipped to his shoulder, then rolled slowly down his chest to fall to the ground at the side of the road.

Raleigh Bacon had gone blind to the pistols.

"You're going to pay for this," he cried.

Raleigh Bacon started digging furiously at Holland's hand, trying to pull it off Calvin's arm. Calvin took hold of his arm.

"Mister Raleigh!" he said. "It's all right, Mr. Raleigh! Please, Mister Bacon!...

At first Raleigh Bacon didn't seem to hear.

"Mister Bacon, suh!"

"What?" Raleigh Bacon said, staring blankly, panting from the effort. "What?" he asked again.

The policemen then took out handcuffs and, without a word, put one pair on Raleigh Bacon. Holland then tried to put the other on him, but couldn't get the cuffs to close over his wrists.

"Shit," Holland said. "But that's okay. I hope you try to run, boy.... I mean Mister Lemoyne, *suh*. I'd just love to shoot your ass right off."

IN THE SQUAD CAR they drove fast away from Bristol, so fast that Calvin had trouble orienting himself by road sign and sense of direction. And then, just as he'd noticed they were heading northwest, and had passed a SR number he'd strained to—but couldn't—read, the squad turned sharply, swerved and raced across the gravel parking lot of a long one story brick building and slid to a stop. They were pulled roughly from the car and pushed inside. He noticed the building was brand new. A brand new State Police Headquarters? In almost every room electric cords dangled from uncapped outlets in the ceilings. A few contained bare light bulbs which shone dimly against the darkness of the windowless building. In the half light his foot scraped metal. He glanced down. Money. No, not money, quarter sized plugs from new, roughed-in electrical outlets lying on the concrete floor. Fool's money they were called, used by smart alec white kids to steal from folks, usually colored kids who didn't know any better. Fool's money....

Something cold reached down, squeezed out his breath.

There weren't any other squad cars in the parking lot! And—he strained to remember—no other cars parked outside either. He stopped, and would have broke the man holding his arm into pieces, but Raleigh Bacon, led by Holland, disappeared through a door ahead into a yawning blackness. He was pushed ahead and they followed. For a ways he couldn't see anything. But then they rounded a corner and climbed down a flight of metal stairs in a dimly lit stairway. At the bottom, in what must have been the basement, he was pushed ahead and then inside a small, dark windowless room.

Face the wall!

Holland's voice.

A light came on. He and Raleigh Bacon were standing together in a tiny room, no more than six by eight, facing a bare, newly plastered wall. Someone had drawn a picture of a huge, erect penis there. Its head dripped semen. The drops grew to basketball size near the floor. Something was written in the last balloon.

Then Holland again. *Take off your clothes! Pile them back of you!*

He didn't move and for a second was ready to...

But just when he started to turn the pistol was jammed hard into his ribs. That made him think. It wasn't just him standing there. So, he started to slowly undress. First his tie and shirt, then his pants. For the drive home he hadn't worn his long johns, just a long sleeved undershirt to ward off the early morning chill. Shining up at him was the gray gleam of the head of his own penis where it emerged from the dark forest of hair, belly and foreshortened legs.

He took off his shoes. Straightening he read the words written on the wall.

'Satan, get thee behind me!'

Next to him Raleigh Bacon was slowly undressing. He could see white arms, red marks on the wrists where the handcuffs had been, a fine silk undershirt, a bowed white crowned head as the man he worked for leaned forward to take off his trousers. Standing on one leg Raleigh Bacon nearly fell over as he tried to slip the baggy khaki fishing trousers over his shoes. Calvin put out his arm for him to lean on.

They stood together, waiting. From the sudden quiet he guessed that Holland and the other one had left. Then, just as he turned, he saw Holland coming through the door.

HOLLAND yelled again.

I told you to strip. Take off all them clothes, nigger. You, too, Mister Nigger Lover. Keep your fucking eyes on that wall.

He took off his undershirt. Raleigh Bacon took off his black shoes and socks. Then Holland left, taking their clothes with him. His footsteps receded down the hallway in the direction away from the stairway. Calvin glanced at Raleigh Bacon. His head hung forward on thin shoulders. He was staring at the floor, covering his nakedness with his hands.

With eyes closed Calvin listened hard, intent on what he could hear beyond the echoes of footsteps. Just the faint sounds of water running. A toilet or an open faucet. He looked around. The room was empty; the door stood open.

He whispered, "Mister Raleigh?"

No answer. He looked over. Raleigh Bacon shook his head.

AT THREE FORTY-FIVE that afternoon they walked naked out of the deserted building. The only car parked outside was the Buick. The keys were in the ignition. Their clothes were in the back, thrown on the floorboard. They dressed on opposite sides of the Buick. One of the car's brake lights had been smashed. Which one of them had done it hadn't bothered to pick up the shattered pieces of red glass lying on the ground directly beneath.

Calvin put the red shards of glass in his pocket.

He waited to be told what to do. But Raleigh Bacon didn't want to talk. It was all the man could do just to open the car's door and climb heavily inside.

They drove straight through to Athena that way, with only one brake light working and Raleigh Bacon sitting silent on the back seat of the big Buick.

F OR WEEKS afterwards, far into a dark November, Raleigh felt sick every time he thought about what had happened at Bristol. He tried hard not to think about it, tried even harder to put it out of his mind when the ugly incident would push its way in. He spent more time than ever at the mill, often working past supper. But nothing helped. No matter how hard he worked, no matter how much he tried he couldn't rid himself of the hateful thoughts. The pictures of shame flashed constantly across the screen of his memory.

How could he have left that hellhole that way? Why hadn't he immediately called the Director of the Virginia State Police? Or at least called Mattingly, his lawyer. To sneak out of the State like a common criminal.... That's what Holland wanted. To humiliate, to terrorize, to make them run.... No, not 'them.' Holland was after him, never Calvin.

Calvin—

He saw himself through Calvin's eyes—naked. Naked and almost helpless. He felt sick, he felt the same deep sense of shame and guilt he'd felt almost every waking moment since their return.

STILL HAUNTED by Bristol, Raleigh left on a long-planned trip to hunt birds with the Jessop brothers. He would rather have stayed at home, but Dot wouldn't hear of it.

"He'll just take it out on me," she said, meaning Eddie King.

And now, as he listened to Eddie King tell Lionel and Ray Boy what to fix them for supper on their last night he was not sorry he'd come. Because the feeling, only a resentful glimmer at first, had persisted and grown to where it had almost taken him over. He knew somehow that the answer to getting free of it was here, in this hunting camp, with these strange men, people like Ben Jessop and his brother, Eddie King.

Eddie King was talented in a perverse kind of way. He knew how to expend the least amount of energy to get pretty much what he wanted. Raleigh had always deplored Eddie King's laziness but had had to accept it because of Dot. Yet Eddie King was anything but lazy on these hunting trips.

There was something about men gathering together in a pine forest, about men being among guns and lots of liquor and the unreality they produced. Those things seemed to make Eddie King a natural if edgy leader. He gave mostly sensible orders that were easy to obey. He chose the pairings and the fields where they would hunt. He was good at repairing what was broken and damaged, whether it was your shotgun or a frying pan or a blistered foot. But most of all he knew how to hunt. They always killed a lot of birds when Eddie King was along.

He also dominated their conversation every night. They let him because it was his right as the best story teller among them. They were the funniest, yet the filthiest stories he had ever heard. Raleigh was a little prudish by nature. But, like most men, he was tolerant of what passed for humor sitting around a camp fire. On earlier trips when Eddie King told his stories he found himself laughing just as loud as anyone about the stupidity of nigras and the length of their men's penises. He found he relished the Paul Bunyonesque stories of Eddie King's sexual exploits. He felt sure that most of what Eddie King said was true. So it was with a voyeuristic fascination that he listened to those tales of perversion and of women worse than whores.

At home, after one of these trips, he was always a little

ashamed of himself. Yet when the time for the next trip came around months later he had all but forgotten what had bothered him earlier and was more than ready to enjoy the hearty companionship of men again. And for this trip in late November he seemed to have new, acutely observant pairs of eyes and ears.

Ben Jessop, who now worked at the mill and who had seemed for the most part to be normal, stayed drunk the entire time. He didn't hunt this trip, not once. He stayed in camp. He cooked a little, helping Lionel and Ray Boy prepare meals. Occasionally he would wander off into the woods to gather firewood only to come back much later with a few twigs. At most other times he was sleeping.

On this last night, though, Ben seemed to have come alive—with a vengeance. He gorged himself with food, with beans and cornbread, tearing through the barbecue and the cold fried chicken as if he hadn't eaten for a week. Even Eddie King, who usually ate in the same almost snarling way, couldn't keep up with Ben. So when Ben picked up yet one more chicken wing with one hand and reached for a slice of cornbread with the other, Eddie King exploded.

"You pig. You are a fucking disgusting filthy pig. You mean to eat everything, don't you? You don't mean to leave a fucking thing for Leigh or anybody else, do you?"

Ben didn't answer, although the obvious answer, the huge still mostly full trays of meats and bowls of beans and potatoes and platters of bread and sweets that Lionel and Ray Boy had been cooking for days rested on tables that partially enclosed and lined the opening where they all sat. Fifteen or so men gathered around a blazing fire, eating and drinking and getting drunk for one last time before going home the next day.

Ben just kept on chewing, but he kept a wary eye on Eddie King.

Then, surprisingly, Ben said, "The hell with you."

"What did you say?" Eddie King said.

"I said go to hell."

"Watch your tongue, you fat pig," Eddie King said, but in a bored way, as if this were the way they always spoke to one another in private.

Then Eddie King lit another cigarette, cupping his hands against what little breeze there was at the moment. Raleigh had noticed Eddie King's hands before, since he used them to talk. Always working, he waved them about to make what he said more important.

They were ugly, blunt and dirty-nailed. Both were stained with nicotine. He held the just lit cigarette in his left hand. He absently flicked the dead ash off the end of the burning cigarette with that hand's little finger. Or so Raleigh thought until he paid closer attention. Then he saw that Eddie King seemed to like to caress the live ash, flicking and rubbing it with his finger before it could die.

Eddie King, who may have sensed he was being watched, came over and sat next to him, pulling the canvas chair close.

Then, out of nowhere Eddie King said, "I've been thinking, Leigh, you've got to get rid of the nigger. He's causing a heap of trouble in your house."

Raleigh was surprised. He looked closely at Eddie King, wondering what had emboldened Eddie King to say such a thing to him. He didn't seem drunk.

He answered cautiously, "Calvin is very valuable to me Eddie King," he began. "In my judgment—"

"Well, Mister Leigh," Eddie King said, "of course your judgment, your opinion, is important. But there are other things to think about. The first is despite what you want Dot wants something different. It beats all; here you got a woman what wants to run her own house and all you want is a lazy good-for-nothing-wife. It's not good for TJ to see his mother shamed this way."

Raleigh laughed, "Shamed? Come on now, Eddie King. You're getting carried away. Dot isn't—"

"I supposed you don't hear so good, Leigh," Eddie King said. "You're like the fellow who drowned when he tried to jump over the creek in two jumps. You only get one jump."

Shocked into silence Raleigh stared at Eddie King.

"I'm giving you good advice," Eddie King said. "You'd be smart to take it."

"Eddie King—," he began, his tone the kind you use with a child or a drunk.

"You remind me of a stubborn old horse, Leigh. Your head is pointy. Your brain has probably shrunk to nothing. You—"

Raleigh leaned into Eddie King's shadow.

"You're drunk, Eddie King," he said, lowering his voice. "Watch your tongue or I'll—"

"Whoa, no need to get riled, Leigh. Family talk, you and me. That's all."

Eddie King laughed nervously, stood, then took his place at the far side of the fire.

Raleigh worked hard to shake off his anger. He took several deep breaths, trying to relax. He drank some bourbon when he'd made a pact with himself not to. The liquor helped, though. So when he could think clearly again he found reason to stitch Eddie King's nasty behavior into what was taking shape in his head.

Then, just as Raleigh was congratulating himself on his

self-control, Ben, with no warning, appeared in front of them in blackface wearing women's clothes. He wore an off-the-shoulder peasant blouse and a full skirt. Like a Spanish dancer he flounced and switched and then twirled open, spinning and stumbling in front of them; the others clapped and laughed. Clearly drunk, Ben slobbered forth a garble of sound, meant, by its rhythm and heavy accent to be colored speech. At first it was funny, if only from the shock. But Ben went on and on, lamely repeating everything he had already done. At long last he decided to quit and tried to leave.

But then Eddie King jumped up, grinning like a Venetian gargoyle. He pushed Ben roughly back into the center of the circle. Certain that it was all part of something planned, everybody laughed when Eddie King made Ben lift his skirt to show the woman's pants he was wearing. But the laughter died when Eddie King ripped the pants off, shredding them in such a frenzy that when he'd finished nothing was left but shreds of cloth, some of which caught fire as they floated onto the blazing logs. Eddie King bullied Ben to his knees; then he pulled out his own penis. He tried to stick it into Ben's hairy anus, directing it with his hands. It collapsed against Ben's flesh like an over-ripe banana. Raging, Eddie King cursed and began to beat Ben about the head and shoulders. Ben sobbed, begging Eddie King to stop. Eddie King shouted angrily for someone to give him a stick. Nobody moved. When that happened, or didn't happen, it seemed to bring Eddie King to his senses. For he stopped pummeling Ben and, still facing into the fire, tried to re-arrange himself as best he could. Breathing heavily, he turned round, smiling pleasantly at the circle of staring faces. He bowed as if it had all been some kind of act. Then, he pulled Ben to his feet and whispered something in his ear.

Ben ran blubbering, stumbling out of the light.

It was then that Raleigh actually thought for the first time about killing Holland. The idea hadn't come to him all at once. He must have been dancing about it in some vague, resentful way for days, all the time refusing to give it life in his brain. But with Eddie King's attack on Ben it forced its way on him with all the fury and the sense of vengeance that was needed to spawn such an obscenity.

To murder Holland: How it could be done, and who could do it.

By the time he got home on Monday, though, the insane idea had loosened its grip. It was nothing he could ever do. After that when the unwanted thought pushed its way into his head he rejected it.

As what? Fantasy?

4

HEAVEN, Sonny always said, was a big old kitchen where biscuits never burn and angels have to do the dishes. Here in Calvin's kitchen the supper pans were already washed, and Papa Bacon wasn't even home from work yet. You might say that Calvin's helpers, Angeline and Polly, were Papa Bacon's angels. Colored angels.

It was getting close to Christmas. Some presents were already wrapped; Elizabeth's gifts to him were in the front hall closet, and had been since Thanksgiving when she last visited. He'd bought a few himself, presents for Sonny and TJ of course. And a secret present for Calvin, a ring from the dime store, which the man said was part silver. But Billy was having trouble finding a present for Papa Bacon. Nothing in the dime store or the drug store seemed quite right.

Calvin had just put on his serving coat, a starched and ironed white cotton waiter's jacket. It whispered its readiness as he forced his arms into starched sleeves. And minutes before Dot Jessop had gone upstairs to change clothes. Some days she got dressed for the first time right before Papa Bacon came home in the late afternoon. Now she would spend a lot of time with her makeup and picking out the right things to wear. Everybody in the house was getting ready like that.

Billy liked being in the kitchen when Papa Bacon came home from the mill. Sometimes Angeline or Polly would shoo him out, but most days they let him stay. He sat either perched on a stool near the door, or in the kitchen window seat, feet drawn up, out of the way.

Today, Pierpont was there to keep him company. The cat spent more time at the Bacon house than at his own house, the Norris place. Most afternoons he hung around outside the back door as if he was in Papa Bacon's waiting party, too. Of course what Pierpont wanted was food (he usually got some), but Billy liked to pretend that Pierpont was a talker, like Zero.

"That's Polly over there, Pierpont," he said. "She's one of the maids here. She ain't been here so long. About a month now. You remember before it was that dumb girl, Charity. She was caught stealing after she had been here only a few weeks. Some of Dot Jessop's cold cream. I mean she up and took a jar and carried it home. I could never figure out what she wanted with that cold cream. Probably thought it was something to eat. She stole other things, too. Food usually. I saw her take it and put it in her sack. So did Calvin. But, he didn't do nothing. And I don't think he would of. You sort of expect folks to take a little food. But, when it came to something owned by Dot Jessop, watch out! Watch out! Boy, she was gone in a minute.

"That's the other helper, Angeline. She comes in to help with getting supper ready. She does most of the peeling and shucking and plucking and all. She snaps string beans faster and louder than anyone. Look…see all them feathers? Angeline plucked those off the duck that's for supper tonight. I hate roast duck. So does TJ. But Dot Jessop will say TJ and me have to eat it, because if we don't some kids in Europe will starve. That'll give you an idea of the way Dot Jessop thinks. But, I guess there really are a lot of people starving over in Europe. There's a big war going on over there now. I hope I get a chance to be in it.

"Well, Angeline washes the dishes, then she and Polly go home. And then Calvin goes home. Calvin lives over on the other side of Calhoun Street. Don't ask me where because I don't know exactly. But, I mean to find out."

There was something special about watching people who didn't know—or forgot—that they were being watched. That's how Billy knew that Charity, the girl before Polly, was stealing food. She would stuff beef or chicken, or pieces of ham maybe, inside her dress next to her bosom. And then later take it out and put it in her sack. He was glad when she was caught. Because he had started to worry. He first worried that she would be caught. And then worried that she wouldn't. After all, it was wrong to steal. And he worried, too, that Calvin might be blamed for using too much food. He also worried that she would see him watching her steal the food. And she did.

"And you know what, Pierpont? She went right on steal-ing!"

She knew he wouldn't tell anybody. It was a relief when she was caught with the cold cream. He could stop all that worry-ing.

Just then TJ crashed into the kitchen from outside heading for the radio to listen to his afternoon serials, shows like *Mary Noble, Backstage Wife, Just Plain Bill, Barber of Hartville* and his favorite, *The Green Hornet.* His tan sweater had snagged on limbs and things in the woods, partly unraveling wool which floated out behind him like curly swirls of dirt. And following, too, were TJ's faint clay footprints, which showed that he'd just cut through the woods down along by Water Moccasin Creek.

"Hey, Billy!" TJ cried as he passed. "Hey, Pierpont!"

THIS PAST SUMMER TJ had been sent off to camp for two weeks, the first time they had been separated in almost a year. With TJ gone the house had seemed empty and boring. He'd complained to Calvin how awful it was for poor TJ that he'd been sent away to a dumb camp just when summer was starting. Calvin had seen through him right away.

"TJ'll be home this Sunday," Calvin said. "That ain't long. I expect Mister Raleigh is gonna give you your turn next summer."

"Naaaw," he said. "I won't be here next summer."

Calvin, sitting in his chair, said nothing.

After a while Billy said, "Elizabeth said this year for sure. She's supposed to send for me. And maybe I'll even go. Tired of it here. Boring…. I forget what this year is, Calvin?"

"1941," Calvin said.

"This year for sure," Billy said.

So with nothing much to do in the afternoons while TJ was away, he'd got in the habit of sitting in the kitchen with Calvin.

For an hour, maybe two, in the dim light of afternoon, Calvin sat, nearly unmoving, up against the kitchen wall between the white metal topped kitchen table and the new electric stove. That was Calvin's place. No one sat in his chair, ever. No one would dare.

Billy had learned that you had to approach Calvin in the right way at the right time if you wanted something at Papa Bacon's. If you didn't he might just treat you like a glob of dried spit. Everybody in the house depended on Calvin for just about everything that had to do with anything. It was amazing. He fixed everything that was broke. Of course he was the cook and dog trainer, but he also drove him and TJ to school every day. He taught them how to fly cast. Not only that he told them when and what to eat, what to wear and sometimes when they had to go to bed. Even things like going to the toilet. Calvin always wanted to know if you had a good bowel movement. That could be embarrassing. At least it was for him, but for TJ it was a chance to use his powers of description. "Round and brown," TJ would say while holding apart his hands to show the length of the turd. Calvin would listen carefully to TJ and then intone a grave and rumbling, "Goooood!"

Whenever Miss Harp was off Calvin changed Emily's diapers. He and TJ would sometimes watch as Calvin cleaned and powdered the giggling girl, leaving her with a friendly pat on the behind. But then, the next day, Emily would hide from Calvin behind Miss Harp's starched white dress. Pretending to be scared of him. Like Calvin never touched her dirty bottom.

Then there was Calvin's magic. TJ was always after Calvin to do his tricks. Calvin knew a thousand card tricks and made coins fall out of their ears or disappear in tightly clinched fists (it didn't seem to matter whether it was his or one of theirs), but it was the other magic that TJ liked the best. One was when he or TJ just happened to walk past. Calvin would grab whichever one of them it was and hold him upside down by the leg. And then take a piece of raw meat out of his shoe.

"Calvin's the best magician in the world," TJ would always say when that happened.

"It's just a trick," Billy would say.

"I guess so," TJ said. "But how does he do it? He don't put it into your shoe ahead of time or you'd feel like you were walking on a piece of raw liver."

TJ cringed.

"And he don't put it in when he picks you up. I know cause I watched close when he did it to you. The question is: How does he do it?"

"A trick is made to fool dummies, dummy. That's why it's called a 'trick.'"

"You really think so?" TJ said. "I ain't so sure."

Billy had scoffed at the time, but then one afternoon during those two weeks when he was hanging around the kitchen with Calvin he'd remembered.

"TJ thinks you're a wizard, Calvin," he said. "Are you?"

"What's a wizard?"

"A wizard is somebody who can make things happen that ain't supposed to happen."

"Then I'm an honest-to-goodness wizard."

"No, you don't see what I'm saying. I ain't talking about your tricks, the things TJ likes, like pulling a piece of meat out of a shoe. I'm talking about real magic."

"Oh, I see."

"When you take the meat out of TJ's shoe it's a trick, has to be. It's a good one, but still a trick."

"You like it?"

"I like it," he said. "I'd like to be able to do it, too." Billy smiled, "Why don't you tell me how it's done?"

"Well, I can't rightly tell you. But I expect I could show you."

"Oh yeah!" Billy said.

This was better than going to scout camp with TJ. TJ would swallow his canoe paddle when he lifted a big hunk of meat out of TJ's shoe. He waited, smiling, looking at Calvin. But Calvin wasn't smiling.

"Ain't you gonna show me?" he finally asked.

"Show you?...You mean you can't feel it?"

"Feel what?"

"Why that ole hunk of meat sitting in your left shoe right this minute."

"Huh?"

"Your left shoe."

Billy's eyes narrowed. He stared across the table at Calvin. You really have to keep a sharp eye on a trickster, he thought.

"Ain't you feelin' it there yet?" Calvin said.

He couldn't stop himself. He wiggled a toe, then two toes. His eyes widened.

"Well, boy?" Calvin persisted.

"I don't think so," he whispered. "...uh...maybe."

"Come round over here, Billy," Calvin said, motioning with his hand.

Calvin's voice sounded kind of hollow, like it was far away. Billy strained to hear. Then he tried to stand up. At first he couldn't move. Then, suddenly, without even trying, he felt himself kind of rise up out of his chair, kind of floating, but not floating, either, more like walking without touching the ground.

And then—this was the crazy part—he saw himself kind of bounce around the table—like a loose balloon—over to where Calvin was. Calvin said something in the same deep, hollow voice.

His heart was beating wildly. At the same time he was very very calm. Calvin slowly took off his left shoe. Bam bam bam bam bam bam bam his heart thumped. With every heartbeat a light flashed at the back of his eyes, blinding him a little.

The shoe's well was dark and empty, but then the shoe tilted and something slid down. Calvin took it and handed it to him.

The next thing he knew he was sitting in the chair at the table like before; and Calvin was in his.

He looked down. On the table in front of him was a piece of meat. It was calves' liver, about an inch thick and three or four inches long.

By the time TJ got home on Sunday the liver was as hard as a rock, and stinking a little. Finally he had to throw it away. He wanted to tell TJ what happened, but every time he began something stopped him. Because this wasn't no little trick; this was special, this was something just between him and Calvin.

IN THE KITCHEN he and Pierpont watched TJ hurry past to find out if '*Just Plain Bill, Barber of Hartville*,' could figure out why the Mayor of Hartville wanted to quit his job and put 'ole Bill in his place. TJ loved the radio and almost never missed listening to his daily serials, which started one hour before Papa Bacon usually came home from work.

Not this day though.

For at that moment Billy heard his grandfather's familiar footsteps on the back stoop. He looked up at the clock. Only five o'clock. What was going on? He grabbed Pierpont and climbed up onto the window seat. Something was happening and he didn't want to miss it. He also kept a hand on Pierpont's bell so it wouldn't ring.

In the back vestibule Papa Bacon took off his hat and coat. He hung them up in the little closet there. Next, like always, he straightened his hair by running his hands once or twice over his head. Papa Bacon's hair was mostly white. But it ran darker toward the temples and sideburns, so that the white part of his hair was kind of a silky halo. It shone. His skin glowed too. He always looked like he did right now, like he'd just stepped inside after a brisk winter's walk.

"Good evening, Angeline," Papa Bacon said.

But he didn't wait for Angeline's answer! He crossed the kitchen, heading for where Calvin stood. Now Billy knew for sure that something important had happened.

Papa Bacon always stopped to ask about Angeline's health. And he always had plenty to listen to because she always had plenty to say. She would complain about the misery in her back or the rheumatism in her knees or something that had happened back at her house. Papa Bacon always listened patiently to whatever Angeline had to say. Like he had nothing else in the world to do.

Not today. And he didn't stop at the stove, either. He always stopped by the stove to see what Calvin was having for supper so he could chat with Calvin about it. Because almost every night they had something Papa Bacon shot or caught as part of the supper. Trout or perch or duck, something like that.

And Papa Bacon always said hello to Billy in some way, by winking or by putting his hand on his head as he passed by. Always. But not this evening. He went straight over to where Calvin was standing at the far end of the room.

Something electric shot up his spine, singeing his ears. Very still now so as not to miss a thing. But he couldn't hear what Papa Bacon and Calvin were saying. He watched their faces. He watched their hands.

That day Blueplate had got out of the run by digging under the wire fence. Afterward he got into the McCauley's chicken yard where he killed several hens before they caught him. That must be why Papa Bacon was early. Blueplate was his best pointer.

He watched for Blueplate's story in their hands.

But what he saw next confused him. Calvin, who never did nothing with his big hands but wipe them with his apron, put his behind his back. And Papa Bacon put his in his pockets. That was something he had never seen before. Papa Bacon with his hands in his pockets! He didn't know what to make of it.

He wanted to get closer. He started to climb down off the window seat, then stopped. With one foot on the floor he froze, for a moment not able to move.

They were talking about him!

Not about Blueplate. About him!

They *could* be talking about something big, like a war starting. It was 1941 and there was talk of America going to war. But there was no war, yet, and wouldn't be at least until after Christmas. Even the Nazis weren't bad enough to start a war at Christmas. And, besides, their hands would shout it to the rooftops that a war had begun.

It *had* to be him. But…but Elizabeth had already decided that he should stay at Papa Bacon's until the school year was over. Or it could be something else, a thousand things.

Whatever it was he didn't want to know.

He grabbed Pierpont and ran outside.

THAT NIGHT Billy lay awake a long time. TJ was asleep in the next bed. At last, when he couldn't hold his eyes open any longer, he slept. But he kept waking up in the throes of jumbled dreams. Somehow he settled on one dream, about a city of cats, where he and TJ and everybody else were the pets, and where Zero wanted to give him away. Nobody wanted him.

When he woke—to keep from being lost to Zero forever—
he was yelling at Zero. His pillow was drenched with spit and
tears. He looked across to the next bed, hoping to see TJ awake.
But TJ was asleep. And smiling. Smiling.

TJ, he whispered. TJ?

"You couldn't wake that boy with a cannon."

Dreaming still. That voice sounded just like Sonny's. He
stretched out his legs, put his arms over his head. Dreaming.

"Yeah, a cannon," he murmured sleepily.

"Or with a tuba, played by a tubby tuba player, tooting his
tuba all night long."

Sonny!

"Sonny," he cried, and threw off the covers. Before his feet
hit the floor Sonny was there, sitting next to him on the bed,
holding a finger to his lips.

"Sonny!"

"I been waiting for you to wake up, Billy. Did you know
you talk in your sleep. You snore a lot too. You know that? Yes
sir, a ten-gun snore it was, but tuneful. Sort of like 'Away down
yonder in the land of cotton, where your feet stink and mine
are rotten, Look away, look away—"

Sonny paused.

"'Look away?'... How does it go after that?"

Billy was dreaming. He had to be dreaming.

"'Look away', what, old man?"

"...Dixieland."

"Right. You ain't so dumb after all."

Billy touched Sonny then. Real. It wasn't a dream. Sonny
was real after all. He started to cry.

"No tears."

"Where'd you come from? How'd you get here? What time is it? Oh!... The hospital. What about the hospital?"

"I escaped from that goldanged place. Flew out of there, fast as my legs would carry me, all the way here to see my Billy."

"You escaped?"

"Yep."

"Oh, Sonny. What's gonna happen when they catch you? Oh—"

"Is that you, Sonny," TJ said sleepily.

"Well, I'll be danged if it ain't ole TJ hisself."

"Where'd you come from?" TJ asked.

"I flew in from Mars, been making candy bars for the Martians. The Mars Bar it's called. Them Martians find Mars Bars mighty munchy."

"He's escaped, TJ," he said. "We got to hide him. Where do you think?"

"Escaped!" TJ said. "From the looney bin?"

Sonny laughed.

"Naw," he said. "I escaped all right. But not over the fence. Not under it, either. No, I'm out because I'm supposed to be out. Got my walking papers. Got my pack. Ain't never never going back. Got my mind ever so fine. Don't never never look behind."

"Let us hide you, Sonny," Billy said. "Me and TJ. I know. Calvin! He could hide you over in Blacktown."

"No, no, honey. You don't get it. I'm out legal, fair and square."

"But—"

"Don't interrupt Mister Blab. Just listen."

"I—"

"Just listen."

"Okay."

TJ climbed across from his bed. Cross-legged, they sat knee to knee in flannel pajamas, too excited for the moment to feel how cold the room had become since they had gone to bed. Sonny, he could see now, was dressed in a big sweater and corduroy pants. Somebody had cut his hair real short so that it stood straight up, making him look a little wild. A little woolly, different from when he'd last seen him over a year ago.

Now Sonny laughed again, not as loud as before, but still loud. A private joke, something he had thought of as they got settled.

"I was just thinking," he said, "about what TJ said. The looney bin. I guess I was one. A looney. But I never thought so. I was sick, see. But I wouldn't admit it so they could fix me up. So you could say that I was Looney Tunes along with everybody else...."

Sonny stopped, as if he were thinking. Next to Billy TJ shivered. Sonny reached behind and took the blanket off TJ's bed. He put it around him and TJ.

"Well, once I started to see that old Sonny could use a little medicine to get well, then I had to get well quick. So I could see my boy. And so I could get out of the looney bin. And so I did.

"I stayed this whole year. I stayed until I was well. But I never could have done it without your letters, honey. Because when I heard that TJ and Calvin were taking such good care of you I could try harder to get well. So, that's what I did—"

"Are we gonna leave in the morning?" Billy asked. "Have you told Kallie that we're coming home?"

"Now wait just a darn minute, Mister Story Interrupter. How can Mister Story Teller tell his tales if Mister Story Interrupter keeps interrupting?"

"But Sonny—"

"Wait!…Now that I'm well there's no reason to be a looney in a looney bin. Right?

"Right? Isn't that kerrect?"

"Kerrect," TJ giggled.

"But I can leave with you, can't I?" Billy pleaded. "In the morning, I mean."

"Well, yes. You could, I guess. But I don't think you'll want to."

Billy stared. Sonny was acting crazy. He felt a little sick, like he'd been punched in the stomach.

"Ain't you gonna go back to Pineville?"

"Nope."

"Why?…Why not?"

"Uncle won't let me."

"Who won't let you?"

"Uncle," TJ jumped in. "Unc…me. TJ won't let—"

"Will you shut up! Will you kindly just keep your mouth shut for once?"

TJ slumped down in the blanket, feelings hurt. But Billy didn't care. He felt worse than TJ by a mile. He wasn't going to get to leave. Sonny wasn't going to take him home.

"Now, Billy," Sonny said. "Be nice to TJ. He's been awfully nice to you…. Because TJ's right, you know. TJ only made one little itty bitty mistake. He ain't the uncle that's stopping me from taking you home. Sam is."

He stared blankly at his father.

"Hey, dumbster, you don't get it do you?"

"No sir."

"Okay, Mister Dumbster. I'll spell it out for you."

He waited just a second or so before saying, "I've joined the Army."

"You did!" he and TJ said together.

"I sure did."

"Wow," TJ said.

"Yeah!" he said.

"Yep," Sonny said. "I marched right down to where Uncle Sam lives and said, "Sign me up, Uncle.""

"You signed up?" he said.

"Yep. The Army. Came back to the looney bin and said, 'I'm Uncle's now and you can't have me no more. You got to let me go.'"

"And—"

"They did!"

"They did?"

"Yep."

Billy didn't know what to say. For something that had started out so sad he was struck speechless by this magical, wonderful news. It wasn't that he felt good. It was so much more than that! It was like he was saved. Not Sonny. Him. Somehow he'd been saved. As for going home to Pineville.... Well, that didn't seem so important now. He would be going home, someday, when Sonny got out of the Army.

Sonny was in the Army!

"But, golly," TJ said then, "what if you get killed, Sonny?"

"Good question, Uncle TJ. After I'm killed I'll come right back here, right here to this room, and tell Mister Billy and Uncle TJ all the ghosts' secrets, who the top ghosts are, how much they get paid and whether a ghost is ticklish."

And with that he tickled them both. Laughing, squealing,

the two of them made the loudest racket anybody had ever made in that house in the middle of the night. It had to be a record. It was also a wonder that they didn't wake the whole house. But nobody came in to see. After that, after Sonny made a big thing about not telling them where he was headed (a military secret) and when he expected to get his first leave (generals don't get leave!) he promised to come back as soon as he could (and not as a ghost!)

By that time though he and TJ were so tired and cold that neither of them hardly knew it when Sonny stopped talking.

One minute he was there. And the next he was gone.

5

BILLY wanted to join the Army just as soon as he could; he might even run away, lie about his age. He would be seventeen when he graduated from high school. He didn't think he could wait until he was eighteen. Not a day passed when he didn't imagine Sonny and him meeting someplace during the war, some place far away, usually in the desert, their tanks lined up nose to nose. He saw Sonny and him facing each other, half out of their turrets, laughing to manly tears at the wonder of having found each other after so many months of war.

Every morning Billy studied the war map in *The Athena News*. Lately it had been the map of the war in Russia. The Russians still hadn't stopped the Germans in the South. The map, with the swastika on the left side and the hammer and sickle on the right, grew blacker each day as the Germans pushed the Russians back toward Stalingrad.

The Marines had invaded Guadalcanal in August. The fighting was hard there, so much worse than expected because the Japanese were so fanatical. They fought to the last man, in caves, in the jungle and—he never forgot this—with the idea that death for their emperor was a good thing. There was no map of Guadalcanal in *The Athena News*. So, he pretty much concentrated on the big map of Russia on the front page. The day before the Germans had reached the outskirts of Stalingrad.

When he'd finished looking at the newspaper he pulled out

Sonny's letter, the first after Sonny joining the Army, and read it again. Maybe for the hundredth time.

D OT JESSOP put on her new Red Cross uniform. She had had it tailored at Mr. Stormeyer's, using a better grade of gabardine than the instructions recommended. But, as Mr. Stormeyer said, it would be hot soon enough. In the spring and summer she would be glad she had decided on the lighter weight. And the tannish/olive color of this material tended a little more toward the beige. That was an easier color for accessories.

There was a small rope of dark gold braid on the cap at the base of the shiny bill. Dot Jessop rubbed the bill of the cap with a damp hand towel, then threw the towel on the tile floor of the bathroom. She placed the cap squarely on her head, making sure with a hand mirror that the tilt of the hat flowed into her hair, which she now wore as a modest bun turned under at the nape.

Next she attached the Red Cross arm band. As always it proved unwieldy. She had to pin it twice before it would lie flat and unwrinkled. She should have the band sewn on, but if she wanted to use the uniform for something else it would mean risking putting a hole in the material when the armband was removed.

She had heard that the new Air Force base outside of Greenville was going to form a USO auxiliary. A lot of the women she folded bandages with at the Red Cross were going to volunteer at the base. She wondered whether her uniform was appropriate for the USO.

She wanted to volunteer. She thought that her Cecile

Underwood print dress would be fine for a while if it turned
out she needed another uniform. She probably wouldn't want
to drive the sixty miles over and back more than once a week
anyway. That meant she would have to wear the Cecile
Underwood dress twice at least before Mr. Stormeyer would
have time to tailor her another uniform.

She tiptoed to check the seams of her stockings. She
scowled at the shoes. That was the only bad thing about uniforms. The awful shoes.

She walked out into the bedroom and was surprised to find
painters, two white men, spreading their tarps against the far
wall. She hadn't remembered that the painters were scheduled
for that week.

They were doing her room today in a warm pink, a color
she'd picked last spring because it matched her New York
underwear. What was the name of that store? Bergdorf
Goodman? Yes, or something like that. She liked the color, a
different kind of pink. Those New York Jews sure knew how to
make clothes. She wanted to go back to New York, but Leigh
didn't go anywhere lately unless it was on business. He was too
busy for vacations. And when he did travel—for the government usually—he couldn't take her. He said Army bases
weren't the kind of places she would like. Maybe not. But, while
she wouldn't be interested in that boring talk about building
barracks for soldiers, she would just love to see some new
places…. Oh, she dreamed about New York all the time. Were
there Army bases in New York?

"Well, I have a meeting," she told the painters. "I got a million things to do."

"Yessum," one of the painters said, smiling at her prettiness.

Or was it the uniform? She had to leave then. Only she didn't have any place to go. Too early for practically anything. She couldn't even go to Five Points. The fountain didn't open until eleven. So she walked out back, got in the car and started it before she thought of where to go.

"GOODNESS, Eddie King," she said, making a face, "aren't you ever gonna learn to make coffee decent? Your coffee tastes like cold turnip juice."

They had got off to a bad start. First, she had had to make him invite her in. And, then, to top everything, he had ignored the uniform. And she was sure he hadn't ever seen her wear it.

She would have liked to leave. But couldn't yet. She'd only been here thirty minutes. She looked at the chipped coffee cup in her hand, empty now except for a puddle of weak tea-colored coffee. A truck passed by on the street outside. The coffee jiggled with the movement of the house, then settled to a point just below a faint brown ring at the bottom of the cup.

"Why don't you ever learn how to make good coffee, Eddie King?" she asked again, demanding that he break his silence.

"Maybe you could teach me," he said.

"Maybe I could," she said.

He laughed.

"When are you going to get a job, like Ben?" she asked in retaliation.

"When are you gonna shut up?"

"Every man should have a job."

"Mind your own damn business, Dot Jessop."

"Don't call me that. I hate it."

"It's your name, ain't it?"

"You could have a job at the mill if you wanted. You know Leigh would give you one if you asked. Just like Ben."

"You can't hunt with a man and say 'yessir', too."

"It don't seem to bother Ben none," she said.

Every time she came over they fought over the same things. But Eddie King wouldn't go to work for Leigh no matter what she said. After one of their hunting trips she'd got Leigh to say that he might be willing to take him on at the mill. But nothing had come of it.

Eddie King just sat around all day doing nothing. If she didn't give him and Ben some of her allowance they would probably have to sell the old house. The house wasn't much and she would like them to sell it. The truth was it embarrassed her. But, if that happened, if they sold it, what would become of them?... Her daddy always taught her that you got to take care of your own. It was funny, she almost worried more about Ben and Eddie King than she did her own children.

"Well," Eddie King said. "You said you got a million things to do back at the house?"

"I do. It's a lot of work running a big house. We're painting today."

"Then you better pick up your ass and get to it."

"You are a vulgar man, Eddie King."

"Look who's talking," he said

"And just what is that supposed to mean?"

"You know what it means."

"I do not."

She still didn't move. She was waiting for him to ask. They sat in silence, Eddie King smoking his cigarettes, she mentally working on improving her uniform by tucking in the skirt, smoothing its lines along her legs. She would ask Mr. Stormeyer to narrow the skirt of the new uniform.

Finally, he said, "Could you lend me a few dollars, Dee? I'm a little short. Could use a dollar or two if you've got it to spare."

This request, this asking for money, made almost every visit, settled her. Eddie King usually asked for a "loan," a loan that would never be repaid. That was important. It showed who depended on who in the family. She felt a momentary flare-up of the old anger and for just a second considered saying no. But that notion was gone as quickly as it came.

"I guess I could lend you a dollar or two, Eddie King," she said. "But, you'll have to pay me back by the end of the month because I have to take it out of my household allowance. Got to pay Harpie, you know, and then there's my other expenses."

That was a lie. Leigh paid Miss Harp, as he paid Calvin and the rest of the servants. She had no real expenses. She got an allowance every week, an envelope with fifty dollars in cash delivered by Masters the mill paymaster along with the servants' envelopes. She never knew what to do with it all. There were envelopes with cash in them all over her bedroom. And in her purse. Her only expenses were what she spent going to the show and buying things at Five Points. She charged everything else. It was hard to spend all her money. She didn't even try anymore. But she couldn't let Ben and Eddie King know that. They would want it. As it was she must give them twenty-five a week, what with paying for the telephone and with all the loans.

She handed him the money, a ten and four fives. His thick eyebrows raised in mild surprise at the amount.

"Thank you, sister gal," he said, grinning, and slapped her affectionately on the butt as she turned to walk to the front door.

She stopped there.

"You didn't say one word about my Red Cross uniform," she said.

"Red Cross!" he said, in mock admiration. "Is that what this is? Why, honey, I thought you'd just been hired as an usherette at the Carolina. I was gonna ask you to sneak me in."

BACK IN HER CAR she headed for home. She looked at her watch, saw that she would arrive too soon. Aimlessly she turned down a street, slowing so she could look at the fronts of the houses. But, they were like what she'd just left. Bungalows, with two brick posts framing narrow porches no one ever sat on. The yards were scruffy, what green there was was weeds and crab grass. She drove over to the north side of town where she picked a street at random. She drove around for a while that way until she finally ran out of streets. At the next intersection she slowed trying to decide where she could go next. She couldn't think of a single place. Slowly she drove around the block. Slower and slower until finally she stopped and let the motor idle.

Sat there.

"Yes ma'am?" a voice asked. She looked up to find a Negro man dressed in white coat and black trousers bending toward the driver's window of the car.

"Oh!" she said.

She tried to pull away but she had forgotten to shift the automobile into first gear, and it stalled. Flustered, she started the car, then stripped the gears in her haste to leave. The car stalled again.

Behind the Negro, across a wide lawn, a door stood open

under the portico of a stately Georgian house. The Negro, white haired, peered at her.

Finally, the car started. She pulled away without looking at the colored man. In the rear view mirror she watched him turn and walk across a lawn toward the beautiful house. The tears came then. More tears. She swore, swore again. GODDAM-YOU, she shouted angrily at a passing car.

She didn't want anybody to see her at the house. She walked around to the front door so she wouldn't have to go through the kitchen. But Calvin was waxing the front hall.

On his hands and knees he looked up and said, "Watch where you step, Miz Dot."

"Don't you dare speak to me!" she spit.

She hurried past, heading for the circular stairway, then slipped. For a moment she seemed to right herself, then crumbled slowly to the gleaming, just waxed floor. She lay there, sobbing.

Calvin hurried to her. She was on her side, curled up, holding one leg.

"Are you hurt Miz Dot?"

"Yes," she said in a small voice between sobs.

"Yes," she said again, to make it official.

By now Billy, Miss Harp with Emily, and Polly, who had heard the noise and had come running, were watching from the edge of the dining room. They didn't approach any closer. They knew from the sound of her crying that Dot Jessop was more mad than hurt. Besides, Calvin was there to take care of things.

"Can you walk, Miz Dot?" he asked.

There was silence as Dot Jessop thought.

"No," she said in the same voice. Then added, "I want to go to my room."

"Yes ma'am."

He bent to pick her up.

As he straightened she had a sensation of lightness, as if she weren't a little overweight, as if the anger and hurt she had just felt belonged to someone else. She was almost giddy from the feeling of...of freedom. She realized, though, that practically the whole house was watching. So she continued to sob a little as if it still hurt.

As Calvin slowly made his way up the stairs she became intensely aware of his hands. She could feel his fist tight against her back and the large hand under her thighs. It was like she was being lifted up by some steel crane. She marveled at his strength. How come niggers were so strong? Some of them, anyway.

But she was not supposed to like what was happening.

"Hurry up," she said. "I want to lie down."

Then, before he could answer, "Are the painters still here?"

"Yes ma'am," he said. At the top of the stairs he shifted his hold slightly, unfolding his fist so that his left hand spread across half her back.

She remembered his hand from before.

She thought she'd forgotten all about it, his hand and all, until now. She had been pregnant with Emily, in her seventh month. And so happy. Happier by far than she had been since. She liked being pregnant. She never understood the women at bridge who complained so much about labor pains. And the delivery and all. For her it was easy. And besides she felt so important. There wasn't anything more important than being a mother. A woman giving birth. It was kind of sacred. Just thinking about it brought tears to her eyes.

And everybody treated her so important. Leigh was so pleased, smiling, saying, well I was starting to worry that TJ wasn't going to have any brothers. Besides being pregnant she was taking care of TJ because Miss Harp didn't come to work for them until just before Emily was born. So she was busy, pregnant and busy.

After she started to show she liked to parade around with her belly sticking out. Somehow it didn't make any difference if you were pregnant. You could do things then you would never dream of doing otherwise. Like the day she was thinking about when they were all in the nursery. They had just finished painting it and everybody, except Leigh, was there. It was like a party.

She hadn't gotten dressed yet. She was still in her nightgown and robe sitting on the chaise lounge when Emily started to kick. When that happened she made everybody come feel the baby kick. The maids, TJ, and Calvin.

Calvin didn't want to do it.

"Yes ma'am," he said without touching her. "I don't need to touch nothing. I can see it! Look at that rascal kick."

But she had insisted. He was reluctant, but she had taken his hand and placed it over her stomach where the kicking was strongest. She held it, pressing down, making him feel the kicks. But then, as now, she was really only aware of the spread of his hand. In the seconds that his hand remained on her belly, she thought she could feel the tips of his fingers through the rayon of the nightgown.

Until now she had forgotten. She remembered now what she had thought at the time.

Was he pressing a little? It was hard to tell. But, yes, she thought. Yes, he could be. And then, finally, she decided that he was. That was when she had let his hand go.

In her bedroom she could hear the painters working in the bathroom.

"The painters," she whispered.

Calvin carefully placed her on the canopied bed. Then he disappeared through the door of the bathroom. In seconds he reappeared, followed by the two men. She watched through hooded eyes as he led the procession around the bed to the hall. No one looked at her. She thought about calling Calvin back to take off her shoes but decided against it.

By the time Miss Harp came upstairs to undress her she had decided that she was hurt more seriously than she thought at first.

She and Harpie quarreled the whole time she was being put to bed.

RALEIGH turned onto Park Drive and drove alongside the Pickney Common. Apple blossoms and occasional mag-nolia trees, their white flowers waxy and virginal, lit the way along the winding road. It was the long way to Victoria's house. He needed the time to consider just exactly what he wanted to say to his sister. But within seconds the snowy profusion of spring flowers took his attention away from that business. To enjoy the scene unfolding ahead he slowed the automobile. Each year it was the same. The beauty of the flowers and his forgetfulness of their beauty. It was as if his memory were as fragile as the flower petals themselves. Still, for some things, like flowers, it was the renewal that counted. That thought of seasons cheered him, reinforcing what the war emergency had already taught him, so when he drove into Vickie's driveway his mind was concentrated again.

"I declare," Victoria said when she saw him in the door, "you have become a virtual stranger, Leigh. You seem to take the war"—she pronounced it 'waaah,' like Mr. Roosevelt—"so serious."

"The war is a serious business, Vickie," he said.

"You know what I mean, dear," she said. "As if we could do anything about it."

She gestured toward the door leading to the back yard.

"At first it was exciting," she said. "My goodness, the Japs were going to invade California! Don't you remember? Ethel Barrington let Mr. Haigaki go because she was sure the little man was going to slit her throat with his clippers. I must say I toyed with the idea of asking him to come work for me. He would be so much better than Shad…. Now it's just tiresome. The war. Four gallons a week. I mean, how can anyone get by with that little gasoline. I say, it's just too tiresome."

"You don't need more gas, Vickie," he said. "As it is you hardly use the car."

"For Caesar's Head, dear, this summer."

"Well, if you need some more gas, I can get you some. Or you can use some of mine."

"Oh yes," she said, opening the back door. "You can get all you want on the Army bases."

"Not all I want," he said as he followed her, "but I am allowed to fill up the car when I'm there."

He was taking a big gamble at Camp Croft. That Army base was spreading over more than twenty thousand acres not far from Spartanburg. Bacon Construction was building four-hundred-sixteen wooden barracks. It didn't seem complicated when he first examined the site and was told what was needed. The big problem was that Bacon Construction had no experience with mass construction. The company, barely three years old, had just one school building and three bridges to its credit. He had always envisioned it as more of an engineering concern than a construction company. All that changed with the war and Camp Croft.

The question was what would happen to Bacon Construction after Camp Croft. Good things he hoped. True, he would have lost more than two-hundred-fifty thousand dollars by then. But since he was the sole owner with sufficient capital he was able to commit earlier and for less cost to the government than anyone else. When he brought in the job ahead of schedule the Army would want to deal with a company who could get things built in a hurry. When that happened there wouldn't be any more competition. Bacon Construction would have more business than it could handle.

It also meant he would be away from home for weeks at a time. He'd already decided to leave running the house to Calvin, to let him write checks on the household account. After North Carolina he had thought he could never feel the same kinship with Calvin again. But that had been before Pearl Harbor. The war—with his scalping a little red clay over in Spartanburg—had changed his life in so many ways.

Victoria led him outside to the garden, to the white-and-green-trimmed gazebo. Their talk followed the familiar pattern—the weather, the family, the mill. Danny, while drunk, had tried to enlist in the Marine Corps at age forty-three. Raleigh had been out of town in Washington at the time so he had been very fortunate to keep reports of the embarrassing scene out of the newspaper. Vickie asked about Sonny, if he'd written the boy. He shook his head, as he did calculating exactly how long it had been. Four months.

"Hasn't it been over four months?" Vickie asked, echoing his thought.

They were silent for a moment.

Then he got to the point of his visit.

Would she be willing to consider buying his Bacon Mills stock?

For just a moment Victoria seemed at a loss for words.

Then, "Why, Leigh, honey, you take my breath away."

"I know it's a surprise, Vickie, but I didn't know I'd be asking until a day or so ago."

"Why—" she began.

"It's a long story. That is, it's been going on a long time. But I can tell you what's happened lately, what brought me here today."

"Please do that, dear. I need a moment to regain my composure."

"As you know, I was going to be away from the mill with my government work and it was decided that Sam should run the Company while I was away," Raleigh said.

"Well, dear Leigh, Sam is the oldest—"

"That's fine with me, Vickie. With the government's orders it would take a true imbecile to lose money now. Remember also that it was my idea that Sam take over…. No, that's not it. That's not why I'm here. What you probably don't know is that because of my leaving Sam has ordered me to sell him my stock."

"Ordered?"

"Yes. He said that if I wasn't going to be working at the mill

I had to sell my stock to a member of the family. Sam in other words."

"He didn't tell me."

"No, naturally. Sam has just enough thief in him to make him a good businessman. That is, if he weren't so lazy."

"Well, if you can sell to Sam—"

"Let me finish, Vickie dear, and your questions will be answered."

"Of course, dear," she said.

"I hadn't thought of selling. I guarantee you it hadn't crossed my mind. But what Sam said got me thinking. I realized that while I would never have considered selling Bacon stock as little as six months ago, my life has changed so much in the last few months that it now made sense to at least think about it. Well, I did think about it. I asked Sam what he was offering. It turns out that Sam was willing to pay five dollars a share—"

"Five dollars!"

"My reaction exactly," he said. "I told Sam the stock was worth closer to fifteen dollars. Since the book value is just under twenty dollars a share I thought that was a good price."

"Well," she said. "You don't have to tell me the rest. I can guess."

"I should have known, too," he said. "But I was trying to be fair. Sam wrote me a little note. Here it is."

She read it aloud:

"'Discussed the stock matter with Danfield. What price family loyalty? For you, apparently, the term is an oxymoron. Better you should sell your stock to the illustrious Jessops of Andersonville.'"

"What a pompous fool," she sighed.

"No question about that. But I'm obliged to Sam for the idea. So that's why I want you to buy the stock."

She laughed, "Really, Leigh, it's absurd. I could never afford it."

"Of course you can afford it. You are a very wealthy woman. What's more you have no expenses to speak of. Your Bacon stock alone gives you an income of over sixty thousand a year.

"My thinking," he said, "is that if TJ someday wants to come to work at the mill you will find a place for his talents."

"I believe that you are dead serious about this, Leigh,"

"Yes I am."

"Then you've come to the wrong place to sell your stock, dear. Because I couldn't afford to buy it."

"I want to sell you my stock for five dollars a share."

To anyone outside the family it would seem that she didn't react. There was no change in her expression, just a quizzical air that came from the cocked position of her head and the slightest of benign smiles. A smile that had followed him politely to the subject of money. But the swing where she sat had stopped moving. In a moment, though, after smoothing her blue dress and patting her hair, she pushed it back into motion.

A throwback, he thought. She should have been a man.

"That's more than four million less than it's worth, Leigh dear," she said.

"I need to sell, Vickie. And I must sell to someone in the family. I can't think of anyone I'd rather have my shares than you."

"What does Dot think about all this?" she asked.

"It's my stock to sell, Vickie. Anyhow, Dot wouldn't be interested."

"You would be giving away more than four million of your family's money," she said.

"I have plenty of money."

"I'm sure. But, Leigh dear—"

She stopped, then continued, "I hope you'll forgive me. But you aren't thinking straight."

"Dot won't care if I sell the stock," he said. "It's not the kind of thing that interests her. I know people think that she married me for my money, but that's not true. She has no real interest in money. Her interests are limited. And, they don't include money. I give her fifty dollars a week and she doesn't spend that."

"I think she would take an interest if she knew what you intended," she said. "And what about TJ and little Emily? What about them? Have you thought about how much it will cost to take care of Emily?"

"Don't you worry about Emily," he said, the annoyance showing in his voice. "I will take care of my family. Now, do you want to buy the stock?"

She didn't answer.

"Well? Please, yes or no?"

"No, dear, I don't."

"If it's a question of payment, I could take back a note and you can pay me over time."

"That isn't the point, Leigh honey," she said. "You can't just sell your stock this way. We need you. Bacon Mills would be nothing without you."

"It's going to have to get along without me from now on."

"Until after the war," she said.

"I'm never coming back."

"Poor Leigh. Of course you'll come back. Don't you see? You don't have any other choice. This is where you are from. Athena is your home. Leigh, dear, we are your people."

CALVIN walked to the middle of the room and stopped. The living room rug was where the partying crowd had left it, rolled up and shoved off to the side under the south windows. The table in front of the window had tilted over, causing the lamp on it to fall. But its cord had caught the edge of the over-turned table, and, still burning, it now dangled upside down, casting long shadows on the ceiling.

His own shadow stretched high against the opposite wall. He picked up the lamp, switched it off, righted the table. In the half gloom he stood still, as if hesitant to see how bad it was. Then he pulled open the drapes to let in the morning light.

Glasses, empty, part-filled, stuck to where they had been left hours earlier. They lined the top of the mantle, filled the other tables and were spotted, like game markers around the edges of the bare floor. Several had broken and glass was scattered about. It had cut someone's stockinged foot. Bleeding, the foot had stamped a series of violent, dark red commas into the floor. Like a mad dancer, they traced a wobbly partial circle half way around the room to where the trail faded, then abruptly ended.

The wood floor, polished and gleaming the day before, now seemed pocked and blighted, the overnight victim of some grim, incurable disease. Together with the blood and glass, marks from the dancers' shoes blended with the blackened remains of ground out cigarettes.

Impassive, he looked around the room, planning the clean-up. Except for a few glasses nothing had been broke. It looked worse than it was—the glass could be swept up and the floor cleaned, the wood re-waxed. In his imagination the room was now almost clean. All that was left was the work.

But first the house needed a good airing.

He walked across the room, through the hall and opened the front door.

To his surprise there were two young men in Air Force uniforms sitting on the top step of the front stoop.

One, reed thin, the youngest looking of the two, stood up and said, "Good morning, mister. We were wondering about our ride? Dot told us she would take us back to the base. We have to get back by eight this morning. Our passes are up then."

Calvin rubbed his big hands on his apron. These boys weren't that much older than TJ and Billy. Only the uniforms said different. Up to now he'd barely spoken to any of the boys who came to the house for one of Dot Jessop's parties. Canteens they was called, receptions where only coffee and soft drinks were served, and where the ladies of the Athena Red Cross Auxiliary moved around among the soldier boys trying to get them to feel at home. At first the parties had been regular, kind of quiet. Then a few months back somebody broke out the liquor. Miss Harp claimed it was one of the soldier boys, but he figured Dot Jessop was the one who had done it.

The airman continued, "Well, we gotta get back. Do you think you could go wake her up and ask?"

No, he said, but he would drive them downtown to the bus station. They could catch an early bus back to the base from there. They grumbled some, especially the second one, but followed him out to the garage.

On the drive downtown the first airman wanted to talk.

"Some party, that was some party."

In the silence that followed he added, "Don't you think?"

After more prodding, the second airman said, "Yeah."

This boy was in a sullen, nasty temper.

"How about you, mister, do you work for Dot?" the first airman asked.

Such young boys. Neither one could be more than eighteen, nineteen at the most. But each was pale, especially around the eyes, as if the long night had sucked out some of their youth. Their uniforms were plenty wrinkled, but both looked clean. They had shaved. Their dark heads, still damp, shone from being just combed.

"She must be nice to work for?" the first boy said.

When he only nodded, the first airman pushed him, "Huh? Is she?"

"Miz Bacon is fine to work for," he said.

"Boy, that was a great party," the first one said. "Fun and, well, you know, wild. Great fun.

"She said she is going to have them more regular," he added. "I hope she does. But, I, myself, probably can't come to more than one or two. I'll be getting my orders soon."

He paused, "At least one party I hope. I want to see that Margo whats-her-name again."

"Old pussy," the second airman said.

"Well—"

"It's all old pussy," the dark-skinned one said. "There wasn't nobody there less than thirty, and most were a lot older than that."

"Yeah, well, so what? That Margo may have been old but you wouldn't have known it."

"She wanted to get laid, bad. I coulda done it to her ten times. But, jeez, man!"

The first airman, embarrassed, looked over at Calvin.

"Anyway Dot sure was nice," he said. "Like I said she picked us up at the base. And, really, she said she would take us back. Isn't that right, Fini."

"I guess so," Fini said.

"Yeah, she said she would take us back to the base. Mister you should please tell her that we waited, but we had to get back."

He nodded, then asked, "Any others from the base with you boys?"

"Oh, sure, there must have been ten other guys there from the base. I didn't know half of them. But, we were the only ones that she asked to stay. Dot. Mrs. Bacon."

BACK AT the house Calvin spent several hours cleaning up the mess in the living room. Miss Harp, wide-eyed, with Emily in tow, stopped to watch him work.

"Ain't you got nothing to do, woman?" he growled. "You get upstairs. She gonna need someone to hold her head when she wakes up."

"What you expect Mister Raleigh gonna say when he get home?" Miss Harp asked, smirking.

"You planning to tell him something?"

"Not me," Miss Harp said.

She twirled out of the room. Her white dress rose up, coving like a pear, revealing the black of legs above where the stockings ended.

When he finished cleaning the living room he went in to check Mr. Raleigh's bedroom. The two airmen had slept in his stripped bed. The white linen spread covering the four poster's mattress had been tossed onto the floor; they'd slept on the bed pad, without sheets, without pillow cases.

He picked up the counterpane, folded it over the luggage stand at the foot of the bed. He spent a moment or two looking at the pillows on the bed. Finally, he picked them up and threw them on the floor with the bed pad. In the bathroom he removed the blade from the safety razor the two had shared, then scrubbed the tub and sink. The used towels went on the pile in the hall. He also found a pair of Mr. Bacon's silk pajamas hanging from a hook behind the door. He took all these things, the pillows, bed pad, the towels and the silk pajamas and burned them all to ash in the metal drum at the back of the kennels.

MISS HARP showed up after each party. To Calvin she was like a dung beetle, eager to skitter in whatever shit she could find. She was attracted by the dirty mess, the bad smells, and, most of all, the promise of trouble. Eyes bright, greedy, she kept her distance. But she was always there, burrowing away.

What would Mr. Raleigh think about what had happened the night before, or the week before, or two weeks before? She seemed to know what worried him most, then picked at it. And that was how to keep Mr. Raleigh from knowing exactly what was happening while at the same time making sure he knew that there were parties, a whole lot of parties, being held in his house while he was gone. Wasn't much more he could do than that. Because Mr. Raleigh knew all about the Canteens. And he'd made it plain that he wanted them to go on.

"Heard you served most of the U.S. Army," Mr. Raleigh had said on his last trip home. "But don't ever skimp, Calvin. Never skimp when it comes to giving those boys the best. Some of them, God's tears, will be dying for us real soon."

Then there was a change. The heavy drinking parties went on for a while. But after one Dot Jessop didn't come downstairs at all the next day. Another time the Canteen had started and was almost over before anyone even noticed that she wasn't there. She was found upstairs, passed out on her bed. One by one the other women in town found excuses not to co-hostess one of her receptions. So, little by little, the big parties were replaced, first by smaller Canteens and then, finally, by USO visits, a program sponsored by the Athena USO to put home-sick soldier boys into real homes.

In early January of 1943 they started to come to the house. Soldiers and airmen, in ones and twos, polite young boys, who seemed real thankful for the chance to rest up over a weekend in a comfortable house and, at the same time, have some good food to eat. Calvin was happy to get rid of the big parties with their heavy drinking and ever present danger of damage to the house. So he welcomed these special guests to Raleigh Bacon's house.

BILLY WATCHED the soldier eat his breakfast. Next to him TJ watched too. This soldier wasn't much different from the others, the soldiers and the flyers who came to the house almost every weekend now. Some were funny sounding with Mississippi and Texas or maybe New York accents, so different you had trouble understanding them. But except for the uniforms they all looked pretty much alike, real skinny, with real short hair. They were young, too, not a whole lot older than him and TJ. Least that's what Calvin always said, maybe to make him and TJ feel good. Because at times they seemed awful old to him. Every single one of them shaved.

They, especially TJ, always asked a lot of questions. If it was a soldier staying over naturally his first question always was did the soldier know Sonny. Nobody had so far. A couple of the soldiers knew where Fort Bragg was, but up to now nobody had even heard of Fort MacClelland.

TJ always asked the soldiers the same things: what it was like to shoot somebody (so far nobody at the breakfast table had ever shot anybody,) or, would he rather kill Japs or Nazis, and always, how old was he when he enlisted. Like most of the others this soldier seemed to not mind answering TJ's questions. His guess was that the soldiers and flyers who came here for the weekend hadn't got this much attention since they joined up. But the best thing was when Calvin came into the breakfast room. That was the absolute best.

In the meantime his watching the soldier eat had made him hungry. He piled some grits on his plate, took three patty sausages off the meat platter. He minced the pork sausages, then mixed the remains into his grits. He ate slowly, savoring the strong, sausage-flavored grits as he half-listened to TJ and the soldier talk.

Although he usually only ate grits and sausage, sometimes hot cereal, the table was filled with a million other things to eat. Happened every Saturday morning, at least every Saturday when they had a soldier for the weekend. There were eggs, scrambled and fried. They could also get boiled or poached eggs if they wanted them. And not just sausage, bacon too. And most of the time either smoked mackerel or trout. There was hash, all kinds of hash, not at once, of course, but a different kind nearly every weekend. And biscuits and toast and English muffins and regular muffins. Coffee cakes, too. And brains. Ugh, brains. Sweetbreads they were called. There was never room on the table for all the food Calvin cooked. It was like he could never cook too much food for his "soldier boys."

Billy stopped eating now to watch as Calvin pushed through. the swinging door. The soldier looked up. His mouth fell open. Stopped eating. Hah! They all acted like that whenever Calvin came into the breakfast room. Like they were having trouble believing he was real. Calvin asked the soldier if he had room for some spoon bread, would he like some pan gravy on his grits, more coffee? Even when they were stuffed to the gills, like this one seemed to be, even when they couldn't swallow another bite, Calvin was offering something more to eat.

Nosir this soldier said. Most did. But some, the really big eaters, said yessir. Give me the spoon bread, give me the pan gravy, I'll have some more coffee. Even the Southerners. Even the boys who never called any colored at home anything but nigger always said yessir or nosir to Calvin. For sure, they had never seen anybody like him. But it wasn't because Calvin scared them. The yessirs and nosirs were right friendly.

It was fun. Everybody had fun, him and TJ, the soldier for sure, maybe even Calvin. Everybody. Until Dot Jessop started coming downstairs.

That must have been the third or fourth weekend. She showed up at the breakfast table and things were never the same after that. Billy was still surprised that she was willing to get up so early. He couldn't figure out why she would want to be seen at that hour. Pale, eyes swollen, her face puffy, pushed out of shape from sleeping hard in one position for a long time, she looked bad. But while she must have felt bad, too, she sure tried hard not to show it.

From the second she showed up at the breakfast table all she did was laugh. It was the kind of laughter that makes everybody else stop talking. Loud, she acted like she did at one of her parties. She was the hostess. A loud, loud hostess. It was grating and made everything she said seem false.

In her frilly and fancy blue silk company robe, with its wavy, stand-up collar, she seemed silly sitting at the same table next to the khaki of the soldiers and airmen.

He and TJ escaped as soon as they could. But the soldier boy always had to stay. He felt sorry for this one, just like he had for most of the others. Because when she came downstairs this soldier, like the earlier ones, would change. From being friendly and open with him and TJ, from smiling and saying his yessirs and nosirs to Calvin, he would become surly, rude acting toward Dot Jessop. It seemed to happen every time.

Wait! Was that the swish of her robe striking the hall banister? He strained to hear. Yes!

"Sure has been nice meeting you, sir," Billy said to the soldier. "If you ever see my daddy, tell him you stayed here. He'll sure be interested."

He kicked TJ's chair to leave, too. But TJ was too slow. He was the only one to escape that morning.

SAM BACON surprised Raleigh. You would have thought from Sam's reaction when Raleigh walked unannounced into Sam's office that the years of bitterness and division were just a bad dream.

"Leigh!" Sam had said. "My, it's good to see you. How have you been? My goodness! And you working for the gov'ment now, too. My, my, our little baby brother's a G-Man."

Then he laughed, in apparent good humor.

"Business seems to be good," Raleigh said, careful to make it a statement rather than a question.

"Business is excellent. Excellent. We got more than we can handle. I been sending what we can't handle over to Woodside. I expect that before long we can send them all the gov'ment business, too."

That alarmed Raleigh. But he wasn't here today to get into an argument with Sam. Just the opposite. In just minutes though and with only a few words, Sam had managed to put him on edge. He had worried that Sam and Danny would do nothing about handling the growth of the business. He had worried, too, that they would passively accept, as they always had, the status quo. They didn't seem to understand that unless Bacon Mills continued to grow it would eventually die. For some reason they were incapable of operating in the future.

Despite having resolved to say nothing that might start a quarrel, he couldn't resist saying, "You don't want the Quartermaster Corps business? It's very profitable. And sole source."

"It's what I call the trash business," Sam said. "We are now in the trash business with this war. Being the gov'ment, it don't want best quality. And the people who tell you what to do are mostly trash. They don't know what they're talking about and some of them are lower than our colored. And that reminds me! I had one here actually ordering me about the mill."

"One?"

"A nigger. He came down from Washington and started poking around, asking questions. I told him to get out and to stay out. You'd think they'd have better sense than to send a nigger down here."

Raleigh started to say something, then thought better of it.

"How do you plan to replace the government business if we lose it?" he asked.

"Replace it? Why we would be at near capacity if we didn't have a dime of gov'ment business. When the war is over we're gonna lose it anyway. It sounds like you are becoming a real honest-to-goodness gov'ment man. I was joking before, Leigh, but I can see that you really do think like Mr. Roosevelt."

Maybe he should just forget it, Raleigh thought, forget what had brought him here in the first place. But he'd never been one to give up easily. He had to give it a try. On a cot in barracks outside San Antonio it had seemed so clear. Both sides were at fault. He hadn't acted so reasonably himself when they criticized his marrying Dot. He should have known what to expect. The key was to forget. Forgiveness wasn't part of this. It was a question of good will, a willingness to wipe the slate clean, to trust the future.

He began slowly, "Sam, I didn't come here today to talk about the mill.... I've been thinking a lot lately...quite a bit...about the family and how we've let things get into a bad state. I figure it's up to you and me to try to fix things. We've been acting like children for so long that we've lost sight of the fact that we are the same blood. You and me, and Danny."

"Well, those are noble words, Leigh," Sam said. "But they seem to say that the other side of the Bacon family should share the blame. The way I remember it you were the one who turned against me and Danny. You were the one who moved outside the family. You were the one who conspired—"

"Now wait one minute, Sam," he said.

"—the one who conspired to rob your brothers—your own flesh and blood!—of their birthright."

"Conspiracy is a strong word," he said. "No one has ever conspired against you and Danny. Yet you could say that's why I'm here today. Let the three of us get together—let us conspire if you will—to heal the family's wounds. We can't do that with all these bad feelings. Do you really want this trouble to go on forever? We have to start somewhere. I'm suggesting a fresh start right here, now, this morning."

"This is hard to believe," Sam said. "You can sit there with a straight face and say that you and Victoria didn't persuade Papa and the stockholders that I wasn't fit to run the mill?"

"I'm sorry about that, Sam. I know you were hurt. But, to call what happened a conspiracy is unfair. It was simply a business decision."

"And that decision was that you were better than me?"

"I don't think this is going to get us any place, Sam."

"I want to know, little brother, how you thought you were entitled?" Sam asked. "Did you think for one minute you could do a better job at the mill? What I want to know is what gave you the right to take my place in the family? How come you took what was mine?"

Sam was breathing hard. His face, flushed a deeper red now, was contorted into half smile and half sneer.

"We're brothers, Sam," Raleigh said, struggling to keep his voice even. "Not only do we have the same blood in our veins we have common interests. When the war is over we will have to work together to make sure that Bacon Mills is ready to adapt to the changes that are coming. I need you, Sam. And I think you need me."

"If you are thinking about coming back in here to run the mill you have another think coming," Sam said, raising his voice, using it as a weapon. "You try to rob me again, Gov'ment man, and…and—"

Sam paused. Raleigh could see from Sam's contorted face that his brother had meant to threaten him physically but somehow sensed the threat would be ridiculous.

Raleigh plowed ahead, "Look Sam, there will be enough to keep us all busy after the war. "The important thing is for us to work together and to be ready to adjust."

"Fine, fine," Sam said, his voice hearty and booming again, as if this ugly glimpse of his underside had never happened.

"But I want a commitment now," Sam continued. "I won't ask for anything in writing. As you say we're the same blood. But I want your agreement that I will keep on running the business after the war is over."

"I think it's likely that nothing will change after the war. I see you staying where you are."

"As President?"

"Yes."

"Then I want your commitment now," Sam said.

"We are speaking of adjusting, of being flexible," Raleigh said. "I can't make that kind of commitment. We don't know how long the war will last. And we don't know what our personal situations will be like."

"Are you refusing?" Sam asked.

"I'm trying to explain."

"What if something happened to you?" Sam asked. "Have you thought about that?"

"Of course," he said.

He started to explain how he had set up a trust that would eventually put TJ in his place.

Quickly, Sam, as if he had long suppressed a forbidden

thought but now wanted to utter it before he could be stopped, interrupted Raleigh and said, "Tell me what's gonna happen if they own your shares."

"They?" he asked. "You mean TJ?"

"You know who I'm talkin' about," Sam said. "The Jessops."

And then, only half aloud, almost under his breath, he let escape, "Those mongrels."

"What did you say?"

"I was asking about the Jessops coming into your stock."

"No, no…no! You used the word, 'mongrels.'"

"Well," Sam said, his tone defiant, "ain't they?"

For a moment Raleigh couldn't speak. His rage was so sudden and so fierce he could scarcely breathe. Helpless, he was helpless in his anger. To have worked this hard for something he really didn't want in the name of 'family relations,' to have put 'good will' ahead of what was best for Dot and TJ and Emily, not to mention the employees and stockholders of the company, was crazy, the worst kind of self-deception. But, these were later thoughts, when his self-flagellation was relentless and merciless. Now he couldn't think beyond his rage.

A rage that was murderous, yet controlled, because he felt afraid of what he might do if it wasn't. He kept very still. He scarcely breathed, swallowing air.

Then with no warning he began to hiccup. This sound, startling yet banal, seemed to mock the seriousness of what had just happened.

Sam smirked. The smirk said he'd won. It said Raleigh was afraid to cross him. To his dying day Sam would suspect but never be sure, according to Danny, that it was at that exact moment—when the hiccups started and what he felt free to say next—that Sam's life changed forever.

"And while we are on the subject of the Jessops, Leigh," Sam said, "I expect it wouldn't do you no harm to get home a little more often. Seems that Dot's Canteen parties belong more to Hollywood than in Athena. But, then again, she probably don't know the difference.

"And it don't look good, you know, what with them soldiers sleeping over at the house all the time. I know that Temp Watertower takes soldiers, too. But, they never stay overnight at the house. You know that they got rooms at the USO? And all the hotels give them special rates. Very low. No need to stay at the house. Looks bad when a wife is alone with young men like that."

Sam paused, then said, "How patriotic can you get?"

Raleigh stood up. He took a step, then stumbled slightly on the corner of Sam's Aubisson carpet, knocking it back from its felt pad. He paused to straighten it with his foot. Sam watched this automatic and reflexive act of housekeeping. Sam was smiling, expectant, as if waiting for Raleigh to say something, to give this meeting its proper ending.

Raleigh left without another glance at Sam. But the picture of his brother's smug, gloating face was burned forever in his mind. Later, when his rage had cooled a little, he decided that Sam was right.

Their meeting cried out for a proper ending.

"WELL she better be waking up pretty soon," Miss Harp sniffed early one Saturday morning a few weeks later.

Calvin didn't listen. He was busy getting TJ's and Billy's breakfasts on the table. He shook the small egg skillet over the hot coils of the stove, balancing the heat against melted butter and the motion of the pan. When the eggs were done just right, a scooch past runny, he flipped them onto the platter of sausage and the eggs he'd just finished cooking.

He was pushing through the swinging door of the pantry, half into the breakfast room, when she said, "Miss Emily's gonna see them there if they don't wake up soon."

He stopped.

"What you talking about, woman?" he said, coming back into the kitchen.

"Well, I don't know if I should tell you nothin'. You too busy with them eggs to worry 'bout some little 'ole thing like this."

"Like what?" he shot back. "You fixing to get me riled up real quick if you don't say what you got to say, woman."

"Missus Dot and that soldier boy are still in the bed."

"What you mean?" he said.

"I mean they is lying nekked without no clothes on in Missus Dot's bed where anybody can see all they got."

He stared at her. She was defiant. She raised her turbaned head in little checkered movements, like a chicken pecking backwards. And for a second or two she tried to hold his gaze, all the time fiddling with a cuff seam of her white uniform. Her face was twisted into what was supposed to be a grave look, but he could see the gleam of pleasure in her eyes for the trouble to come.

"I don't want my chile to see it," she said aloud.

"Don't move!" he said.

First he served the boys. While they were busy jabbering and eating he slipped out into the dining room, then went upstairs. He stood in the upstairs hall for a minute, listening. Then he eased open the door leading from the outside hall into the little bedroom hall. But he couldn't see much. The bedroom itself was dark, the drapes pulled shut. From where he stood he could only see a portion of the east wall. The foot of the chaise lounge jutted across his view, and some clothes were on it, but it was too dark to see whose they were or what kind.

He waited, trying not to make a sound.

Deep breathing sounds from the unseen part of the bedroom. Then a light snore, a snore that broke off a moment later when she coughed. She cleared her throat, murmured, coughed again. And then quiet. He stood still, waiting. Finally, they were back asleep, the sounds of breathing deeper than before.

He backed out, closed the door. He looked up to find Miss Harp coming up the spiral staircase. Without stopping he grabbed her arm and dragged her down to the first floor. She let out one yelp. Then his hand was over her mouth. He pulled her into the hall closet.

"You see what I done told you?" she said. "You see now I don't lie Mister Calvin, sir. That woman ain't no better than a barnyard bitch."

He hit her. He struck her hard and sharp across the right side of her face. As he hit her, he measured the force, calculating just how hard was enough.

Her head flew back. She tried to pull out of his grasp, but she didn't make a sound. She only turned her head away. She was breathing hard, close to panting.

"Now, Miss Harp, you listen careful," he said. "Look at me," he said again, shaking her. "Look at me, woman, I'm talking to you."

She knew she didn't have a choice. She turned, faced him. But she was dry-eyed. Undisguised hate filled her narrow face.

But he was satisfied with what was there. Next to fear, hate was best.

"Listen careful. You are gonna go back upstairs and walk just as quietly through Miz Dot's room as you walked through before. If you make even the littlest sound and them people wakes up you will wish you had never heard of this house. You hear what I'm saying, woman? And then you will get Miss Emily up, dress her for the day, quietly, and then you take Miss Emily and come back through the room, with you keeping between Miss Emily and the bed. I don't have to tell you to keep the child quiet do I? Then you will carry Miss Emily on down. After she is downstairs you will go back upstairs, take the hall door and shut it hard. Do I make myself plain, woman? You will slam it. One time. One time only is just fine.

"Now, woman, I told you to stay put in the kitchen. You came right upstairs after I done told you to stay put. If you don't do exactly what I'm telling you now I will take your ugly body and stuff it in my furnace. You hear me, woman? And when Mister Raleigh comes home if he ever finds out about what's upstairs I will know who told him. And then I'm gonna fix you for good."

He shook her, forcing her to look at him again. Her surly face was a mixture of hate and fear—and now greed. She was greedy for this trouble. She liked what was happening. He stared at her for a few more moments. Finally, satisfied that she would do exactly as he said, he let her go.

Sometime later that morning the young soldier appeared for breakfast. But Dot Jessop stayed upstairs. The house and the people in it went about their business that Saturday, as always.

A T WERTHEIMER'S TIRE & BATTERY Eddie King pulled a bottle of Orange Crush out of the ice cold water of the ice chest and let the lid fall shut with a thud. He wedged the cap off in the opener and sat down. One by one the other men in the room chose something to drink and took their places around him. As he waited the repeated thud of the lid reminded him that he was supposed to have a plan by now.

But, with everybody in place he still said nothing. Instead he lit a cigarette. Around him matches flared as Lucky Strikes, Camels and Chesterfields were lit. He took a deep drag, and waited. There was always somebody who wanted to run off at the mouth.

Toppy Black, a deputy over at Sheriff Henderson's office, with one son already in the Army, said, "I cussed out two boys just last Saturday. They'd been over at the base and stole some wood. Said the Army give it away. Now they'll just turn right around and sell it. Things like that all over. There's a thousand ways to make money off the war now. Can't tell me they'll go back in the fields for twenty cents when they spend that much now on a pack of these here Camels…. Those boys sassed me. I was wearing my gun, too."

"There's been enough talk," Hank Sims said. "It's past time to do something."

They all turned toward Eddie King.

"I love America," he said. "All the time, all the time I was bragging about the South and how the goddamned Yankees had stole everything we had I loved the USA and didn't even know it. This is a beautiful beautiful country and it took the yeller belly Japs to make me see it. I don't mean to say that I don't still hate what the Yankees did to South Carolina—that goddamned motherfucker Sherman and his murdering

thieves—because I still do and always will. But what I am saying is that we got to let bygones be bygones—at least until the
war is over.

"Next to South Carolina I love the USA best. I hate the Japs
and the Nazis so much I would like to kill every fucking one of
them with my bare hands. String 'em up. Take your time, line
'em up, do it one by one so the one's behind can watch. That's
justice. Oh, I wish I could get in this war…everybody here
wishes he was in the fight—killing Hitler and his crowd and
every fucking Jap alive, killing them all—"

"I wish I could," somebody said.

There was a rising murmur.

"But we're too old," Eddie King said. "They won't take us."

He paused to light a cigarette.

"I tried to enlist. The Navy, but shit, the Navy is picky. They
wanted to see a birth certificate."

He waited, wondering who here knew he was lying. He
looked around the room at the faces. No way for anybody to
know anything. It would just be a lucky guess.

"Fuck the Navy," he said, meaning anything they wanted it
to think.

"But one thing we can do," he continued. "We can make
sure everybody in this town does his part. Can't have no shirkers. Can't have any fucking shirkers living off the labor of
another person," he said, thinking about an article on Eleanor
Roosevelt he'd read in *Liberty* magazine at the barber shop.
"You all know who I'm talking about…. No nigger lovers like
Eleanor Roosevelt are going to tell Eddie King Jessop how
much to pay his help. Keep your nose out of my business you
ugly old bitch."

He stopped talking. Somehow he'd messed up what he'd

meant to say. But it must've sounded okay because everybody started to talk at once. The voices were raised, angry. They fed on each other until something close to rage filled the room, hot, near-hysterical voices that meant he could tell most anyone there to do most anything, just point his finger, and it was done.

"But we got to be smart about it," Eddie King said. "Everybody is watching. Uncle Sam is watching—"

They all laughed.

"So—? So we get smart. And how? I'll tell you how. We make sure no coon escapes, no coon runs. Do their duty. We'll see to that. Can't have shines dodging the draft while boys like Kenny Black are risking their skin, maybe dying.... Shines can't fight worth a shit. Run at the first fucking shot. But they can clean the toilets, they can cook, they can deliver what has to be delivered. A nigger can make it so's a white boy can kill Japs and Germans.

"Wertheimer here is on the draft board. I don't have to tell you what the problem is. Niggers who don't want to fight. All the fucking niggers want is a free ride. Like Wertheimer said, the second they get a notice to register most of them hop a bus up north to some nigger-loving city like Chicago or New York, then...then....

"Where was I—"

"The niggers escaping."

"Oh yes. Well that's it. Simple. That's it in a nutshell. That's our plan. We make sure not one fucking nigger dodges Wertheimer. We make sure he gets them all."

"Dead or alive," somebody said.

` They all laughed.

"That's right," he said. "And we'll start with Captain Coon himself—"

D<small>OT</small> J<small>ESSOP</small> fought it, but, little by little, the comfortable, misty lassitude of half-sleep was pushed back and back and back until she was awake. She kept her eyes closed, hoping to go back to sleep, refusing to think about anything. She felt ironed flat to the bed. Arms, legs...heavy, too heavy to move. Like?... Sore, she was a little sore. Yes, she felt battered, spent, like after a night of making love. Oh, ohh! She pushed an arm out to the side, searching, searching.... And then she remembered what she already knew. She was alone. "Ohhh," she said aloud, the sound half-whimper, half-groan, echoing, without knowing it, thoughts of love, of men and what they always did to her and would always do to her and what she had become obsessed by.

Her hand, undirected, moved to the new damp between her legs. The sound of longing grew into frustration. She groaned. His picture, the latest one, unnamed, burned in her brain. She sucked in her belly.

She suddenly remembered. Friday. It was Friday. Leigh would be home tonight. Only until Tuesday, but the thought of Leigh coming home killed secret longings. She was annoyed, then frowned. It was all so...so...hateful. Better not to think about it, better not to think about what could happen...better to think only pleasant thoughts.

Before she fell back to sleep she brought the picture of the soldier back, but he was a different one this time.

WITH HER thin arms around his neck, surprisingly strong, like the sinewy arms of a young primate, Raleigh carried Emily from the backyard into the house. There, she still refused to let go. Warmed by this affection, he carried her through the length of the house to his sitting room. In the carpeted and draped silence he sat down next to the fireplace. He arranged the child's thin legs to get the two of them comfortably seated. They sat that way for a few minutes, a portrait, he imagined, of normality, of fathers and daughters everywhere.

"Oh, my you're getting so big, Miss Emily." he said. "And so heavy! What a big girl! Would you like to take a trip with Daddy? We could take a choo-choo train and eat our supper on it and sleep on it. Don't you think that would be fun?"

Emily giggled, buried her face on his shoulder.

Had she understood?

He waited for her head to rise. He longed to see the intelligence in her eyes.

Then Miss Harp was standing in the doorway.

She crooned, "Did you and your Daddy have fun on your walk?"

At the sound of the nurse's voice Emily squirmed in his arms. She began to whimper. Strong arms, so recently clamped around his neck, now pushed him away. Emily held out her arms to Miss Harp.

"Oh, sugar, sugar," Miss Harp said.

Yet the nurse didn't move. She looked over to him for approval. For a moment he said nothing, then he nodded slowly and raised the wiggling child for Miss Harp to take.

"Emily and I were just having a little talk," he said. "I was just telling her how much she has grown. You've been taking real good care of her, Miss Harp."

"I does the best I can, Mister Raleigh," she said.

"A fine job," he said, absently.

Miss Harp, with Emily's legs dangling, the child lying heavy on her shoulder, retraced her steps out of the room. She stopped in the doorway and turned back.

"What is it, Miss Harp?"

"I just want to say that this here chile needs you, Mister Raleigh. She needs her Daddy." Then added, "And her Mommy."

"Well, that's true, Miss Harp. Certainly that's true. It's the war. What with the war we're all so busy."

"Yessuh, this here war done takes up a whole lot of your time."

"And Miss Dot's," he added.

"Yessuh," Miss Harp said.

He'd heard this tone from Miss Harp before. A Negro trying to be important.

"Are you trying to say something, Miss Harp?"

"Oh, no suh!" she said.

"If you've anything to say, say it."

Miss Harp, wide-eyed, said, "My chile has to take her nap now."

She scurried out.

Raleigh was relieved. Yet he felt he'd been unfair. Without realizing it he had taken offense when, he was sure, none was intended. Just the way nigras were sometimes.

LATER that same morning Raleigh was working at his desk, listing the things that had to be done before he went back to Texas on Tuesday, when Calvin came in. They went over the household accounts, which, as always, were in good order. Perfect order. In the face of this efficiency his own tiredness seemed a weakness. He listened for a while longer to Calvin's report then, interrupting, said, "Black Jim is getting fat. You're feeding him too much, Calvin. Pretty soon he'll be worthless."

"Yessuh," Calvin said. "Black Jim needs to be hunted. Not gettin' out of his pen enough. Wouldn't do you no harm neither, Mister Raleigh."

"I ain't got time to hunt," he said, reverting to country language in his fatigue. "You know that."

"Yessuh," Calvin said.

"I expected things to run better here than they have. I spoke to Junior Warden down at the bank and you haven't spent near as much for household expenses as when the account was first opened. I didn't mean for you to skimp. That isn't why I put you on the account. If I was worried about how much money you were spending I would have put a limit on. The idea is to spend what you need to keep my house up while I'm away. Do I make myself clear?"

"You sure do, Mister Raleigh."

"All right?"

"I got plenty, Mister Raleigh. The way I see it the money is there to pay your bills. If you want me to spend ten dollars more or a hundred dollars more than I got bills for I guess I could put in some more coal if I can find it. There could be a shortage next year."

Raleigh was annoyed with himself for making an issue of the household account. But, perversely, he changed the subject to something he cared even less about.

"And what is happening to my talc? It's almost all gone. You know how hard English talcum powder is to find. What with the war and all."

"Well…well, now Mister Raleigh," Calvin stammered, "I got a can put away and I looks for it whenever I goes to the store. I asked Mr. Conway to find us some. I sure did."

"Are you using my powder?" Raleigh demanded.

"No suh!" Calvin said, his tone shocked. "I shore ain't!"

"Well, I'd be surprised."

He waited in vain for some explanation.

"Well?" he insisted.

"The soldiers," Calvin said.

"What?" he said.

"The soldiers. The soldier boys."

"Oh…the soldiers."

"Yes suh."

"Oh, I see," he said. "Well that's all right then."

"Yessuh."

With that the big black man took a questioning half step in the direction of the door.

"It's fine with me," Raleigh said.

"Yessuh."

"My first thought was that I didn't like it. But, it really isn't that bad. There's nothing wrong with those boys sleeping in my room while I'm away."

"Oh, no suh," Calvin said. "Ain't nobody sleeping in your bed, Mister Raleigh. I wouldn't let them."

"Why don't we have the young men use the bathroom upstairs?"

"Yessuh, I'll see they do that for sure."

"Then we'll have to get them some talc of their own. No need to come looking for mine. Johnson's. Johnson's just fine for our visitors."

Calvin nodded.

Raleigh knew he was making a fuss over nothing. Talcum powder!

Yet he could feel his blood quicken. His face warmed. And the silence in the room grew so that it was noticeable. Heavy, almost palpable, it seemed to drag down everything, including the light.

To his front Calvin waited, a frown of concentration on his earnest face. That familiar frown of wanting to do the right thing.

With a nod and a wave Raleigh sent the colored man back to his kitchen. After Calvin left Raleigh got up and walked into his bathroom. He took the near empty can of English talcum powder off the shelf and sprinkled a little in his palm. He rubbed it between his fingers, feeling the fine powder's silky smoothness.

Afterwards, he washed up for dinner.

O NE SUNDAY MORNING more than a month after the soldiers stopped coming to the house Calvin turned the station wagon into the Bacon driveway. He'd just taken TJ and Billy to All Saints for Sunday school. He noticed that Dot Jessop's gray-green Packard coupe wasn't parked in its usual place. Relieved to find her gone Calvin hurried into the house; he wanted to finish his Sunday chores and leave before she got back.

The soldier visits had stopped for good. Miss Harp said that Mister Raleigh had called the USO and told them to stop sending the boys. Supposed to be too much work for the servants, Miss Harp smirked, looking at him. For once he let her say whatever she wanted. But with the soldiers gone Dot Jessop started getting up a lot earlier, even on Sundays. She complained that she couldn't sleep. As often as not she would come downstairs and without even having a cup of coffee drive off in a big rush, showering gravel and cinders on the rose bushes in the driveway turnaround as she spun the Packard's wheels. When she came home she usually made a show of that, too. Sometimes she would wander all over the house looking for one of the other servants. Then she would give strange, mixed-up orders, telling the girl to do this or that, often changing her mind a minute later. Then Mattie or Polly, or one of the others, would come to him, asking him to explain what Dot Jessop wanted done. Nothing he could explain. He couldn't say the woman was crazy or even that she was sick without causing Mister Raleigh shame. So he didn't say nothing. Yet this kind of thing was awful troublesome. Worse thing that can happen in a house is for the help to lose respect for the people they work for.

In the back vestibule he put on his furnace stoking clothes, an oversized railroad engineer's coat and rubber galoshes, and went downstairs to the basement to stoke the furnace to the boiler. He checked the smaller of the two furnaces. The fire he'd fed on coming to work still glowed hot. Its orange light flickered against the sooty and windowless walls of the basement. He threw two or three more shovelfuls of coal into the pit, then banked the coals, arranged them so that they would burn as slowly as possible. The water in the boiler would stay hot. It always did, but he had yet to find a live coal on Monday morning. He pushed the coals about anyway, and, as he had many times, considered coming in late that night to add a few coals to the fire.

He laughed to himself, shaking his head in wonder. It was

strange that he liked to come down into this low dirty basement to shovel coal. Why would any man like such a thing? Maybe it reminded him of being young and working on the railroad. Or was it because without anybody saying so they all depended on him to do it?

The fire now glowed from the bottom up, as it should, like the banked coal in the fire pit of an old steam engine. As the flames licked up through the pile of coals a pocket of coal gas ignited, flared up, and a tiger-striped flame beat for a few seconds against the furnace walls. For a moment he stood transfixed, waiting for the rogue fire to burn itself out. After a bit he neatened things up, shoveling the loose coal back on the pile. When he'd finished he tramped back upstairs. The harsh, metallic sound of galoshes' buckles rang out with each step.

In the back hall he removed the engineer's coat and stored it away with the galoshes. He went into the kitchen. At the sink he stripped off his tie and shirt and carefully laid his glasses on the window sill.

He splashed cold water on his face for a few seconds. Then he picked up a white bar of Ivory soap and vigorously scrubbed his head and neck working hard to raise suds in the cold water. Every now and then he blew through the growing suds like a breaching whale. With the suds thick and white, shrouding his blackness, he rinsed. Splashing about he ducked his head under the faucet. He made loud noises, puffing and snorting more than needed to keep the soap out of nose and mouth.

He began to hum. Eyes closed his voice searched itself, traveling up and down, and had just turned satisfying when he felt somebody else in the room.

As if this feeling were a switch, the lights blazed on. Through a film of water he saw Dot Jessop standing in the doorway of the kitchen. She was in her nightgown. Just out of bed. She looked bad, real sick. That was his first thought—that she was going to get sick any second—so he didn't even notice that she was close on to being naked.

He only became aware of that when—seeing himself through her eyes—it dawned on him that he was standing in front of her, half naked, too.

"Yes ma'am?"

He didn't wait for her answer. He grabbed his things and retreated to the back hall where he dried himself and dressed. While he was putting on his shirt and tie he listened, hoping she would go back upstairs, hoping he could leave without having to see her any more. But no. In only seconds she was calling out to him. Calvin, she said. Over and over. Calvin. Calvin.

He came back into the kitchen. She was holding on to the kitchen door. It swung back and forth under her weight.

"Calvin?" she said, her voice both faint and demanding.

"Yes ma'am."

"I'm fixing to take my shot."

"Yes ma'am," he said warily.

She swayed against the door, trembling. She was struggling to stay upright.

"I thought you was gone, Miz Dot," he said.

"Gone?"

"Thought you had done gone someplace in your car."

"Oh," she said. "Eddie King needed to borrow it."

"Yes ma'am…."

He nodded, unsure what would happen next.

"You gonna have to give me my shot," she said. "Miss Harp won't be back until late."

"Your shot, Miz Dot?"

"That's right. Since Harpie isn't here you'll have to give me my shot."

"Oh, no ma'am. I ain't giving no shot."

There was no mistaking his tone. His voice dropped, a hard flat certainty. It matched his eyes, cruel without the glasses lying on the window sill.

Dot Jessop began to cry. At first he was suspicious. She pretended or hid what she felt all the time. Crying was her favorite way to do that. But these were pure sounds of distress. They were real, cries from the heart, painful sounds of anguish. Still, he hoped it would pass. So he just stood there. He said nothing, did nothing. The smallest movement might in some way give her the idea that he was willing to give her the shot.

Dot Jessop, with a half-muffled, whimpering sound, stumbled across the room over to the sink. She grabbed it, holding onto its edge. Her legs shook with weakness. She bent over, half-lying on it. Then she slowly crumpled onto the floor.

She lay sprawled on the linoleum. face down, sobbing. Tears fell onto the floor so that, soon, a little lake glistened under her nose. Her nightgown had twisted in the fall. It was caught under her outstretched legs. The nylon stretched thin over shaking buttocks. The top lacy part of the gown was pulled down, too, completely exposing one breast. As she sobbed its nipple kissed the floor over and over.

There was nothing he could do to help her. He couldn't touch her. He couldn't leave. He was trapped by this crazy woman.

After a while she stopped crying. Several shudders and deep sighs later she lay still.

"Couldn't you help me?" she asked in a small voice. "It's not hard. TJ could give me the shot. It's that easy."

"You best wait until Miss Harp gets back," he said.

Ah, that was a mistake. A big mistake. He shouldn't have said nothing at all. Just his talking about it was all she needed. Because now she said, "Help me up."

He held onto her arm. She wobbled to her feet, then leaned forward as if she might fall against him. But he tightened his grip, keeping her at a distance. She winced but said nothing. It took her a while to steady herself. Finally, she pulled loose from his grip. Rubbing her arm she walked slowly but more or less steadily back across the room where she stopped.

She said, "You boil the needle and syringe two or three minutes. You'll find the bottle in the icebox. Bring them to my room and I'll show you how."

WHEN CALVIN walked into her bedroom she was lying on the canopied bed, eyes closed. She had put on her blue dressing gown. He noticed that the bottoms of her feet were dirty. He stood there, just a few feet inside the room, waiting. Finally, she opened her eyes.

"Oh!" she said, as if surprised to see him. "Well, we need the alcohol."

He carried the sauce pan with the needle in one hand, the syringe case and bottle in the other. The sealed rubber-capped bottle didn't have a label. Someone at Five Points had pasted the pharmacy sticker on the neck and had written "VITA-MINS" in capital letters in lavender ink. He put it along with the rest on her bedside table.

He helped Dot Jessop into the bathroom. Breathing hard she sat down on the lowered toilet seat. For a moment she didn't speak.

"There," she said indicating the medicine cabinet.

He took down a bottle of alcohol and several cotton balls. He balanced the little white balls on the edge of the sink. Most of the balls rolled to the bottom of the basin and got wet. He took several more out of the cabinet. Dot Jessop leaned against the wall next to the toilet. Eyes closed, she stayed that way for a few seconds.

"Bring in the hypodermic," she said.

He went back out into the bedroom and picked up the bottle and the parts of the syringe. When he came back into the bathroom she had taken off her robe. It lay spread on the floor at her feet. She peered up at him.

"You rub some alcohol on my arm here and put the needle in at the same place," she said.

"But, Miz Dot—"

He stopped. Her eyes had closed again. She leaned heavily against the wall. He hurried, trying to attach the needle to the syringe. It was balky, wouldn't slip on, but finally he was able to get it right. Then he tried to fill the syringe the way he'd seen Miss Harp and Dot Jessop do many times. But as he tried to push the needle through the rubber membrane, the bottle, too small for his big hands, bounced off the end of the needle and flew out of his grasp, falling to the tile floor where it bounced around. It didn't break.

At that moment, as he bent to pick up the bottle, Dot Jessop slid off the toilet onto the floor. She collapsed in waves, in slow motion, with her parts settling easily and softly onto the robe. Just when he thought it might all be play-acting her head hit the tile hard. It seemed to bounce.

"Good God almighty!" he said.

Eyes closed, on her back, she lay wedged in the narrow space opposite the toilet, up against the wall. Her legs, sticking out of the nightgown, were pointing at him. Above the knees, just inside the thighs, the legs were discolored with bruises, the flesh a splotchy mixture of nut-brown and nicotine yellow.

She said something.

"Yes, Miz Dot?"

But she had fainted again.

He tried to pick her up. Too narrow there. He needed to slide her back to a wider part of the room. He pulled on her legs, moving her as carefully and as gingerly as he had ever slid a cake from his oven. All the while he tried not to look at the growing expanse of flesh.

Finally he moved her to where he could get a hold. He carried her into the bedroom. She was more alert now, making the carrying easier.

"Oh, what happened?" she whispered.

"You fainted, Miz Dot," he said. "I'll call Dr. John right away."

"I don't think I need a doctor," she said.

"Oh, yes ma'am," he said. "You got to have a doctor."

He leaned to put her down on the bed. He tried to be as gentle as he knew how. As their weight shifted she slipped her arm around his neck for support.

"Thank you," she whispered in his ear. "Thank you for helping me."

In his mind he'd already left the house. Flustered by the voice in his ear he tried to think of ordinary things. Then he could feel that she didn't mean to let loose.

"No trouble, Miz Dot," he said, his heart thumping a mile a minute. "No trouble at all."

"Lie down a minute," she said, swallowing the words, her voice choked.

Good God almighty!

He pretended he didn't hear.

"No trouble. Well…I better be going."

She held on, her arm tight around his neck, her head close to his.

"Just for a minute, honey," she said.

Her breath roared in his ear. By now Calvin was terrified, terrified to be their witness. He couldn't think beyond his fear.

She strained upwards, at the same time pulling him down, down. Disaster had overtaken them. He knew it…but she…she….

Finally Dot Jessop's eyes, unfocussed, pleading, opened. She was staring right through him, back to somewhere deep inside herself. Her head shook slowly from side to side. Eyes closed again. Then, for the first time, she seemed to sense that something was wrong. She stopped moving, became still…. She must have noticed he wasn't doing anything back. Hands off to either side he was supporting most of their weight.

He wasn't doing anything back!

She stiffened, sucked in her breath. For a moment or two she froze in the midst of understanding. Then she let go. She fell back heavily on the bed, her arms and hands hurriedly covering herself. She straightened her legs. She looked at him through wide eyes.

Still, she lay very still. Calvin edged slowly away from the bed. As he moved away Dot Jessop's gaze shifted. She stared at the bed canopy overhead. He slid sideways around the bed and down the little hallway until he was out of sight. Now he expected the worse, for the rage to explode into screams. He ran downstairs. Quickly he gathered his things to leave; he paused at the back door to listen one last time.

Nothing. The house was deathly quiet.

6

LOOKING BACK Billy figured it had all started about a month earlier, that day when Dot Jessop had walked into Stone School and had moved TJ from there over to Dexter Elementary in Alta Vista. They'd come in from morning recess that day, and there she was. No warning, nothing. Just showed up. She told TJ to fetch his things. In a loud voice she told all the kids that TJ was leaving and wouldn't be back. TJ was mortified. But he did what she said. He left with her without taking any of his things. Like his mechanical pencil. He was so embarrassed he just left it and the rest of his stuff there. He didn't put up even the littlest fight.

If TJ had been willing to raise Cain about being moved out of Stone school, it might never have happened. But TJ didn't say anything, not a word then and nothing a week later when she split them up at the house. She made Billy move out of their room into the guest room down the hall. There wasn't a peep out of TJ. When Billy got mad about it TJ acted like he didn't care. Like it didn't make any difference, for instance, whether they made their model airplanes together, as they always had before, or built them apart in separate rooms as they did now.

TJ had just finished a model of the German Stuka dive bomber and was trying to decide whether to build the Messerschmitt 109 or the Jap Zero fighter next. TJ really wasn't much of a model builder. Mainly because he was too impatient. He broke a lot of the pieces. He was always asking Billy for some of his balsa wood.

So TJ came into Billy's new room and said he had decided on the Messerschmitt, and, sure enough, could he borrow some balsa. TJ always seemed to be building enemy planes. That might be okay once in a while, but to do it all the time was queer.

"I don't think so," Billy said. "Can't have you building no 109. That would be giving support and comfort to the enemy."

He wouldn't have cared if it hadn't been for the way TJ had been acting, like a mama's boy who did whatever Dot Jessop wanted whether it made any sense or not. When the fact was that nothing she did these days made any sense at all. She had been on a rampage for weeks now. From the moment Papa Bacon left again for Texas she'd been acting like a crazy person. The slightest thing set her off—one of the maids not answering quick enough, a door slamming when she was trying to sleep, even if anyone asked her if she wanted something to eat. And just seeing him seemed to be enough to make her mad. She cried and stamped her feet all the time. It was so bad he'd taken to hanging around over at Beth McCauley' house.

"I've lent you my balsa lots of times," TJ said.

"Well, that's true. But I always paid it back. You never do."

"I'm going to pay you back. You know that."

"How would I know that when you never do?"

"I'll get mama to buy some today if you'll just give me that one piece there."

"This ain't Lend Lease, you know."

"I'll pay you back."

"I bet."

"What makes you know everything? You think you're so smart. Well, you ain't. There's lots of things you don't know."

"Yeah, like what?"

TJ looked like he could bawl at any second. Over some dumb balsa. He should give him a piece. He had it to spare.

"I'll give you some if you promise to make a Navy Corsair with it."

"You're mean, Billy. Mama's right. You're a mean kid."

"So I'm mean because I won't let you make a Nazi plane with my balsa. Huh! And so Dot Jessop thinks I'm mean. Is that what you're saying? And you believe *her*?"

"You are mean. You know mama don't like anybody to call her 'Dot Jessop.' But you do it all the time."

"I never say it to her face."

"But you'd like to, wouldn't you? Just like I said. You like to hurt people."

"You're crazy. You're a crazy Nazi."

"And at least I got a mama. She takes us to Five Points all the time. And you never say thank you squat."

"What do you mean by that, when you said 'at least I got a mama'? Is that supposed to mean something? Like I don't have a mother? And a father, too."

That was his ace in the hole, talking about Sonny. To have your daddy fighting for freedom on the other side of the world was hard to beat. It always put you on top. Since he got the letter from Sonny from North Africa just over a month ago he hadn't stopped talking about it. He might have gone a little overboard with his bragging. Still, Sonny was the reason he hated it when TJ built only Axis planes. It was kind of disloyal.

TJ said, "Sonny's not...."

TJ stopped right in the middle of what he was going to say.

Like he'd thought better of it. And it was a good thing. Because if TJ'd said one word against Sonny he would have had to do something.

He picked up his balsa, put it away in his box. For good measure he put the cap on the glue, leaving the sharp smell as the only thing in the room between them now.

"Thanks," TJ said with a ton of sarcasm.

"And thank you, Herr Schicklegruber."

That did it. TJ rushed at him, pushed him, tried to get an arm on him, while at the same time reaching for the model box. TJ's weight carried them onto and over the bed. TJ, his face as determined as he'd ever seen it, rolled over him and reached again for the box. He hit TJ then, hit him harder than he really meant to. Blood spurted out of TJ's nose.

God!

At first TJ didn't know he was bleeding. But the second TJ saw the blood on the back of his hand he started to bawl. TJ ran out of the room, crying so loud you could hear him all over the house. And Billy knew then that he was in a heap of trouble. So he ran for the back stairs and escaped from the house. He hid in the bathroom of the garage. That's where Calvin found him an hour later.

YOU WOULD HAVE THOUGHT he was an ax murderer. From the way Dot Jessop reacted, TJ's bloody nose was worse than Pearl Harbor, and he was worse than the Japs. Bully boy! And he was an ungrateful know-it-all. She must have said how ungrateful he was a hundred times. And then she separated them. They weren't supposed (sometimes she forgot) to do anything together ever again.

All that did was make them best friends again.

On his own TJ couldn't stay mad at anybody for longer than fifteen minutes. He couldn't stand to have anybody mad at him. So within a few days of their being officially separated TJ had snuck into his room at least ten times. "I ain't mad anymore," TJ'd said. "Are you still mad?" "Naw. I ain't mad." "I've decided to build a *Corsair.*" "That's good," he'd said "I'm awarding you the Navy Cross."

By the next Saturday things had calmed down even more, to where they did most things together. But TJ made the mistake that morning of asking if they could go to the circus together. And she erupted again; so Billy had gone back into hiding.

A FEW DAYS after the circus left town Billy came home late one afternoon from Beth McCauley's to find Miss Harp waiting for him. She pounced on him to say that Dot Jessop wanted to see him right away. He searched around for TJ, for protection, but TJ was nowhere to be found. The last thing he wanted was to have to see Dot Jessop alone. So he waited, stalling, until TJ came home. But then Miss Harp came down again and he had to go upstairs.

He found Dot Jessop in her dressing room. She was dressing. Or undressing. He couldn't tell which. Dot Jessop was sitting in front of a triple-mirrored dressing table at the far end of the narrow room. Dozens of dresses and suits and blouses and gowns and other clothing things hung from hangers on both sides of the room. It looked almost like Belk's Department Store. He hadn't seen most of these clothes before. Dot Jessop had her favorites, things she wore over and over, leaving the rest in her closet. One favorite was the fancy blue silk robe. She had it on now. Its skirt was so full it had to be arranged every time she sat down. It swirled around the bottom of the stool like a small blue pond.

She was putting cold cream on her face.

"You wanted to see me, Dot?"

"Sit down," she said.

Huh oh, he thought.

But then she seemed to forget he was there.

A cloth band of some kind was tied around her head to keep the cold cream out of her hair. With three fingers she dipped into a blue jar and took out another glob of cold cream and smeared it all over her face, even over her eye lids, all the time holding her mouth open in the shape of a capital O. But she rubbed too hard, or got careless. Because some of the cold cream got in her eye. That made her swear. She jerked a tissue out of a box and dabbed at the corners of the eye. When she'd finished cleaning the cold cream off her face she leaned back and looked at herself. She stretched her lips over her teeth, then flared her nostrils like a snooty movie star.

She happened to glance up then to see him watching her.

"What are you doing here?" she snapped. "Are you spying on me ?"

"I ain't spying, Dot," he said. "You wanted to see me."

"Oh, yes," she said. "Well, you shouldn't lurk around like that. It isn't polite. And by the way, stop saying 'ain't'. You act like you don't know any better. What will people think about how your grandfather is raising you?"

"Yes ma'am."

"Where is TJ?" she asked.

"He's around here someplace. Should I go get him?

"Yes…. No, wait. No, it's you I want to talk to. Your mama has sent a telegram."

"She has?" he said. "Where is it?"

"She wants you to come to Cleveland."

"Oh yeah?" he said. "When did it come? Can I see it?"

He'd never received a telegram. He'd seen them of course, but they were the kind that congratulated you on having a baby and things like that. When Beth McCauley's little sister had been born eight months ago he had read the telegrams of congratulations posted on the McCauley's bulletin board. And there were the terrible telegrams that were sent to the families of the soldiers who were killed in the war. Some gold stars had begun to appear in windows around Athena. He thought about the telegrams that had arrived in those houses, picturing them, not on some bulletin board, but crushed in the hands of the boys' mothers. What if the family had moved? Or if nobody was at home? Did they just slide the telegram under the door?

Thank goodness his telegram wasn't one of those. Only a month ago he would have dreaded getting a telegram from Elizabeth. Not now, though. Something had gone wrong here in Papa Bacon's house. Just what he didn't know. But what he did know was that something bad was going to happen. Or had happened already. It might, but he didn't think it had anything to do with him….

Just then TJ ran in, out of breath.

"Polly said you got a telegram!"

TJ's smiling face was flushed with excitement. It was real hard to hide how you felt when TJ was around. TJ had this way of exposing true feelings. So, he began to join in TJ's excitement.

"Can I see it?" TJ asked. "Can I? Please?"

"I ain't seen it yet," he said.

"It's out by my bed," Dot Jessop said to TJ. "Go get it, honey."

TJ ran out and came back with an envelope in his hand. Then, with a big smile, like he was the Western Union delivery boy himself, TJ handed it to him with a flourish. He felt the envelope, felt for the raised words that would take him away from here. They would be blue, blue words printed on narrow, heavy strips of yellow paper, the strips lined up and pasted on. You could feel how important the words were before you even opened it.

TJ was now so excited, jumping around, making faces of anticipation, that he felt he had to say something.

"Okay, I'm gonna open it."

He turned it over. The flap was loose, having already been torn open. He carefully took the message out, read it and started to put it back.

"Hey," TJ said, "don't I get to see?"

"Sure, I guess so."

TJ took it and read it aloud. "'Billy, darling. Expecting you seventh July. Ticket follows. Love Mother.'"

TJ handed it back, "Golly, on your birthday."

When he didn't say anything, TJ said, "Well, ain't you gonna say anything? Ain't you excited?"

"Not much. I figure this telegram was meant for somebody else."

"Don't be a dope," TJ said. "There's your name in the window, plain as day."

"I figure it was meant for some other William Smithson," he said.

"Are you crazy?" TJ said.

"Must be some other William Smithson. Else why would it be open? If I was the right William Smithson wouldn't I have opened my own telegram? If it's your telegram nobody else gets to open it. Ain't that right? Ain't that the rule?"

He didn't look at Dot Jessop. He threw the questions at TJ, his voice chock full of the disgust he felt. At first a bewildered TJ didn't get it. TJ didn't understand who he was talking to. When he did his sunny smile collapsed into confusion and he began to slowly back out of the dressing room.

Still clutching the telegram he brushed past TJ to leave.

"Stop!" Dot Jessop cried. "Come back here."

He tried to ignore her. But she wouldn't let him, screaming now, "Billy! Billy Smithson! You better get your tail back in here! I'm talking to you, boy!"

He stopped in the doorway. But every part of him oozed defiance.

"Yes?" he said.

"Yes, *what* you rude, rude thing you."

"Yes, Dot Jessop…ma'am."

"Don't you dare talk to me that way. Don't you dare!"

She was panting with anger.

"I've never in my life had to deal with such a boy as you…you rude, rude thing you."

"At least I don't go around opening other folks mail," he said.

She looked at TJ, then at him. Her eyes were wild. Suddenly, he was half sorry for what he'd said. More than half. Not that he would ever say that he was sorry. But he wished now that he had kept his mouth shut.

She was staring at him, batting her eyes, in a state somewhere between hysteria and murderous rage. Without eye liner her eyes seemed small and amazingly like a rabbit's, pink at the edges. She was about to cry, but trying hard not to.

"All right," she said in a choking voice. "If that's how you want it...you ain't the only one.... Want you out of here. I do. I'm not gonna wait two whole weeks. I'm gonna send you back to Pineville today, tonight, whenever there's a bus. I'm gonna have Calvin put you on it, on the first one. I can't wait to get you out of my sight...."

She paused, breathing hard, then said, "How do you like that, Mister Bully Boy?"

He looked at TJ. TJ was staring at the floor. Like before TJ wasn't going to help. Without TJ on his side he couldn't hold his own with Dot Jessop.

He tried to retreat a little.

"I'll be gone in two weeks. I'll stay outta your way until then, Dot."

"You're an ungrateful child."

"No, I ain't. Not really."

"We have done everything for you. We took you in when you didn't have any place else to go. We gave you food and clothes, we treated you just like TJ. And TJ has been so nice to you—"

She stopped, the way she felt about him written all over her face.

"I really appreciate everything—"

"I mean," she interrupted, "we couldn't have done more if you were our own son.

She paused, then said, "You'll never know."

"I know about all those things, really I do. I just didn't like you opening my telegram. That's all."

"I opened it for a good reason."

"You did?"

"Yes."

"What reason was that?"

"I can't tell you."

"Sure you can. What was it, Dot?"

"Well…I thought it might be about Sonny."

"Mama!" TJ cried. "Don't!"

"What about Sonny?" Billy said. "Is Sonny all right? Did something happen to him?"

"Mama, what are you doing?" TJ said.

She shook TJ off.

"Well, you oughta know anyhow. I did think it was about Sonny. I thought the telegram was about him."

"Has he got killed in the war?"

She laughed, "No, nothing like that. I thought he'd hurt himself, or something. Besides, you weren't supposed to know…so it was perfectly fine for us to open your telegram. It would have been wrong if we hadn't."

"Mama," TJ yelled, then turned and ran out of the dressing room.

Billy looked at her, saw she was going to tell him something, tell him whether or not he wanted her to. Suddenly, fear flooded through him like a sudden drenching wave. His heart was skipping around in his chest like it had come loose from its usual place.

"Sonny isn't any more of a soldier than I am," she said. "The Army don't take crazy people. Boy, your daddy is still up in North Carolina. He's still in that asylum. He never left. You see? You see? Now, mister Bully boy, I guess you can understand why I opened your precious telegram."

H E DIDN'T BOTHER about most of the things in the mattress. Baby Ruth candy bars and compasses seemed foolish now, things a kid might use. Instead, he stole some of Dot Jessop's money. He waited until she went to the movies the next afternoon and crept about the room pulling open drawers and going through her purses, looking for the envelopes. He found three. The first one was empty, but the second, folded and stuffed into a beaded purse, had twenty-five dollars in it. He almost missed the last one. It was lying right on top of her dressing room table. Fifty dollars in crisp new ten dollar bills. He was careful not to do anything else that might make anybody suspicious. He didn't take any clothes or the flashlight, or anything else that could be useful. As far as anybody else was concerned—especially TJ—they were supposed to think that it didn't matter to him one way or the other whether Sonny was at the hospital or in the Army. After all, he'd said, you never knew what to expect from Sonny. One day he's a soldier. The next, a civilian. So what?

But it was especially hard to pretend with TJ, who he knew now must have known about Sonny all along.

"I hope you ain't mad," TJ'd pleaded over and over.

"I'm not mad," he'd told him. "You can forget it. Forget it the same way you did before."

THE NEXT AFTERNOON, right after the midday dinner, at a time when he wouldn't be missed for hours, he walked through the woods over to Tigerville Road, and from there all the way downtown, dodging off the road into bushes or behind trees when he heard a car coming. It took him almost an hour. At the bus station he had to wait until five-fifteen for the first Trailways bus to North Carolina. The schedule in the glass case next to the ticket window said it was six hours to Raleigh-Durham. From there it was at least another hour to Rocky Mount.

He sat down to wait. The bench he was sitting on was a few feet away from the door to the men's room. From where he sat he could see anybody who came into the station. If Dot Jessop missed her money, if they came looking for him, he could hide in the toilet.

The waiting room slowly began to fill up with passengers. Every once in a while somebody would look at him curiously, as if he didn't belong there. After this has happened a few times he figured out why. He should have brought a suitcase or a sack or something to look more like a traveler. He must look like he felt: out of place.

Time dragged. The black arrow hands of the station clock never seemed to move. What with trying to keep still so as not to call attention to himself and looking at the clock hundreds of times he got so tired it was hard to even sit. But somehow the time passed. Finally, he looked up to see that his bus was due in a few minutes.

Now, a lady about Elizabeth's age was staring at him. He pretended not to notice. But out of the corner of his eye he could see that she was pretty, like his mother. She acted like she wasn't going anywhere, like she was sitting in the waiting room only to watch the passengers. She had a calm, serene air, as if all the rising commotion in the waiting room had nothing to do

with her. He had the strongest feeling that she would speak to
him at any second.

But nothing happened. And then she seemed to lose interest
in him. Finally, the ticket agent shouted through the grill of his
cage that the bus was coming in. He hurried to buy his ticket.

"One ticket to Raleigh-Durham, please," he said.

"Will that be one-way or round trip?"

He froze.

"How much is that?"

"Is what?"

"The ticket."

For the first time the agent looked at him suspiciously.

"Do you have the money to buy a ticket, son?"

"Sure I do."

He took the money out of his pocket and put it on the
counter. When he'd finished it was kind of strewn there, and he
knew that that was wrong, that either he should have handed it
to the agent or stacked it neatly on the counter. This man, who
had a scarlet birthmark on the right side of his throat that crept
up his jaw to just below his ear, had to know by now that he
was not a real passenger. He'd probably guessed that he was a
criminal, a thief…at least a runaway.

"Well, you got the money all right. What'll it be?"

He drew a blank.

"One way or round trip?"

"Oh, how much is one way?"

"Sixteen fifty."

"One way," he said, hurriedly gathering up the rest of Dot
Jessop's money and stuffing it into his pocket.

THE BUS STOPPED in Gastonia long enough for him to buy a hot dog. He hadn't eaten since breakfast and he was starved. He bought a second one to eat on the bus, but the bus driver, a big man with straight black hair combed straight back and a pot belly, wouldn't let him bring it on the bus. With the passengers watching he had to eat it quickly, standing on the street next to the open door of the idling bus. The driver, who—like the ticket agent—had probably figured out by then that he was a criminal, angrily slammed the front door shut behind him. As the driver pushed the handle into its locked position it squeezed the sounds of the world outside—the roaring motor of the bus, its heavy shifting gears, shouted good-byes—to almost nothing. His ears popping a little Billy made his way down the aisle.

Someone, a farmer in overalls, had taken his seat. He didn't dare make any kind of a fuss over it. He picked his way slowly toward the back, looking for an empty seat. At the back, in the row right in front of where the nigras were supposed to sit, was one last seat. Except it had an open wicker picnic basket and a white starched and folded linen napkin resting on it.

The pretty woman who looked like his mother was in the next seat. She smiled as his eyes met hers.

"Could...could I sit here, please?"

"Why, of course, honey," she said, leaning up to look back down the aisle. "I guess somebody took your seat."

She moved the basket and napkin and he sat down. He made sure to mind his own business, to keep as still as possible. He leaned out over the aisle to watch through the front windshield as the winding road marched through the scrubby red clay foothills of North Carolina.

During the trip from Gastonia to Charlotte the lady slowly ate her supper, cucumber sandwiches with the crusts cut off and something that looked like chicken, only whiter and smaller than Calvin's fried chicken. Every now and then she stopped eating to smile sideways at him. But he was afraid to say a word, and then he was too tired. So, although he tried hard not to, he finally fell asleep in the darkened bus.

When he woke up the bus was stopped. More than just stopped, the motor was shut off and they were sitting in darkness off to the side of the road. He thought he could hear the chirpy croak of tree frogs. Confused, he tried to figure out exactly where he was.

"What time is it?" he murmured aloud, although he believed he'd only thought it.

"Oh, around two," the lady next to him said.

Startled, he looked over at her.

"What happened?" he asked. "Why are we stopped?"

"The bus broke down," she said. "A gasket or something like that. The bus driver is looking for a house with a telephone."

"How far is Raleigh?"

"A ways yet. I'd say fifteen miles or so."

He started to get up, "I've got to get off."

She put her hand on his arm. He stopped.

"Honey, you'll get lost out there," she said. "This is tobacco country, nothing but cure houses for miles and miles. At least wait until daylight. By that time I bet the bus will be fixed and we'll be on our way. But if it isn't at least you'll be able to see."

She paused, smiling. "Doesn't that make good sense?"

He nodded sheepishly and sat back down.

"Where are you from, honey?" she asked. "But, first, what's your name?"

In the darkness of the bus he felt his heart begin to thump.

His name? Then, without really thinking, he said, "Tommy... Tommy Carpenter."

He couldn't see her eyes in the darkness.

But her voice sounded like she believed him.

"Tommy. That's a nice name. And where are you from, Tommy? Athena?"

"No, ma'am. I was just visiting some people there. A cousin of mine. I'm taking the bus home."

"Oh, really? Where do you live?"

"Uh, Pineville. It's between Tarboro and Bethel?"

"Oh, yes!"

She seemed to know Pineville, at least where it was. Maybe she knew some folks there.

"Where are you going, ma'am?"

"Raleigh. I live just outside Raleigh in a little town called Eagle Landing. I bet you've never heard of it."

"No ma'am."

"It's an awfully small town. Even folks in Raleigh don't know where it's at. I bet Eagle Landing is littler even than Pineville."

"Yes ma'am...but Pineville is an awful small place."

He wanted to keep her talking. She had the most...well, the prettiest voice. It was kind of musical, it rose and fell like a song and at the same time was so soothing. Not only that she had a kind of magical way of speaking, with a noticeable lull before she said anything, like it was to be the most important thing anyone would ever say in the entire world.

"Do you have any children, ma'am?"

Her dark outline, framed against the window, moved with his question, and he knew that she was thinking how much to tell him.

"No, honey. I don't. I wish I did. I wish I had a child just like you."

His face warmed with embarrassment—and pleasure. He was glad she couldn't see it.

"You are a beautiful boy," she added. "I'd be proud to have a son just like you."

In the darkness he hung his head, real embarrassed now to have made her feel she had to say these things.

"How old are you, dear?" she said.

He was going to lie again but then found he couldn't. He owed this nice lady the truth.

"I'm twelve. My birthday's next month, though."

"It is? So's mine. We're Cancers, did you know that? No, what we really are are soul mates, brought together by God for some wonderful reason."

She reached over and patted his hand. Tears welled in his eyes. She was right. God had meant for the farmer to take his seat. God had meant for him to come sit by a lady who was part angel. And so…and so everything else could be all right, too. Even the lies, even stealing Dot Jessop's money.

He could feel her eyes on him.

"You've run away, haven't you, honey?" she said.

Feebly, he shook his head.

"That's all right. You don't have to say a thing. But I know. Really. Remember, we're soul mates. I know things about you no one else could ever know. Besides, you looked so sad back in Athena sitting there in the bus station. And young boys don't travel all night by themselves, especially not carrying anything. But I suppose you could have just lost it. Your bag, I mean."

She had stripped him clean. This angel lady had looked

inside him and had seen all his lies and now was forgiving him even though he was a terrible liar and an awful thief.

"Now, darling," she said, "wouldn't you feel a whole lot better if you told me everything? Isn't that what a soul mate is for?"

And so he told her everything; he told her that he had run away, and why, he told her everything that had made him sad from the moment he had left Pineville so long ago. He didn't tell the good things—about TJ, Calvin, Black Jim, Papa Bacon—because angels are needed to give you what you don't have. And for now that was Sonny and Pineville and Kallie and Zero and all the things he missed so much. And needed so much.

He was still talking when the bus driver came back, only stopping a minute to listen to the driver explain how the bus was to be fixed right away. And hardly stopping when the mechanic came to start the bus. When he finished talking he was exhausted, so tired he could scarcely lift his head. It was a wonderful feeling, though, to be free of all the heaviness. And the hurt.

"You poor darling," she said and took his hand. "Come here."

She pulled him down to her, folding him into her sweetness. He gratefully sank into the bliss of being taken care of, of being loved as only angels can love, without pain.

"Oh," she said. "Your hands are like ice."

She rubbed them between her own soft palms. He could smell the soft lotion sweetness of her. He closed his eyes.

She rubbed his hands, one after the other. As he lay there, in her embrace, both child and man, the same, both needing her angelic sweetness and feeding on her beauty, he was happy, yet at the same time as confused as he'd ever been in his entire life.

Soon he was hovering at the edge of sleep, tasting it, yet fighting every step of the way. Vaguely, as if in a dream, he felt her take his right hand, then lift it to her lips. She seemed to kiss it lightly...so lightly. He'd just thought he'd let go, that it was really okay and not a bad thing to go to sleep in this good lady's arms when—without his hardly realizing it—she had slipped his hand into her blouse between her breasts. Just like that.

God!

Stunned. He was at first, sleepily, then confusedly, stunned—yet not surprised at all. It was a time for feelings of strangeness and paralysis—yet it seemed the most natural thing in the world. So...right. Still, his hand seemed to belong to somebody else. It rested there, fingers numb, no longer his to command.

"There," she whispered in his ear. "That'll make it better. Don't you think?"

He waited, could only wait for what would happen next.

She seemed to gather herself then, to embrace herself with her other arm, folding the mounds of warm flesh over the top of his hand.

After a while she whispered, "Does your hand feel warmer now, honey?"

He nodded.

"That's good...that's good...."

"And can you feel that?" she asked. He nodded again.

"Tell me. Say it."

"I...I can feel your heart beating."

"I have a warm heart."

"...Yes."

There was a long silence.

"You know what I think?"

"...No...what?"

"I think that when the bus gets to Raleigh you had better come home with me. We'll go to my house in Eagle Landing where we can rest. We'll take a nap together at my house, get rested and warm and all. And then you will feel good when you get to see your daddy."

He didn't say anything.

"What do you think?"

He couldn't think. All he could do was nod, work his face up and down a little in the warm crook of her neck. He dared not...dared not move more than that. And then he must have fallen asleep for the next thing he knew he was coming awake. At first he thought he might have been dreaming. But, no. He was still in her embrace. She was sleeping. His hand had dropped free of her blouse to her waist. It lay curled there, pink, dirty nails. Above his hand her partially exposed breasts lay heavy and without mystery just inches below his gaze. He flexed his fingers slowly, carefully, trying to get some feeling back without waking her.

He raised his eyes to look out the window. Dawn was beginning to break. Streaks of gray flat light bounced off telephone poles, off the tin roofs of barns and off the roofs of passing cars as the bus drove toward the not yet risen sun. Stiff from being in the same position for so long he didn't trust himself to move at all. Agonizing minutes crept by.

Now....

Slowly, slowly, an inch at a time, he slid free of her embracing arm, holding it, lowering it carefully.

She lay half on her side, facing him. With a movement of the bus she swayed a little. She began to snore softly, a breathy, raspy sound. He sat watching her face, barely breathing, afraid she would wake up at any moment. When at last they reached the outskirts of Raleigh he crept out of his seat. He went to the front of the bus and asked to be let off. The driver grumbled but stopped the bus. He jumped down to the street. The bus sat, idling. Through the open door he could see the driver comb his hair, put something in his mouth. Finally, the door closed and the bus pulled slowly away, toward the center of Raleigh.

North Carolina State Hospital, Rocky Mount Asylum.

The name was chiseled out of gray stone set above the entrance way. From where he sat Billy tried to figure out which floor Sonny might be on. Opposite his bench, across the wide scruffy lawn, the hospital building's top floors were still shrouded in mist. A staggered line of old swoopy-limbed, untrimmed pines blocked his view of most of the lower floors. What windows he could see were ivy covered. Behind the green of the ivy dim black grids told him the windows were all barred.

Billy stood and walked back down the gravel road, past the gladiolus filled turn-a-round, almost as far as the highway. From there he could see through the rising mist another side of the whole building, all five stories. It was just like he remembered. The only floor where the windows weren't barred was the fifth. That's where Sonny was most likely to be. That's where he would start. But first he had to get inside.

Couldn't just walk in. Too risky. Someone was bound to notice. Still, getting in was nothing compared to getting out. Going in alone he had a good chance of not really being noticed but escaping with Sonny was something else.

He had to have a plan.

But when he sat back down on the same bench his brain just up and quit. Too tired to think. What he really needed was to stretch out on the still damp bench and sleep for a minute or two. He was tempted, but what if somebody saw him and started asking questions? He sat up as straight as he could, trying to concentrate on the entrance to the hospital, trying to think.... People came and went. Quite a few of the hospital folks, the people in white. And there was also a good number of visitors, men in suits and hats, women carrying purses, passing by, heading in and out, going in and out.... Going in and out, in and out...in and...and....

He woke up with a start. He'd been sleeping sitting up. In a kind of panic, his nerves jangling in a way he'd never known, he jumped up and ran half way across the gravel oval before he really knew where he was. He spied a family walking up the walk toward the entrance. The man wore a fedora and the woman carried a large sack in one hand and her purse in the other. They were followed by two kids younger than him. He just stepped in behind and followed them in. Inside he found the same polished bench as before, the one at the end closest to the front door. Safe now he exulted. So easy! And it would be easy getting Sonny out, too. God was always behind you when you were doing something good.

Nothing had changed. The inside of the hospital was just as dark and dreary as before. He sat there for a while, letting his eyes get used to the gloom. From where he was he could see the entrance to the stairway to the upper floors. Not far from the stairs an old elevator was operating, and although he couldn't see it from where he sat, he could hear it ring out when it reached the lobby.

No one was paying him any attention. Everybody, the staff, visitors, were all too busy, too much in a hurry to notice a loose kid like him.

He got to his feet and walked down the hall. When no one was looking he ducked into the stairway. Quickly he ran up the stairs, counting the doors until he reached the fifth.

Fifth Floor. 'Watch Your Step!'

The door wouldn't open. There was no lock on his side of the door. What kind of a jail was this? Did the loonies just let themselves in and out?

"Sorry, Sonny," he whispered. "Didn't mean it."

He tried to think. If the fifth floor stairway door was locked they all had to be locked. Almost sure to be. As he walked slowly back down to the first floor, trying to figure out what to do next, he tried them all. Locked.

As he came out of the stairwell door an older, pleasant faced, apple-cheeked woman walked by right in front of him. Her long gray hair was fixed up in braids, held in place by big, tortoise shell hairpins sticking way out of her head, like a circle of amber horns. She was carrying a purse. And she was heading for the elevator. The door slid slowly open as she walked up to it. But she hesitated to step on, as if the one or two inch raised gap between the corridor and the elevator floor was a real obstacle. The elevator operator, an older white man dressed in a white coat, leaned toward the lady, motioning her in.

Billy hurried to her side.

"Can I help you, ma'am?" he said, touching her arm lightly.

"Oh," she said, smiling brightly. "Thank you young man."

She made it easy for him. She kept nodding and smiling, thanking him several times for helping her. He was able to keep his hand on her arm, like they were together. The people who got on and off, some visitors, mostly staff, didn't give them a second glance. The elevator rose slowly upwards, its doors clanking open and shut on the second, the third, and, finally, the fourth floors. By the time they got to the fifth floor they were the only passengers left on the elevator. He was practicing his polite escape from the old lady when the door opened.

Two heavy-set men, both dressed in the short-sleeved, white uniforms of orderlies, were standing there, like they had been waiting to take the elevator down.

"Oh, ho, there you are, Rosie," one said when he saw them.

"You've got to stop this, old girl. If you don't we'll have to strap you to your chair. And you know how bad that makes you feel."

"And give us nurse's purse, sweetie," the other orderly said, smiling, prying it not so gently from her. "Nurse gets madder'n hell when you take her purse."

They were beginning to lead her away when the first turned back to look at him.

"And just who are you, boy? You some kin of Rosie's?"

AT FIRST Billy lied. To the same woman as before, Miss Rindquist. He'd seen right away she didn't have any idea who he was. So, he'd said his name was Tommy Carpenter. He was visiting with his aunt, Elizabeth Carpenter, come over from Bethel to see his aunt's friend—here he made up a name on the spot—Herman Randall. And it worked for a while: he was good at lying now and she didn't know offhand if there was a Randall in the hospital or not. Of course what he was doing was much more than a game, but that's sort of what it became. But a game in which it was hard to figure out just who wins and who loses. The game required that he keep on lying, required that he keep playing for time. If the game could be won, how to win it would come to him later.

During all this, the time waiting in her office, while she asked her questions, the time she took to check, he came awful close to forgetting about Sonny. The game itself was one reason. But a bigger reason was that he kept wondering if Miss Rindhurst would remember that she had seen him before. The suspense gave everything that happened a special, edgy, got-to-survive feeling.

He was also, at the same time, fast becoming Miss Rindhurst's tarbaby. The hospital's Assistant Supervisor wanted to get rid of him quick. She wanted to find his "Aunt Elizabeth", to get him off her hands. But every time she went out of the room to check something he'd lied about, he got stickier and stickier. She would come back into the room, try to appear calm and would ask him to repeat one of his lies. First, no Aunt Elizabeth could be found. And, just now, unluckily, it turned out that there wasn't even one Randall in the asylum.

"Tommy," she said, "Are you trying to fool us? Is that it? There hasn't been a Randall in this hospital for years. So I think you must be having some fun. I think you must be trying to play some trick on poor old me."

He shrugged, "That's what she said. Herbert Randall. She said his name as clear as day. Course I never met no Herbert Randall so—"

"You talking about your aunt?"

"'We're going to see Mister Herbert Randall. He's an old, old friend of mine.' That's what she said, as clear as day."

"But you said, Herman. *Herman* Randall."

"That's right, Herman. Never heard of the man until this very day. So you can see why...."

He shrugged again. He tried to look at Miss Rindhurst steadily, like Bulldog Drummond would've, tried not to blink. Don't smile. Don't ever smile. Or she will know. And then the game will be lost. Still, he felt the corners of his mouth tugging upwards, defying him.

Miss Rindhurst had lost her vacant, can't-be-bothered look. Her mouth was set. Her dark eyes had narrowed under the ridge of her bangs.

"Look, boy, if you think we don't have anything better to do than to chase down your stories you have another think coming. This is a hospital. And we have sick people here...who have to be taken care of. So, we don't have time to fool around with you on this."

The game said he should look innocent.

"Do you understand me? Do you?"

"Yessum. I sure do. You are busy and don't have no time for the likes of me. Maybe I should go now?...I got to find my Auntie...Auntie Elizabeth."

He leaned forward in the chair to stand up.

"Sit down!...I want to know exactly what you are doing here!"

She was yelling now. The game had got a little out of hand.

The best thing to do at a time like this was nothing. But he couldn't stop looking around for a way out. The orderly who'd brought him down here might still be around, outside her door. Or maybe not. Still, from everything he'd seen she could call somebody to catch him without much trouble. Besides, if he ran away he would never see Sonny. So he had to keep on with the game.

"Really, ma'am, everything I told you was true. I can't understand where Auntie is. I really should go try to find her though."

"I hate smart aleck boys like you," she said. "Because somebody is nice don't mean you can take advantage. I've got a good mind to turn you over to the police. Maybe you're more than a smart aleck kid. Maybe you're more than just a liar."

"All I want—"

"Shut up, boy. There is no Aunt Elizabeth. You lied about that. Why, I don't know. But you lied. Probably everything you said was a lie…. Tommy probably isn't your real name. But the police will find out what—"

She stopped, looked at him closely. His heart skipped a beat.

She cocked her head.

"I've seen you someplace before."

He stared down at his feet.

"Yes. I know you from someplace."

The game had got out of hand, and he was about to lose. He slumped a little in the chair.

"Where do I know you from?"

He didn't answer.

"From here, right?"

She didn't wait this time.

"You've been here before, haven't you?"

The game was over. But he still couldn't bring himself to admit it to her.

"Tell me who you are? You better."

Well, now that there wasn't any other choice he would have to try the truth.

"I'm Billy Smithson. I'm here to see my daddy."

She acted like she didn't know who he was talking about.

"Sonny Smithson. Really, Walker William Smithson? My daddy? I'm here to see him."

She sat back on her chair.

"I didn't mean to cause you no trouble...honest."

"Yes."

"So, please ma'am, can I see my daddy?"

"That's gonna be hard, boy. Your daddy died more'n a month ago. That man's dead and buried."

7

RALEIGH sat at the dais in the Chairman's chair, waiting to call the Special Meeting of the Shareholders of Bacon Mills to order. He'd decided to hold the meeting in the First National Bank's large board room because the Bacon Mill's board room was likely to be too small for the number of shareholders who might want to attend.

He could see already, with a few minutes to spare, that he'd been right. Almost every seat in the bank's board room was taken. The buzz of conversation was much louder, more expectant than usual. Many of those waiting hadn't been to a shareholders' meeting in years. Mrs. Paul Gossett, for example. She was in the second row, and had been for over forty minutes. She was with her good friend, Mrs. Farris. Winnie Farris was Doctor John Farris's second wife. While he knew the doctor well he hadn't met the Farris woman until today. And there were many others like those two. Yes, no question about it. Interest was high. But as the fates would have it, his own feelings were mixed.

They'd found Billy at the Rocky Mount asylum. Except it wasn't exactly accurate to say he'd been found since he'd run away—or maybe been chased away—from there, too. A woman named Rindhurst had called from the hospital. She'd been in a state, so excited that she seemed to think she could order him around. Come right away, come now, she'd demanded. But then he found out that Billy wasn't there. And why—why the boy had run away.

He couldn't leave for North Carolina then. This board meeting had been planned for weeks. In his mind it had simmered for many months before that. There was no question of his missing it. So he'd sent Calvin. There hadn't been anybody else. Besides, Calvin had made it plain he wanted to go.

But he felt real bad about Billy. More than bad, he felt guilty about his part in the whole business. Just thinking about it now made him uneasy, a nagging reminder of his failure. So it was with relief that he looked up to see Sam Bacon walk into the board room. Now he could turn his attention to the business at hand.

Sam was with his lawyer, Tommy Edmundson. Sam stood there for a few seconds at the back of the room looking unsure about where to sit, up on the dais with him and the other directors, or in the roped-off section of the front row. He watched Junior Warden of the bank, as planned, hurry up the aisle to guide Sam and Edmundson to their assigned seats in the front row. Thank you for coming, dear brother, he thought. It wouldn't have been the same without you. Now that everyone was in place he could open the meeting. But there wasn't any hurry. Another ten minutes or so of waiting would help to increase the tension.

He smiled to himself with grim satisfaction at what was to come.

He looked at his watch. Just past two. By this time Calvin should have reached the North Carolina line. But he still had hours of driving ahead.

Why is it that sometimes our best intentions can turn out so badly? He was sure that there wasn't a soul at the house who would want to cause the boy harm. They all—he, Calvin, and later, Dot, who managed to find out on her own—felt they couldn't tell Billy that Sonny had been sent back to the hospital.

Sonny had begged him to pretend to Billy that he'd gone into the Army. And he had said they would. At the time it had seemed the right thing to do. For one thing he had done it all through Calvin; only Calvin had actually talked to Sonny. For another he had wanted to settle the matter and get the man back up to the hospital. But it had turned out to have been a terrible mistake.

They hadn't thought about all the lies that would be needed to make the first one work. The false addresses, the elaborate deceptions to make sure that Billy didn't see where Sonny's letters came from, their efforts (again, mainly Calvin's) to try to make sure Billy never mailed any of his letters himself. And those times when the damn fool forgot his own scheme—and didn't write. He would go for months at a time without a word. That was uncomfortable, even painful at times. Almost inevitably—he could see that now that it was too late—it all led to the worst possible ending for Billy.

Raleigh was in Oklahoma when Sonny died. While he'd heard the words, while he understood the man had died, he had failed to do anything about it. He still didn't know why. Even when he got home last week he hadn't told Dot or Calvin, although one of the first things he did was call Vickie. Part of his problem was that he had not wanted to have to tell the boy his father was dead. Another was figuring out how to do just exactly that after all their lies. But a lot of it, his slowness to act, was because of a strange detachment that settled over him away from Athena. He had heard the news of Sonny's death in

Tulsa as if someone had told him of a construction set-back on the job. Something to deal with, but in its turn.

He looked over at Sam, sitting, chatting with Edmundson, only a couple of yards away. At the sight of his brother he felt the familiar heat rise in his throat, spread to his chest and upper arms, warm his face. His breath quickened.

Ahh, revenge. That lust still made his blood sing!

He had Danny's proxy in his briefcase. Danny wasn't to get the money for his stock until after the meeting.

Twenty-five dollars a share, a rich price to have paid, especially to someone in the financial trouble that Danny was in. It had been necessary for his lawyer, Mattingly, to buy Danny's defaulted mortgage from the bank and then to threaten foreclosure before Danny would sell. Now that it was a fact Danny was downright cheerful. But not so happy that he had had the courage to attend the meeting.

Vickie was there though.

"They will hate you for this you know," she'd said.

He hadn't answered.

"What will you say to TJ when he asks why everybody on that side of the family hates him, too?"

"That can't be helped."

"Whatever happened to your grand plan for a Bacon reconciliation, for one big happy family, Leigh? I sort of liked hearing you talk that way...awfully naive, of course, but nice."

"You vote any way you want."

"Oh, don't be silly."

It took just seven minutes. In that time the Board of Directors accepted Danny's resignation and elected Mattingly as a director in his place. That was followed by Mattingly's terse motion to suspend payments of dividends until further notice, in the words of the motion, "to permit a build-up of reserves to meet the capital demands of the Athenian community when the war is over."

That was step one.

Then Raleigh moved the election of Mattingly to be the new president of Bacon Mills. Sam, who hadn't said anything to that point, jumped to his feet, claiming to be surprised, demanding time to consider the election of this "outsider." At first Sam was half-way calm, but then the years of stored resentments took over. From a kind of rambling, self-serving, whiny, yet half-way reasonable complaint he went (as Raleigh had hoped) in just a few minutes to red rant. His face blazing, Sam began to accuse him and Vickie of family crimes that had nothing to do with the motion: they were thieves, they had conspired together, they had robbed him and Danfield of their birthright.

Vickie was looking pointedly at Raleigh. She was obviously horrified at this airing of the Bacon family's underside. But although he could have stopped him he let Sam go on. He wanted dear brother to do their dirty work for them. Under the circumstances he could almost enjoy being called a robber. But then, amid all the charges and finger-pointing, Sam abruptly stopped talking. He staggered a little. He looked fixedly at the floor. The eerie silence that followed seemed unreal as they all held their breaths watching him struggle for his composure. The blood had left his flaming red face all at once. It was as if the plasma and cells had rushed to invade his brain, short circuiting it. Now he weaved back and forth, as if he was having trouble keeping his balance. He had to be helped back to his seat by Edmundson.

Sam's mouth worked still, but soundlessly now. Raleigh

began to worry that Sam might have had a stroke. He hadn't meant to harm Sam, only ruin him.

But at that moment his brother seemed to rouse himself. Sam looked up at him. Their eyes met. Sam's ashen face flushed red, refilled with hate. It was a lovely sight.

OUTSIDE the Board Room Vickie said, "Well, you have to be pleased, Leigh. Not only are we finally rid of Sam, but even your Elizabeth sent her proxy and voted with us."

"Yes."

"Well, I certainly wouldn't have expected that."

"No, I didn't either. Perhaps she's through avenging her mother. I hope so. But revenge—as you saw today—is very important to the Bacons. No one is allowed to trample on us. Even us. So for her to forgo her revenge is more significant than a simple proxy vote. Maybe Elizabeth is finally growing up. Maybe she's finally capable of caring for Billy."

He stopped for a moment, looked at Vickie, then said, "When we find him…."

"Has Calvin left yet?"

"Yes. He should get to Rocky Mount in a few more hours."

IN PINEVILLE Calvin turned the station wagon onto the county road running alongside the vacant Smithson house, then drove east. Unpaved, the road was only a little worse than some of the highways he'd taken driving up to Pineville. It hadn't rained in this part of the state for days and the surface was dry and dusty, leaving a choking cloud in its wake whenever a timber truck passed going the other way. But it was straight; it went to Ramey, where Billy's Kallie was supposed to live.

His first stop had been the hospital in Rocky Mount where he'd talked to the Rindhurst lady. She'd told him some of what she'd told Billy. When she said his daddy was dead the boy had run out of her office in a terrible state, sobbing, only to be stopped by one of the hospital people, one of them orderlies. She claims the orderly thought the boy had stole something, or was trying to escape, and that was the reason the orderly had 'cuffed him some.' She wouldn't have told that much if Mr. Raleigh hadn't got on the phone. Mr. Raleigh had said something that made that woman's face go pale.

Poor Billy. All alone, traveling all night, the boy had to have been wore out. Probably hadn't had a whole lot to eat, either. Tired, hungry, on his own and full of his own special kind of devilment. A game to be played? Maybe. Could be why he had snuck into the hospital and then lied about who he was when he was caught. But he didn't think so. Most likely Billy had some idea of taking Mister Sonny out of there.

To be told your daddy is dead just when you thought you were going he help him fly free could make you act kind of crazy. Even if you was only twelve years old.

IN RAMEY he got out of the car and walked stiffly across a dirt yard toward a small, unpainted house. Like most of the colored houses he'd seen in that part of North Carolina this one was raised a few feet off the ground. It was set apart from the other houses on the road by a small plot of land. New corn was growing on one side. There was a chicken coop sitting at the far edge of the other.

A scrawny rooster roamed about under the wooden porch, scratching, looking for anything to eat that might have slipped through the cracks. The door of the hen house, he noticed now, had been propped open for good. Any layers had long since been eaten by the folks here or by foxes. The porch to the house was empty except for a stubby worn cane broom. It leaned against one of the posts. At first he thought that nobody was at home, but then he noticed white kindling smoke starting to curl out the chimney.

He stepped up on the porch. The screen door flew open. A wide-eyed boy, about the same age as Billy, peered suspiciously from around the edge of the door frame.

"What you want, mister?"

"Who are you, boy?"

The boy just stared.

"Is your mama at home?"

She came out then, moving from the shadows into the light. So, this was Billy's Kallie.

She looked at him, then at the station wagon.

"Your name Sallie?"

She didn't answer.

"I'm looking for Billy Smithson," he said. "Figured you might know where he's at."

She looked again at the car, maybe to make sure he was alone.

"You must be that Calvin fellow. The one that works for Mister Bacon?"

"That's right. Mister Bacon sent me to fetch the boy home."

"Well, he ain't here. That's for sure."

"Have you seen him?"

"No."

One look told him she was lying. And a bad liar at that. She dropped what had been a strong gaze to look over at the boy, to warn him. But the boy didn't notice. He was still glaring at him.

"Woman," Calvin said, "I didn't come all this way to take no foolishness off'n you. You better tell me where Billy is. If you hiding him it's gonna be mighty hard for you."

She stared up at him through fierce eyes for a few moments, then backed inside the house, pulling the boy with her, and then slammed the screen door shut.

HE SAT WAITING in the car for over an hour. No one came or went. The only sounds were the buzzing of crickets and an occasional bark of a dog. He looked up at the sky. It would be dark in less than an hour.

He stepped back up on the porch and knocked.

"Listen, woman," he said through the door. "If Billy Smithson ain't here, fine. But I got to know. And if I don't know in the next five minutes you had better get out your knife, or a gun if you got one. Because I'm coming in."

He waited, shifting about, walking up and down the porch. Finally, the door opened and she came out on the porch, walked to the end and spat.

"Don't know where the boy is," she said turning toward him, wiping her mouth with the back of her hand. "Go see if you want."

He went inside. Food was cooking on the wood stove, green beans simmering in one pot, potatoes boiling in another. He could smell cornbread in the oven. It was a clean kitchen, and there was no place to hide. Through a screen on the back door he could see a privy and a vegetable garden where a scarecrow stood guard against thieving birds. He looked out there, then searched through the rest of the house. Smaller than his place in Athena; there wasn't anywhere for anybody to hide.

Back outside he said, "Well, I guess he ain't here. But you know where he's at, don't you woman?"

The boy came part way out of the house then. He stood in the open door, half in, half out. He was holding something in his hand. He seemed to cup it, to be hiding it against the side of his leg.

Billy's Kallie shrugged, spat one last time and walked inside. The boy sidled in after her. This time she latched the wood door. He knew now that he could scalp this nigger woman, pull out all her teeth with pliers and she still wouldn't say nothing.

He hated to, but there wasn't nothing to do then but leave.

HE HAD TO SPEND the night in the car. It was dark by the time he pulled off the road at the Smithson house. It was empty, Geraldine Smithson having gone home to her folks after Mister Sonny's death. He drove the car into the small field back of the grape arbor. No one would see the car parked there. He left the back window and his side window down so he could hear the noises off the road.

And settled down to wait.

At least he knew Billy was alive—although after what Dot Jessop and that Rindhurst woman had done to him the boy probably figured he was better off dead. Yes, Billy was alive…and probably somewhere close by. But where? That woman could be hiding him someplace. But he didn't think so. And they couldn't bring in the sheriff. That would make things worse. Had to find Billy himself. By now the full moon had risen over the trees to his left. A silver light flooded the space between the grape arbor and the pine break. Beyond the pine trees was a big cotton field, just like the fields he used to pick in when he was a boy. He'd noticed earlier that this field was ready for a second picking, the spotty white of the new cotton waiting until the pickers didn't have nothing better to do with their time.

He was tired, wanting sleep, but not willing to close his eyes on this day. He climbed out to stand beside the car. It was very quiet now. The only sounds were his breathing, the murmur of his thoughts breaking through, the faint squeak of the car's springs as he leaned back against a fender. After a while he straightened and walked across the narrow space to the pine wood break. It was pitch dark there. A few feet to his front the big cotton field lay cool, silvery. Unreal. At the far end of narrow rows the moonlight gathered to a more intense brightness and seemed to cover that part of the field like a bright, glowing blanket of ice. At his side his hands smarted, remembering on their own the hours of picking in furnace heat and the few pennies paid for back breaking labor. In this reverie he imagined picking at night, or even in snow. His hands seemed to cool with the fantasy.

Overhead a solitary, dark, scutty cloud chased itself off the moon's bright face. Looking skyward he searched for other signs of rain without finding any. When he lowered his head he felt a little dizzy.

He walked back to the car, climbed in, and before he was half settled felt himself give in to sleep. When he woke later he couldn't have said how long he'd slept or, for a moment, where he was. All he could see in front of him was an inky blackness. He lay still, not wanting to wake up. It was then that he felt it, whatever must have woke him in the first place.

A prickling pressure, a warning sign. Hairs on his neck tickled.

He stopped breathing.

He sat straight up, flung out an arm, roaring at the unknown. With the other he cupped his head protectively as he came upright. He flailed about, striking something. Then, a sharp pain, like scalding grease, seemed to splatter across his hand. He yelled, pulled back, knocking his hand hard on the car's roof post.

Sounds now from outside the car, like a tire rolling over dry sticks, then silence.

He pushed open the car door and rolled out to kneel on the ground beside the car. He looked at his hand in the moonlight. It was bleeding. The blood was black, reminding him of the old darky's story about niggers who bleed in the night.

He listened. But like before the only sounds were his own.

He slipped across the yard to the dark of the pines, then picked his way through the trees back out to the road. He crossed over, jumped the flood ditch, then half-ran, half-walked the length of the field, keeping as low as he could. The moon seemed even brighter than before. As he moved his shadow moved. He stopped to catch his breath. Kneeling, he brushed his fingers over the top of his hand. Couldn't tell if there was any fresh blood. He pushed on. When he finally reached the end of the second big field he paused to listen. Nothing. Then he bent low and scuttled sideways back across the road to the other side. Breathing hard, he sank down to disappear completely into the dark shadows of twin cotton rows. He lay there for at least ten minutes, maybe more. Still no sounds other than leaves scraping and muffled grunts every time he had to move his big body. He was about to give up when he finally heard a different scraping sound, this one like a mule switching its tail back and forth against the dried stalks. It was coming right at him.

He waited until the sound was right on top, in the next row, then jumped up, at the same time reaching through the stalks at the moving shadow. He grabbed an arm, roughly pulled it around, then clamped on to the other arm just as the boy let out his first and only yelp of surprise. It was the woman's youngun. He went limp and kind of curled into a ball on the chalky soil, covering his head with his arms. He didn't make another sound.

He searched the boy's overalls first but he didn't find the knife. Then he half carried, half dragged the boy all the way across the fields back to the car.

He put the boy inside the car.

"I ain't afraid of you," the boy said.

Full of sassy beans. But he was trembling, too. This boy reminded him of Billy, just as stubborn, and maybe just as hard to handle.

"You got a name boy?"

"My name's Jefferson…and I ain't 'fraid."

"I can see that. Your mama send you?"

The boy sank lower on the seat without saying anything.

"I expect that your mama counts on you to take care of her?"

"Me and my brother."

"Who be the oldest?"

The boy gave a younger brother's shrug.

"So, was it your mama who sent you to find me?"

He went back to looking at his hands.

"Or did you come all by yourself?"

The boy started to say something, then stopped.

"I expect I was awful hard to find, hid away like I was back of Mister Smithson's grape arbor."

"I didn't have no trouble."

"So, you was the one? You was the detective?"

"I knowed where you was all the time. Followed you all over town. First, you stopped at Miz Strickland's, after that you drove over to the Texaco on the highway. After that you come back to Miz Speed's boarding house. You left your car in front of Miz Speed's and then walked over to Ranger John's General Store. You bought a can of peaches there. And a loaf of bread.… I knowed where you was every second."

"All right then. You followed me. Now I expect you'd better say why. Or I'll have to turn you over to the Sheriff. You don't want to go to jail do you?"

The boy began to look worried. But all he said was, "I ain't scared of you."

"Guess there ain't nothing to do then but turn you over to the sheriff."

He reached to start the car.

"Wait, mister," the boy said. "I didn't do nothing."

"You call that nothing," he said, reaching over and putting his hand right under the boy's chin. "Look at what you done. They'll probably put you in jail for at least ten years."

"Oh," the boy said.

"That all you got to say?"

Before Calvin could stop him the boy opened his door and got out of the car. He ran over to the house where he climbed up on the back stairs. Then he came back, carrying something. It was a cat.

The cat struggled to get loose. Jefferson had to hold tight to keep it from escaping.

"This cat done caused your hurt," the boy said.

"This here cat?"

"This here's Billy's cat. Zero? I figured, well...she's Billy's cat."

"So this here is the cat named Zero. I sure am surprised to hear that. The Zero I heard about was supposed to be a smart cat. Yessir, the smartest cat, the bestest cat on the face of the earth. Not wild like this jungle thing....She sure is scrawny looking."

"That's cause Mama makes her hunt. We give her cow's milk. But she's got to catch her own supper...mice and birds and things."

"All right. So it wasn't you who cut me. It was this fool cat. How come she was in the car in the first place?... Now wait a minute. It's coming clear for me now. If I was to find Billy Smithson he'd want his cat. Wouldn't he? Is that what you thought?"

"Will you take her, mister? Please."

"Maybe I could. But that means I've got to find Billy Smithson for sure. What if I don't? Couldn't keep her. Probably have to drown the damn fool cat."

Jefferson mumbled something .

"What was that? What'd you say, boy?"

"Mama...Mama says you'll find him sure enough. She say no way you won't. She say that you'll find him and take him away. As soon as you find him you'll put him in this here car and take him away. That's what she say."

"Well, that's natural, ain't it? Nothing to keep me here once

I find where he's hid. But Billy wouldn't want to go home without Zero. And you was putting her in this here car when I woke up. Is that how it happened?"

"Yessuh."

"You been keeping Zero all this time?"

"Yessuh."

"Feed'n her her milk and giving her her pets?"

"Yessuh."

"Why, I expect a boy like you could get pretty attached to a cat like Zero. I expect it might be hard to let a smart cat like Zero go."

The boy hung his head, wouldn't look at him.

"Well, boy, I've been thinking. A cat as smart as Zero is probably too smart to drown. Even as mean as she is. So, I guess you just better tell me where Billy is hid. To save time, you know. No need to hunt all over town if I'm going to find him anyway, is there?"

"Nosuh."

He waited.

Jefferson looked at him, on the verge of tears.

"He's hid over at Cotton's cousin's place, over near Bethel. He's staying over there."

"I guess I don't know where this here Cotton lives."

"Over by the railroad, in the house on the other side of the tracks, just as you come into town."

"Maybe you could show me?"

"Yessuh."

"And then I'll drive you home, honey. Too far for a good boy like you to walk at night time."

WHAT MADE her say something like that? Raleigh looked over at Dot, sleeping now after their love-making. It had been months…so long an abstinence as to be almost embarrassing if one thought about it. He was amazed, really, that he thought he could live as a celibate. Even an unthinking one. After tonight he didn't believe he could ever think that way again.

Still, what on earth would prompt her to say such a thing?

It had begun as an argument.

He was asleep in his bed when she slid in beside him. Slowly, he became aware she was there and needed his attention. He murmured Yes Yes I'm awake and fell back asleep. When he woke the second time he realized that she had been talking for a while, and that he was supposed to have been listening.

"What?" he said. "What did you say, dear?"

"I said you act like I did something wrong. I mean, I'm supposed to be your wife. But you don't ever come to my room to see me anymore. Like tonight. I expected you and you went straight to bed."

"I was very tired, Dot. Nothing to do with you."

"You acted like you're still mad about Billy."

"I was never angry with you, dear. Anyway, Calvin thinks he knows where the boy is. He hopes to find him and start driving back home tomorrow. Everything will be fine. I'm sure of it."

"But you still think it was my fault—that he ran away."

"It's late, Dot."

"Well, it wasn't my fault."

She moved into his arms. She kissed his chest, then settled tight against his side. She drew up a leg, put it partially across his. This was so mannered, so self-conscious that his skin seemed to burn at her touch.

For a long time neither of them moved. Her leg became heavy. He shifted slightly, then eased away, hoping for peace, to be allowed to get back to sleep.

"It ain't my fault, goddammit!"

She was near tears. An alarm somewhere from the back of his brain went off.

"It's the war," she said, her voice quivering. "It's so…so, well, you know, nothing's the same."

He pulled himself up on the pillow a little, but didn't turn on the light. He somehow knew that both of them would be better off in the dark.

She lashed out, "It's your fault. You left me. You left me all alone. You—"

"Stop this!"

She started to cry. Soon she was sobbing. He could feel the slickness of her tears between her cheek and his chest.

"I said stop it," he said, pushing her away. "What is all this about?"

"Okay," she sobbed. "I…. Okay."

It came to him then. She was getting ready to tell him that she'd let one of the soldiers make love to her. Could that be it? Was she going to confess that she had betrayed him with one of the soldiers who had come to the house?

Yes…yes, that was it. She was going to confess. He was so tired, and she was going to confess. Oh, he thought, please don't. Don't make it so something has to be done. Her making love to one of those boys had crossed his mind once or twice, but he had been too busy then to worry about it. Was he going to be made to think about it now?

What did he think? What did he think about the infidelity of Mrs. Raleigh Bacon with a boy soldier? Was he outraged? He should be outraged. Some boy in khaki coming into his house and making love to his wife. He was outraged. Or was he?

The sorry truth was that he didn't seem to care at all. It all seemed so removed. So would he care if he caught them in the act? He tried to imagine that but couldn't. She was right. It was the war. The war had changed everything. Things would return to normal after the war.

He would care after the war.

Silently he implored her not to say anything. Once she said the words he would have to react in an honorable and decent way. He would have to do something, punish her. She'd even expect it herself. Everybody would. They'd say he was justified no matter what he did. He could get rid of her if he wanted. Is that what he wanted?

Still crying she shifted towards him. It was coming, her confession.

Before she could say anything else he pulled her to him and kissed her hard. After that they made love. For the first time in their married life he—fired by his imagination—was physically rough with Dot. In silence he ordered her and used her in ways he would never have dreamed of before. And she responded with a release of passion that was astonishing.

Neither of them were themselves, but the sex had never been better.

In a short time the rough, selfish contest swung to Dot. He finished, but she held him tight in a fierce embrace. Then, bucking and heaving, she rode to the top. She was blind now, intent only on her need, a need so deep inside her that he knew she had lost all sense of what was happening outside the innermost linings of her body. And she sang, a mélange of nonsensical words and sounds, baby talk, love words.

Suddenly, she stopped moving, looked down at him with unseeing eyes.

"Know what I need," she said. "You know what I need, baby? I need you to do it to me like a nigger would.

"Come on you nigger," she said. "Come on. Come on!"

With that her eyes glazed over. She stopped, simply stopped like a wound-down toy. Then she collapsed on his chest. In a moment she had rolled over onto the bed and was asleep.

TIRED, so tired. That must be it. Too tired to sleep. He looked at the clock on the side table. Four o'clock. Nothing could be done for a few hours anyway. He'd have to wait.

He had always thought of himself as a man of reason. He always carried that idea of himself with pride. That kind of pride wasn't sinful, wasn't even bad, like arrogance could be. Every good man, no matter who he was, had to have pride to exist. Otherwise he was no more than an animal.

But pride in what? His love of books and ideas, the mill of course. And this house and everything in it. And in certain standards. Standards were important. Not only for him, for everyone in Athena. He was supposed to set an example.

That kind of pride was part of everything he was, everything he did. Take Blueplate, for instance. That fine old dog, destroyed on his orders. The McCauley's hadn't asked him to shoot the dog, but he had ordered Calvin to do it anyway. A matter of pride. A man doesn't keep a dog that kills chickens. It didn't matter that Blueplate would probably never do something like that again. He'd already done it.

So very tired. Exhausted, really. More than that. He was

tired to the bone, close to a feeling of despair of ever being rested again.

...It wasn't what you owned. Everybody owned things. That wasn't it. It was what was yours and nobody else's. That wasn't owning anything. That was who you were.

He looked over at the figure sleeping next to him.

After a second or two, he reached out and touched her, then shook her roughly.

"Wake up, Dot. You and me, we got to talk."

THE INSIDE of the station wagon was boiling hot. All that afternoon the July sun had been like a furnace. Heat shimmered off the flat roads, making oncoming cars seem to wiggle through a curtain of wavy glass. And the cane seats, heated up by the west sun, were almost too hot to touch. Every now and then Calvin leaned into the rushing air of his window in a futile effort to get some relief.

He figured he had to get as far as Charlotte. At least. He had wanted to drive all the way through to Athena today, but they'd got too late a start. Him and Billy and the skinny, mean little cat.

Billy was in the far back of the station wagon along with the cat. He was lying curled up on a spread Cotton's people had given him for the trip.

Billy had seemed all right at first. He'd come out of the cousin's mill house in Bethel without any fuss and climbed right into the car. And he looked pretty good, too, a little thin maybe, but as good as could be expected. Only thing was Billy had walked right past him without saying one word.

That's the way the boy had been acting ever since, kind of

like only half of him was there, like he was sleep-walking. Because of that he'd expected Billy would want to sleep once they got started. But so far the boy hadn't closed his eyes. And if Billy had moved more than a couple of times in the last four hours he hadn't seen it. As for the cat, she was just the opposite. Nervous at first Zero prowled all over the back of the car. She had finally settled down on the spread near the boy's head. She must have finally decided just exactly who he was.

That was the most worrisome thing. Billy didn't even seem to see Zero. He acted like his cat wasn't even in the car. Because of that—it had made him want to get them home just as soon as he could—he'd started off driving too fast. It was only after he'd almost driven off the road while passing another car that he got some sense and slowed down. He was resigned now to stopping at Charlotte.

They'd just passed the Randolph County line. They had at least two more hours before they would get to Charlotte. Driving through tobacco country. Cure houses, their plain side boards gray with age, set a scant inch apart to let in air, rose up one after the other under tin roofs so much alike that sometimes the sameness of those houses made it seem like the automobile was almost standing still.

"WHERE are you?" Raleigh asked, when Calvin called.

"We's in Charlotte," Calvin said into the phone. "We got to town about a half hour ago. This place is a colored hotel not too far from the train station. It's called the Abe Lincoln Hotel. We's in room 5-1-4. You got to call the front desk to get ahold of me."

"That the only place you could find? A colored hotel?"

"Yessuh. Won't no other place. We could've slept in the car, but I wanted to call and let you know where we was."

"I would have worried if you hadn't. You did the right thing. Tell me, how is Billy?"

"He ain't good, Mister Raleigh."

"What's the matter with him?"

"I ain't sure. As far as I can see he ain't hurt. Nothing wrong that way. But he ain't right."

Alarm crept into Raleigh's voice.

"What do you mean not right?"

"Maybe you'd better call Doctor John, Mister Raleigh."

"Doctor John? John Farris? But you said Billy wasn't hurt."

"Yessuh. He don't have a broke arm or a busted head. But he definitely ain't right. I think Doctor John ought to look at the boy."

"Calvin."

"Yessuh."

"I sent you to bring the boy home. That's all. Leave the decision about what to do with my grandson to me. Do you understand."

"Yessuh, I do."

Neither man spoke for a bit.

Then Raleigh said, "If he's really sick, we could get a doctor in Charlotte?"

Calvin didn't answer.

"What do you think?" Raleigh said.

"Well, that's up to you, Mister Raleigh."

"I'm asking you for your opinion."

"The way I sees it, Mister Raleigh, the boy needs to get home. He needs to see TJ and have something to eat. And he ain't sleeping too good. I left him in the room, but he still wasn't asleep. He looks awful skinny to me. That's worrisome enough. But mostly he's got to sleep some so he can see that things ain't as bad as they seem."

"All right. I'll have Doctor John here about ten in the morning."

"Yessuh."

"But mind well what I said," Raleigh said.

With this odd remark Calvin wondered what more Raleigh Bacon had meant to say. Whatever it was had been powerful enough to make him believe he'd already said it.

CALVIN went upstairs to check on Billy. The boy lay on the room's only bed with eyes closed, not moving, as if he might finally be asleep. And yet it was almost too hot for sleep. A fan in the window rotated back and forth. It hummed, clattering rhythmically with each change of direction as it struggled to cool the hot air. Beneath the window an old mustard-colored muslin sofa was pushed up tight against the wall. Its worn arms showed years of hard use. The coarse matte horsehair padding was missing down to the wood in places, bulging out in others. The sofa wasn't near long enough for the likes of him, but tonight it would do, especially if the boy slept some. He went over by the window. He wanted to pull the shade down, to keep the waning daylight out of the boy's eyes, but it was missing. The screen, too. He stood there for a few seconds, then sat down on the edge of the sofa. He waited, watching the boy to make sure he was really asleep. After a minute or so he became aware of the sound of voices drifting up from the street below.

He turned and leaned out the window. Below, in front of the hotel, colored soldiers stood in little knots at the edge of the sidewalk. They were talking just loud enough so that if you listened real careful you could make out a few words now and then.

He'd left the cat in the car. He leaned further out the window to look down the street to where it was parked, but couldn't see it from where he was.

There were still chores to be taken care of. The cat was one. She had to be fed. Glad he'd left her in the car. It would have been a lot harder for the boy to get to sleep with Zero in the room. When they had arrived, though, he'd made a big show of what to do about her. He'd hoped Billy would complain. He'd hoped Billy would want the cat to come into the hotel with them. But it turned out his show was for nothing. The boy acted like he didn't even hear him.

Of the two, of Billy and Zero, only the cat seemed to remember.

Calvin checked Billy one last time, then stood up to leave. His foot knocked against a free-standing, metal ashtray. It tottered, then settled back with a loud tinny clatter.

He held his breath.

Billy didn't move.

DOWNSTAIRS the tiny lobby was crowded to overflowing. The idea that there were Negroes—not railroad porters, not niggers like him—who traveled to strange cities and had to stay in hotels like the Abe Lincoln was something he had trouble getting used to. But here was the proof. Soldiers—there must have been nine or ten of them—were standing around in the narrow hallway, near the front desk. It looked as if they meant to go out together to supper. They were plenty loud, with much good-natured name calling back and forth, voices rising to be heard, voices vying—so different from any Negro voices he'd ever heard before.

Two older colored men sat over by the door. They were dressed fancier than Sampson Thompson ever dreamed of. Ironed and starched they both wore black and showed lots of jewelry, making him think of Mr. Reno, Blacktown's gold-crazy undertaker. When Mr. Reno buried you he always asked your family if he could keep any gold. No one ever said yes but that didn't ever stop Mr. Reno from asking.

Mr. Reno would never want to bury these soldier boys. It was plain that they didn't have anything. They were just recruits. Their khaki uniforms were brand new, without insignia, without rank. There was nothing to tell one from the other. But seeing them here like this, as nameless, as low as there is in the Army, he was struck by how different they were from the two fancy undertakers sitting just a few feet away. Not one of the soldiers was acting like a nigger. Not even like a Negro. Fact is they weren't acting like much of anything at all. Like all soldiers everywhere they were just being young— young soldiers having a good time.

He asked the little pretty woman at the desk to lend him a water bowl. There wasn't one, but she let him take a glass ash-tray from the lobby. She gave him directions to a nearby store. He went over there and bought milk and bananas, some sardines and a box of crackers. Then he walked back to where he'd left the car. Zero, he was glad to see, was doing just fine. More than that, she was ready to be friendly once she saw he was going to give her a little milk. So he stayed for a while, making up with her. He even let her out of the car for a few minutes on a rope. He imagined how Billy might act when he saw them together, getting along just fine. The most natural thing in the world then would be for him to ask, why not me, too?

It was cooler at last. As he walked back to the hotel he could feel the change. With cooler weather it would be easier to get a little sleep tonight. The drive tomorrow would also be easier. The cat was going to be a help, too. Sooner or later she was going to remind Billy of something beside his hurt. Yes, things were changing for the better. By the time they got to Athena tomorrow morning Doctor John might not be needed.

He realized then how hungry he was. A couple of doors down from the hotel he climbed to the top step of a closed dry goods store where he sat down and keyed open the lid of the sardine can. Using his fingers he dipped out the sardines onto crackers, eating hungrily until they were all gone. His fingers smelled of sardine oil, that smoky fishy smell that reminded him always of the galley on the Azalea. He was licking them clean when he turned to look down the street, in the direction of the hotel.

The sidewalk and curb in front of the hotel were clear of soldiers. He idly imagined the soldier boys invading some cafe someplace nearby with their loud voices and new ways. And so he didn't see anything wrong at first. Instead he felt it, a stab of alarm which told him the picture in his head was false. He turned to look again. Something drew his attention and he looked up. Fat rolls of dark smoke were billowing out of an upstairs window.

Lord God almighty!

He jerked himself to his feet and half-fell, half-stumbled down to the street. He ran toward the Abe Lincoln, counting the floors. But even as he counted he knew whose room was burning.

The same girl was behind the desk. She was leaning forward, talking to someone. He didn't really see who, only that it was a colored man and he wasn't wearing a uniform.

"There's a fire on the fifth floor," he shouted as he went by. "Call the fire department."

The woman's eyes grew wide. She didn't move. He had to stop.

"There's a fire in this here hotel! Fifth floor! You understand?"

The man with her said, "There's a fire upstairs, Cincy. Better call the fire department."

"Oh!" she said and reached for the telephone.

He ran up dimly lit stairs. On the third floor he started smelling smoke. Fire! he yelled. Fire! he shouted as loud as he could. At the fifth floor he went down the hall knocking on doors, shouting there was a fire.

At the room he stopped to feel the door. Warm but not red hot. He fumbled with the room key. Finally, he got it inserted. But the lock only moved part way. He tried again, but it still wouldn't open. It seemed to be bolted. Like it was locked from the inside!

"Billy!" he shouted, pounding on the door. "Billy, open the door!"

He was vaguely aware that people were standing in their doorways peering anxiously at him, then these figures began hurrying toward the stairway.

By now the smoke had started to funnel out from over the top of the door in little sheets. A little puff of smoke leaked out of the keyhole.

"Don't you have a key?" a voice shouted.

He turned. The man from downstairs.

"Help me," he said.

They kicked together at the door, aiming at the lower panel and the lock. But it held fast. By now the smoke was thick enough that he was beginning to have trouble breathing. A few seconds later the other man had to stop. He kicked at the door a few more times, then stopped, too. With his pounding stopped he could hear a siren. Faint, much too far away. The firemen weren't going to get to the hotel in time.

He hurled himself at the door, then again, and again, only to bounce off each time. But on his last try there was a cracking sound at the hinges. Then, with his last all-out assault, the door gave way, splintering inward. Dark brown smoke flowed out and streamed toward the stairs.

In the room he couldn't see a thing.

Billy! he yelled, groping to where he knew the bed to be.

Empty!

Blind, he again swept the sheet with his hands, then felt under the bed. Nothing.

Had he got away?

His lungs hurt. He stumbled over to the window, tripping over the ashtray. The window was still open. But for some reason the smoke was even worse there. And then he felt the intense heat.

The sofa! It was burning, smoldering from inside. He gasped for air but instead swallowed thick heavy smoke.

Gagging, he ran out to the hall, took two or three breaths, then went back into the room. He dropped onto the floor. He could see the sofa now, see the smoke billowing upward, see a lone flame shoot up from one arm then die back. He crawled over, took hold of the closest end only to burn his hands. He had to let go. The whole sofa seemed alive. But as he felt his way along he found a cooler part. Finally, he was able to move the couch away from the wall, but by then he had to quit. He ducked outside again to the hall to breathe.

The man who had helped said something, something about the firemen. Were they here?

He crawled back into the room. The flame was licking up off the arm again, but it seemed to be eating up some smoke. He started kicking at the nearest arm. When nothing happened he stood up and, holding his breath, jumped on the front rail until it broke. He kicked the closest arm off. Smoldering pieces fell to the floor. And now the rest of it, weakened by the fire, broke apart too. Coughing, choking, he threw the smoking pieces one by one out the window then crawled back out to the hall where he lay on the floor, coughing his insides out.

In no time at all the smoke started to clear. A few minutes later what smoke there was in the hall was collected at the ceiling in a two or three foot thick band. By then he could breathe again. He went back inside the room. From head height to the ceiling the room was as black as he was. And empty. He leaned out the window, as if Billy could be down on the street somewhere. Below, pieces of the sofa, still smoldering, lay scattered on the street. Just then the fire truck arrived. It came around the corner, its siren tapering off to nothing just as it came to a stop. Firemen jumped off the truck, ran over to the burning parts of the sofa.

Calvin turned back into the room. Then for the first time he saw a closet door tucked behind the little dresser. Heart pounding he walked over, took hold of the corroded brass knob and, murmuring a prayer, jerked the door open.

Billy!

The boy was sitting on the floor hugging himself tight to his knees.

"Billy, honey! You all right?"

The boy didn't answer. His face was sooty, near as black as his. Big white eyes stared, but at nothing. Calvin reached out a hand. Billy pulled away, pulled back deeper into the closet. Yet the boy didn't resist when he took hold and lifted him slowly to his feet.

As the boy straightened a book of matches fell off his lap onto the floor.

Calvin stood there, struck dumb, still holding the boy's hand. They both just stared at the matches, like ape men must have at the first fire.

A THENA MEMORIAL. The hospital was on State Road, too close some said to the honky tonk parade of cheap liquor stores and auto parts yards that lined that part of town, but nobody north of Main Street had been willing to have a hospital in his back yard. Despite its location the original clinic had grown—largely from Bacon family contributions—to a full-service hospital that rivaled any in the tri-city area. It had replaced Greenville General as the hospital of choice. Nobody who was anybody in Athena now would even consider going over to Greenville to have his appendix or tonsils removed, or to have a carbuncle lanced.

Raleigh, as he always did, entered the hospital through the old entrance off State, walked down to the clinic level then followed a series of expanding corridors to the newer wing. He'd neglected to ask Dot for Billy's room number, but found

Doctor Farris waiting for him in the new wing at the first nurse's station.

"Hello, John."

"Hello, Leigh. I hadn't expected to see you here today. I thought Dot was coming."

"Yes, I know. But I wanted to talk to you about Billy."

"Of course."

John Farris at eighty-one was an amazing example of good health. With his ruddy face and limber frame (he chopped wood daily for exercise) he could have passed for a man of fifty. He had been the family's doctor since Raleigh could remember. Farris was getting on in years—and maybe was a little forgetful—but he wouldn't trade Doctor John for a dozen Duke medical school graduates.

"Dot tells me you want to send Billy home today," Raleigh said.

"That's right. I want you all to take him off our hands. Take him home, fatten him up some and then give him a good whipping for playing with matches."

Calvin had saved Billy's life, no question about that. John Farris knew it. Most of Athena seemed to know it too. Of course what had happened in a colored hotel in Charlotte three days ago would never get into the newspaper, but it was probably all over town by now. The heroism part was fine. But he was worried: it wouldn't take much to turn what Calvin did into vicious gossip. Everybody might start asking how come Billy happened to be staying at the Abe Lincoln in the first place. Questions like that always led to more questions.

And the way Dot was acting was no help at all.

She was afraid that Billy would try to burn the house down. He had treated that as absolute nonsense. Still, he had to admit that the only show of emotion he'd seen from the boy was when Billy first laid eyes on Dot. That look on Billy's face could have meant anything. Still, it was a look of awareness, of making sense of exactly who she was. He hates me, she'd said then. If she'd said it once since she must have said it fifty times.

He wondered how much of what she'd told him the other night was the same kind of wild talk....But the boy had seemed to save that look of intensity just for her...and it didn't make any sense for her to tell him about...about...that unless it was true—at least unless she thought it was. No white woman would ever admit to such a thing otherwise.

So to keep Dot on an even keel he'd reluctantly agreed that it wouldn't hurt to have Billy stay at Athena Memorial until he left for Cleveland. And now John Farris wanted to discharge Billy today.

"Do you think that's a good idea, John?" he said. "I mean is he really ready to leave?"

"Well," the doctor said smiling, "I expect you had better wait on the whipping. But there's no reason to keep him here any longer."

"I see...well, if you're sure...."

The doctor's smile faded to a questioning look.

"Elizabeth called this morning," Raleigh said.

"Oh yes?"

"She asked me to ask you if Billy was well enough to travel. He's leaving us next Tuesday, going to Cleveland to live with Elizabeth. She's worried. So am I. We got to make sure he's fit to make the trip."

"Tell her he's fit enough. Unless she's planning to make him walk."

The doctor smiled in appreciation of his own joke.

"I'm serious, John."

"Yes, Leigh."

"We just want to make sure you don't release him too soon. After all he did breathe in a lot of smoke from that fire."

"He took some in. But his lungs are clear now. Swallowing that much smoke did affect his appetite some. That's probably one reason he don't seem to want to eat."

"That's what I mean. We're not sure it's all physical, are we? The boy may not be himself, not mentally strong enough to come home just yet."

"He suffered a considerable shock of course. But, he's young and strong. Yes, I can see why you might worry about that. But he knows who he is, knows who I am, knows where he is. All that. And I asked him if he knew what had happened to him, you know that he had got lost and about the fire. He did. He knew all about that. He answered all my questions.... Now, I had to prod him. But he did answer.... Another thing. He didn't mind me asking. Which is one of the things you look for, the lack of anger. That's important."

"He's not mad at anybody?"

"That's right. Or himself."

"You mean he could've hurt himself?"

"That happens sometimes."

"What would you say the chances are that he will try to burn something else down?"

"Almost no chance."

"Almost?"

"Nothing is ever certain when it comes to figuring out what people will do. But if you ask me all this boy needs is to get home. He'll probably snap out of his funk in a day. I would bet on it."

CALVIN WAS WAITING at the front entrance with the Buick. They put Billy in back. Pale and unsmiling the boy seemed listless. They hadn't gone more than a block or two before Billy stretched out on the seat. In another minute he was sound asleep. Now, Raleigh had planned to have Calvin drop him at the mill, then take Billy home. But after seeing the boy....

Before he could decide they came to the Tigerville Road turnoff. Calvin slowed the car, clearly expecting to be told to take Billy home first. When he didn't say anything, Calvin brought the car to a stop at the side of the road. Raleigh could feel Calvin's questioning look.

A sudden, burning, disorienting anger, stunning in its fury, surged up from somewhere, literally blinding him. He struggled to hide it, to push it away enough to think a little. Just then a car sped past. Its wake and sound seemed to shake the Buick. He watched—they both watched in silence—as it receded into the distance.

Raleigh breathed deeply trying to calm himself.

Yet despite everything he began to shake inside.

"Mister Flynn at the Buick called to say they had a low-mileage car come in," he said, his voice wavering only a little.

No new cars were being built during the war. But it was understood that when the Buick agency got a similar low-mileage sedan in they were to call. He had talked with Calvin many times about making this kind of trade.

"What do you think?" he added.

Calvin nodded slowly, carefully, but didn't say anything.

Raleigh had trouble keeping the anger out of his voice, "Well, come on man, I'm waiting."

"I reckon you got me stumped, Mister Raleigh," Calvin said warily.

Again the anger. He swallowed hard against it.

"You own a car?"

"Well, yessuh, I do."

"What kind is it?"

"It's a Chevy, Mister Raleigh."

"Don't you think you should have told me?",

"Told you about the car, Mister Raleigh?"

"Yes, the car. What do you think we are talking about?"

"Mister Raleigh—"

"I've been told you keep the car not too far from where we're sitting now. What I would like to know is why you don't drive it up to the house? Why do you need to hide it?"

He stopped talking. In the idling car he was suddenly aware of his own shallow breathing, the clock ticking in the dash.

Calvin's answer was slow, deliberate.

"I guess I should have told you, Mister Raleigh. If I'd have knowed how important it was I surely would've."

He erupted, "Are you mocking me? Don't you dare mock me! Drive home right now! This second. You hear?"

BY THE TIME they drove into the yard Raleigh had got control of himself.

"I need to talk to you alone," he said. "Take Billy down by the gazebo. This'll only take a minute."

"Yessuh. I'll just take him and his suitcase inside and then come right back."

"Don't argue with me. Follow my instructions exactly. Take him down by the gazebo."

"Yessuh."

Calvin woke Billy and led him down the gentle hill to beside the gazebo. The boy seemed a little dazed. But he sat down willingly enough. Then Calvin walked back up and got back into the car.

"I want you to take Billy for a few days." Raleigh said abruptly.

"Take Billy, Mister Raleigh?"

"Yes. Elizabeth called to send him on Tuesday. So it wouldn't be more than three or four days."

"I don't think I understand what you're saying, Mister Raleigh."

"I want you to take Billy home with you for a few days."

"Home? Home with me? You mean over to Blacktown?"

"Yes."

"But why, Mister Raleigh? Why in the world would you—?

"Why do you keep questioning everything I say!"

"But, Mister Raleigh, I don't have no place to keep a youngun. My place ain't fit. And I got to come to work over here every day."

"Bring him with you. As long as you know where he is and what he's doing I don't think there will be any trouble."

"But...but, Mister Raleigh.... What about Miss Vickie? She could take him."

Raleigh didn't bother to answer. He looked down the hill at the boy. Billy was sitting in the chair swing. He was sitting quietly, not moving. He should, he realized, feel something. Guilt. Remorse. Even more anger. But he didn't seem to feel anything. Then Calvin surprised him.

"I suppose I could ask a friend to take him. She has two childrun of her own."

"Yes," Raleigh said. "But take him right now. Don't go into the house at all. It'll be better that way."

RALEIGH WATCHED as they drove out of the yard. The car was moving much too slowly. Calvin was giving him a chance to change his mind.

"Calvin!" he called.

The car stopped.

He raised his voice, "Tell your friend I'll pay some rent."

He thought for another second before adding, "And come to my den tonight after supper. There's some things we got to talk about."

RALEIGH SPENT a few restless, aimless minutes in the house doing nothing. Then he drove over to the mill. When he got there he called Miss Christopher into his office. For thirty minutes or so he worked on answering his mail. Then, when he was finished, Miss Christopher looked at her note pad.

"Mister Mattingly is to get ready to go to Texas next week if you're not able," she said. "The way it looks now he will be making the trip in your place. Is that right?"

She looked at him, as she often did, with a polite question on her face. He was allowed to explain, really to complain, if doing so would make him feel better. Impossible of course. But he was touched by her willingness to shoulder some of his burden. How much simpler, how much more satisfying his life was here at the mill.

And then Vickie called.

He hadn't seen her for over a week, not since the board meeting at the bank. He'd spoken to her on the telephone once or twice, but she expected his visits.

But she didn't complain about his neglect. Instead she asked about the children and Dot. She also wanted to know about Billy. How was he getting along.

"I just spoke to Elizabeth this morning," he said. "She wants us to put Billy on a train Tuesday. In place of her driving down to get him. That means we have to drive him up to Ashville to catch the Cleveland train."

"Oh, I see .... And?..."

She held her question, as if the subject was too delicate to talk about.

"She knows all about that," he said, annoyed now at her constant innuendo.

"I think it was shock," she said. "Billy was too young to handle so many terrible things happening at once."

"Well, he's doing fine now."

"Will he be coming home from the hospital soon?"

"...Soon...yes.... Vickie, I'm awfully busy. Was there something you wanted? Did you have anything particular in mind?"

There was a pause. As it grew he realized that she was hurt by the way he'd acted. But he didn't even consider offering an apology.

At last she said, "I did have something I wanted to talk to you about. I was gonna wait and tell you when you came over. But now I think you should know what happened."

"What was that?"

"Yesterday I was sitting at Junior Warden's desk at the bank, you know, up on the mezzanine. Junior was checking the certificate numbers of my shares against his list before I put them back in my box. That's how I happened to notice. Junior was busy and I was watching the door. Well, Calvin came in. It kind of surprised me, and I wondered out loud what he was doing in the bank. Well you would have thought I had said the bank was being robbed. Because Junior Warden said, 'What?' and when I pointed out Calvin down below, he said, 'Oh my goodness, I forgot.' Well, Junior jumped up and ran down stairs. He sneaked up behind Lettie Stapleton's cage and whispered in her ear. Calvin didn't see him because he was busy writing out a check. Then Junior Warden came back so I had to stop watching."

She paused, "Poor Calvin. I felt sorry for him. I still do.

"When he got back to his desk, Junior was purely mortified. He had forgotten. He had clean forgotten your order to cancel Calvin's authority to write checks on the household account. Of course I didn't know what he was talking about. How would I? I never heard of such a thing—giving a nigra the power to write checks. My goodness! But I had to pretend that you had told me. Yes, I said, I knew about it all the time.

"Now, I promised Junior I wouldn't say that he had forgot. You understand?"

When he didn't answer she went on.

"It was embarrassing. You think you can do things nobody else would ever do, Leigh, at least in their right minds. Only you would allow a nigra to write checks like you did Calvin. Only you would figure that nothing bad could ever happen. Because it was you doing it …. Still, while I never would have done such a thing I couldn't help feeling sorry for poor Calvin."

"None of this is your business, Vickie. I have been listening patiently to all this. But my patience has just run out."

"The trouble with you, Leigh, is that you've had your way too long. You are rich and powerful. Too rich, too powerful maybe. Men like you don't need anybody else. You don't seem to have any loyalty to the people who care about you. You should be an unmarried woman like me, a woman who has no one but a brother to depend on. You should be one of your mill workers. Or a nigra. Then—"

He hung up. Sitting there at his desk, breathing hard, he

tried to think, but he couldn't seem to concentrate properly. She'd get over it. As she'd once said he and she were kin. There wasn't anything either of them could do about it.

When he looked up Miss Christopher was gone.

THAT EVENING, Raleigh was still distracted by thoughts of what had to be done in Texas and what he needed to say to Mattingly, so he wasn't really prepared for what he wanted to say to Calvin when the black man walked into the study.

Without any preliminaries he barked, "Sit down!"

Calvin, clearly startled, dutifully sat down. But just as quickly stood again.

"If you don't mind, Mister Raleigh," Calvin said. "It don't feel right for me to sit. I can listen just as good standing up."

"Suit yourself," he said. "Did you get the boy settled all right?"

"My friend said she'd take him. As I said she's got her own younguns."

"That's good. And I'll pay her some rent for doing this. Did you tell her that?"

"She don't want no money. She was happy to take Billy."

"And how is he? How is Billy?"

"Well…."

"Yes?"

"Excuse me for saying so, Mister Raleigh, but I wonder if Doctor Farris should have let Billy go out of the hospital. The boy still ain't near being hisself. He needs more time to—"

"You're a doctor now, too, are you?"

"No, suh, I ain't no doctor. That's for sure."

"But you know better than Doctor John?"

"I'm just saying what I seen. And my friend thinks so, too.

We both got to work. Billy would be better off where he's got somebody looking after him all the time. He ought to be over at the Memorial—"

"Are you telling me what to do?" he said. "Eddie King was right. You don't know your place no more. You think you can tell the people you work for what to do. Well, that's at an end. We are finished with that business for good."

Calvin rocked back, as if struck. But his face was expressionless.

Raleigh looked at his hands lying still on the desk. Strange hands, they could have been somebody else's.

He started slowly, deliberately, "Now, I got something to say. To you. Something that's important. So listen careful now. And be ready to answer my questions."

He plunged in, "There are some questions that I got to ask. Personal questions that are as hard for me to ask as they will be for you to answer."

He paused for a moment, then said, "Mrs. Bacon has told me that you put your hands on her and tried to take advantage—"

"Oh, Mister Raleigh—"

"Don't interrupt me. That ain't all. That's just the beginning. It's the end, too, but it's where I got to start."

"But, Mister Raleigh—"

"Keep your mouth shut! I'll tell you when you can talk…."

But then he didn't trust himself to go on. He waited for a second or two, trying to get himself under control.

He began again, "She said you took advantage of her being sick. She said…she said you…you…took off some of her clothes. She said you touched her and would have done more if she hadn't come to her senses."

"Mister Raleigh—"

"Shut your insolent mouth when I'm talking to—"

"Stop, Mister Raleigh. Don't say no more—"

"—you, you ungrateful—

"This is wrong, Mister Raleigh. Too much been said already. No more. Please don't say no more."

Somewhere toward the other end of the house a door slammed. They both half turned in that direction but neither moved. For the first time through the open window he heard the sounds of dusk, the full-throated croak of the frogs singing in the creek from across the road, the muffled flapping of what he'd always imagined were bats coming awake to hunt, the constant buzzing of insects. All so indifferent to him and Calvin.

He looked across at his servant.

"You see," he began, "the drinking is…. When a woman drinks it's hard on the husband. Her drinking and this other thing—the stimulants—have changed her. Not that she hasn't tried to be a good wife. She has done the best she knows how. Maybe she was too young when I married her, too young… and…."

He stopped, trying to find his way.

"I worry about the children, especially Emily. Poor Emily. And I worry about what Dot could do."

He looked at Calvin. His face, his broad, coal-black, ugly-beautiful face was blank, a mask.

"Emily…and the war…and…and everything—Eddie King and Ben—have given her good reasons to drink. And with me being gone so much…."

He looked at Calvin. He had to understand.

"So it's perfectly reasonable that she got mixed up. She and you have never gotten on too well. She went to the picture show, or read something in the paper about one of the northern colored taking liberties—because of the war—and she had too much to drink and just imagined it. Just imagination. That's all it was...her imagination?"

His question—if it was a question—hung in the air.

"All you got to say," Raleigh said, "is that it's not true."

Calvin didn't move. He could have been a black stone statue.

Raleigh waited, then said, "But you got to say it. Out loud.... Out loud you must say that it is not true."

Calvin still didn't move. As Raleigh waited his hand nervously, absently, searched for the letter opener on the desk. And then, just as his hand closed on its handle, he understood.

Calvin was not going to answer. Would never answer.

Every part of his being seemed to rush to his head. Lights jumped in his brain, blinding him. He struggled to bring himself under control. Little by little he pushed back the black rage; and at last he could breathe again.

But it was too late. When he could see again Calvin was gone.

Hello, Eddie King?

Why, ain't this a damned surprise.

I've got something I have to talk to you about.

Go right ahead.

This is something I'd rather not discuss on the telephone.

I'll come right over.

No. Best we don't meet here at the house.

I see. I suppose you wouldn't want to come here?

Isn't there someplace else?
Come to Wertheimer's today, after five. I'll be out back.

ON SUNDAY AFTERNOON Calvin took Virginia May and her girls for a ride in his car. He put Billy in back with Towhee and Phoebe. At the last minute he decided to bring the cat along, too. So he put Zero and her wooden cage in the trunk, propping the door of the trunk open for air with one of the damp dish towels Virginia May had brought to cover the food bucket.

The partially open bucket rested on the seat between them. She'd put it there without a word, as if it was understood that you never got into a car for a Sunday drive without some food to eat. The escaping smell of freshly fried chicken and just-baked cornbread soon filled the car. Before they had gone five miles the little girls were clamoring for something to eat.

Virginia May tried to quiet the girls down. As she shushed them Calvin saw her look over at the boy.

Calvin caught her eye. Virginia May answered his silent question with a slight shake of her head.

They headed south, toward Gaffney. The highway descended gradually to a mostly flat stretch of road that passed through cuts of raw red clay. On both sides of the car scrawny, sunburned pines showed what that summer's drought had done to the land. It wasn't long before they had the highway pretty much to themselves. Most of the Sunday sightseers were on the other side of Athena, heading north toward the cooler mountain air.

They came to a town called Cowpens. Its main street, a part

of the highway, was almost empty. One man leaned against what looked like a closed-up store and two brown-and-white dogs lay panting in the heat under a wooden porch. In the middle of town Calvin turned west toward Jackson's Church, a town he knew, figuring to head back to Athena from there. Then, not more than a mile outside of Cowpens, they found what looked like a colored motel with several picnic tables scattered among four tiny dilapidated cabins.

They stopped and everybody but Billy got out of the car. They walked around to see if this was where they could stop. They peered through the dirty windows of the little cabins, trying to see inside. At the last one Towhee pushed open the door to a tiny room no bigger than a good-sized chicken coop. In it were an old metal frame bed and a stained, dirty old shuck mattress that every animal in the vicinity had lived in at one time or another. The floor was dirt.

"No wonder," Virginia May murmured, peering into the room.

It was plain enough that the place was deserted and had been for a long time: there was no office, never had been; the motel's faded sign ("For the REST WEARY") was propped up back of the first cabin.

Excited, Towhee and Phoebe ran back to tell Billy. Clamoring with their news they pulled him out of the car to sit on its running board. As they had for days they plucked at him, with their hands, with their questions. They tried to climb onto his lap. They vied to tell him what Towhee had found. But the boy took no real notice of the girls. Didn't try to hush them. Didn't try to push them away. He just sat there until they got tired and lost interest.

"What you think?" Virginia May whispered.

Calvin shook his head.

"I was hoping seeing his mama would help," she said. "But now that Miz Elizabeth ain't coming...and, by the way, why ain't she coming?"

"Don't know why. Called to say she couldn't come. That's all. So we's supposed to put him on the train from Ashville."

"What does Mister Raleigh think?"

He shook his head in a way that made her not ask again.

By now Towhee and Phoebe had the car's trunk open. They let Zero out of her cage. The girls chased her for a few minutes. Then Zero, as if she *knew* something was wrong, went over to Billy and rubbed up against his legs, getting nothing in return. Virginia May watched all this, then called over, "Now, Billy, honey, let's get going. You and me got to get the food ready."

He did whatever she asked willingly enough, but only did exactly what she asked. And, while she cleaned and set the table, chattering away—trying to get him to talk—he wouldn't say anything but "yessum."

The chicken, fried in Crisco, went around the table twice. And the cornbread, so good that nobody hardly wanted to take the time to butter it or to pour on the molasses. But everybody's favorite was the buttermilk. Virginia May had brought two quarts, the jars covered by damp cloths pulled tight over the lids by half inch sections of an old bicycle inner tube. It was still hot, so the special cool of the buttermilk kept them drinking until it was all gone. The girls begged for more.

Billy hadn't touched his. The girls got after him to give his buttermilk to them.

"Now you girls mind what's yours," Virginia May said. "That's Mister Billy's buttermilk. He's just saving it. Ain't that right Mister Billy?"

She waited. The girls stopped talking. With mouths open the girls watched to see what Billy would do.

Without a word Billy reached for the glass. Slowly he raised it to his lips, and then, even more slowly, drank about half the buttermilk. It was almost painful to watch. Then he paused, took a breath and started to drink again. Calvin stopped him. He took the glass and gave it to the girls.

But the heart had gone out of the party.

ON THE WAY HOME Virginia May said, "They be sleeping now. Billy, too."

He nodded.

A little later she asked, "Did you like my chicken?"

He nodded, "Mighty good. And the cornbread was good, too."

"Did you know," she said, "that I ain't never been on no picnic before?"

He looked over at her.

"I don't believe I have either, Virginia May."

"Towhee and Phoebe can say that they have been on a real picnic and that they took a drive. They can say all that."

He nodded again.

IT WAS LATE AFTERNOON when they turned off Calhoun onto Sycamore. At his house he took special pains with his parking, not saying anything until the car had come to a complete stop.

"I was wondering," he said, "if I could park this here car on your lot. As you could've heard I've had some trouble with some folks over it. I expect it would be a whole lot safer if it was off the street. And, as you know, I don't have no place."

"That'd be fine," Virginia May said.

"Maybe you'd want some rent?"

She laughed.

"You, too? Just make sure you keep it clean. I don't want no dirty car on my place."

EARLY TUESDAY MORNING Calvin received the first of several telephone calls from Elizabeth about Billy's leaving. She wanted to know exactly when he was to arrive in Cleveland on Wednesday and such things as what he was bringing with him and what she needed to buy. She argued a little against the cat, but that had already been decided. Afterward he was too busy helping Billy get ready, buying new shoes, packing, picking through and washing the last of his clothes, building a new crate for Zero, to worry much at first about the way the boy was being shipped off. But at Miss Polly's travel desk at the Tolliver Hotel on Main Street he opened the long accordion-like train ticket to check it. And when it fell, cascading down to reach almost to the floor, like one of the hotel's retractable fire escape ladders, he stopped, not able for a moment to answer Miss Polly's question about whether every thing was all right.

"Calvin?" she prodded.

"Yessum," he said. Looks just fine.

He carefully refolded the ticket. He nodded to Miss Polly, left the hotel, and drove back over to Aiken Road.

RALEIGH drove home from work early. When he got to the house the Ford station wagon was being packed; its rear door stood open. Billy's large cloth bag and the cat's empty cage had already been loaded. No one seemed to be around, though. He went inside the house. The kitchen, also empty, showed signs that supper was being prepared. Peeled potatoes sat in cold water in a big bucket in the sink. And he could feel the added heat from the stove's oven. He walked into the front hall, then paused at the foot of the stairs to listen. No sounds from upstairs. He thought he could smell the faint scent of Dot's perfume, as if she'd recently passed this way. Good. He hoped she would stay upstairs for a while. Then, as he was passing through the living room toward his end of the house, he saw them, Calvin and the boy. They were outside, standing on the front lawn about half way down to the road.

Calvin was talking and pointing at something. Billy stood close by. For just a moment or two he thought that Calvin was talking to the boy. Just then though Robert's head appeared over the rise as the old colored gardener walked slowly in the direction of the house.

Calvin kept talking to Robert, gesturing in a general way. Calvin had on his apron. He was bare-headed. He kept shading his eyes against the afternoon sun as he spoke. Then Calvin walked ten or twenty feet along the middle ridge, pointing at something. Billy followed along behind. The boy had that same dreamy look.

Robert said something to Calvin, wiping his sweat-stained face with his hat as he spoke. Even from this far away he could feel the familiar agitation start up again, the same burning sensation at the pit of his stomach. He went into his bathroom, drew a glass of water from the tap and drank it while looking at himself in the mirror.

He didn't look that different.

WHEN RALEIGH walked into the kitchen an hour later it was at its busiest, near the point when everything was coming done at once. In the midst of oven-like heat and the smells of roasted chicken and baking pastry everybody seemed to be talking at once. Calvin certainly knew he was there, but he didn't stop what he was doing.

Calvin moved around the kitchen pulling open drawer after drawer, looking for something. Lordy, Lordy, he kept saying as each drawer failed to reveal whatever he was searching for. Then he found it and held the thing up, smiling in triumph. It was an engraved silver-plated butter knife from the Azalea, famous in the house as Calvin's pie-testing knife. He used it now. He slid its blade through the warm brown crust and deep into the heart of the rich, sweet filling. A little steam escaped.

Calvin had tested hundreds and hundreds of pies in this way, but never had one been tested so completely, so carefully. Raleigh was as courteous as his being would allow.

"Calvin, I'd like to speak with you back in my rooms. Now if you please?"

He was scarcely seated at his desk when Calvin came in.

He picked up the brass letter opener, pointing it at the black man.

"I'd hoped it wouldn't come to this," he said. "I'd hoped that you would come to your senses, that you would come to me…. But we don't have to go into all that again. You know what I'm talking about. What I do want to talk about now is your future in this house."

He studied Calvin's face, waiting for some reaction. There wasn't any.

"Alright, then," he said, "I'm gonna be blunt. I could fire you. For what you've done no one would blame me for throwing you out of my house. What's more if I wanted to I could see that you never work in Athena again. And no one would hire you in Spartanburg or Greenville if I asked them not to. For what you've done, for the disrespectful way you've acted alone—not to mention the other—I could send you away from these parts for good. I could if I wanted give you no notice, no reference and, if somebody called, I wouldn't have any choice but to tell anyone who might want to hire you the truth about what's happened here."

He paused for a moment to let what he'd said sink in.

"I am at times, as you know, a hard man. Just a few weeks ago I went to great lengths to teach my brother, Sam, a painful lesson. But I like to think that I am not unjust. Sam deserved his punishment. I don't want to punish you, Calvin. I hope you'll believe that. But if you won't help me now you'll leave me no choice."

Calvin swayed a little. He shifted his weight to spread his legs, to brace himself, as he once must have on racing trains.

"Mister Bacon?"

"Yes?"

"You asked me to carry Billy up to Ashville to put him on the train. And I mean to do that. Yessuh, I mean to do that for sure if that's what you say to do. But the boy truly ain't well enough to travel now. We should keep him here…a least 'til he's himself."

A sledgehammer was pounding in Raleigh's head. He could scarcely see past the blood-red curtain that flashed across his vision with every breath. At that moment he seemed to leave where he was and, suddenly, he was back at Two Holes, fishing. But he was naked and Calvin and the policeman, Holland, were both looking at him with disdain. They seemed to be laughing as he tried to cover his nakedness….

"Why are you doing this?" he said. "I'm trying to meet you half way, more than half way. I wanted to give you another chance to help me make things right. And you treat my kindness with...with this rudeness."

"I ain't sassing you, Mister Raleigh."

"Defiance then."

"I always give you my respect."

"That's better. That's more like what I would have expected from you, Calvin. Now, I don't want to go into that whole thing again, but—"

"I'm leaving, Mister Raleigh."

"What?"

"I can't stay here no more, Mister Raleigh."

Stunned, Raleigh sagged speechless against his chair.

"I'm thinking that it's best if I leave," Calvin said. "If it's all right with you I'll get Billy off on the train to his mama. If you'd let me take the station wagon I could bring it by the house tomorrow. I'll leave it parked in the garage...if that's all right?"

And then, as if this nightmare had doubled in stark horror, Raleigh saw Billy's face in the doorway.

Billy edged a foot or so into the room, staring at Calvin. There was a stricken look on the boy's face. It was as if Raleigh's feeling of horror had found expression on Billy's pale face. Calvin turned, put his hand on Billy's neck and gently steered him out of the room.

RALEIGH SAT UNMOVING for a long time. Finally, he stirred. He was still holding the letter opener. He went to replace it on the blotter, but his fingers wouldn't open. He had to pry numb fingers off the handle. Its imprint lay across his palm. Parallel to his life line there was a faint red streak. As he watched the line grew, swelling with its own life as his ebbed. Then the line of blood broke, flowing, erasing his palm.

When he couldn't stand it any longer he put his head on the desk and sobbed like a child.

BILLY had hold of a piece of cornbread. By now it was cold, but he held tight, as he'd been told. He was to eat it if he got hungry. The car's sound was funny, different from when they had driven over to the house. And there were other new sounds. The cat's cage kept hitting the back wall of the car every time it started up. And the cat was crying. It wanted to get out for some reason.

The car slowed down, then stopped. Another traffic light. He watched and counted. After a long time the light changed to green. The car started forward. He looked back to watch the light change to red. Like the others. Green changing to yellow and then to red. But this one didn't switch colors before they turned onto a new street.

Calvin was driving. Big hands on the wheel. He was wearing a hat. Humming.... Calvin was humming. He tried to listen. Off to his right something made a big screeching sound. He didn't know what.

Calvin looked over at him. Billy put the cornbread in his mouth and took a bite.

"You hungry, honey?"

He looked at the cornbread in his hand, kept on chewing.

They came to another turn. He'd seen it before, something about it reminded him of something. He tried to remember.

There were smells, different from the big house. These were the smells of people like Calvin.

His heart beat faster. They were close. But when the car stopped he didn't move. Calvin got out of the car. He walked around to the curb, came to beside his window.

"How'd you like to step out a minute, honey?"

He nodded. He waited to be let out of the car.

The two little girls were inside. So was Virginia May. They smelled like pecans. Virginia May said something to him but he didn't hear what. She came over, stood right in front of him. He couldn't see Calvin. He wanted to see Calvin. The little girls were holding his hands. He couldn't move.

Virginia May laughed very loud. The sound hurt his ears. Then the little girls let go his hands and ran into another room. He could move again. He went over to his chair and sat down. He was still holding tight to the cornbread. Soon Virginia May took the cornbread away and gave him a glass with milk in it. He held it so it wouldn't spill.

IT WAS dark now.

Calvin said to wait for him. Virginia May was gone. The little girls were there. They were playing next to the back door, near the light. He had to go to the bathroom, but he had been told to wait.

The oil lamp on the table flickered. Who had lit it? Billy tried to remember. He liked to watch the flame. He liked its color. He liked how the glass was warm to his touch. He ran his hand up and down the hot chimney. His hand made shadow patterns on the wall.

Suddenly, he was afraid. He looked at the girls. They were

the same, playing on the floor, their heads together. He wanted Calvin. He called out for Calvin but the girls didn't seem to hear him. They didn't move. Where was Virginia May? Where was Calvin?

The oil lamp flickered again. He looked at the wall. A shadow plunged across it. He looked at his hands. They were in his lap. He was terribly afraid. He wanted to run, but he had been told to stay.

Now lots of shadows danced together on the wall. Their big black tongues stabbed the orange light. The room was orange all over, brighter, so bright. He didn't need the lamp to see anymore.

There was a crackling sound behind him. He turned. Calvin came through the door. He jumped up and ran to Calvin. So did the little girls. They were crying for some reason.

Maybe because their faces were orange. Calvin was orange, too. Calvin was staring out the window. Billy turned to look.

Outside, a few feet away, hot flames shot skyward as they poured across from the house next door. The sky was raining fire. A river of hungry flames seemed to be arcing down on their heads. He ran to the window. He reached his hand out to the fire. Calvin grabbed him and pulled him back, then carried him into the front parlor. The little girls were there. They were crying. Phoebe wanted to be held.

The fire was burning Virginia May's house. He could hear it eat the house alive, like hundreds of rats gnawing through its wood. He was afraid. He wanted to run. But Calvin didn't move. He was looking out front.

There, blazing as hot as the house, a black car was changing color before his eyes. It dissolved from a dark green to a lighter color, and inside it was all lit up. So bright, too bright.

Suddenly the fire took hold of the seats and steering wheel and smooth cloth lining of the walls and exploded. The eyes of the car popped, first one then the other.

Somebody grabbed his arm.

"Time to leave, Billy," Calvin said. "Follow me."

Calvin picked up the little girls, turned to him.

"Follow me!" Calvin said.

He couldn't move. He watched as Calvin carried the girls over to beside the door. Calvin looked around at him.

"Come on, honey," Calvin said.

But now he could hardly see them. Calvin and the girls. He was afraid. He sat down on the floor. Then, Calvin was squatting next to him.

"All right, honey," Calvin said. "Now listen careful. I have to take the girls out. But I'll be back. Promise me not to move. Count to twenty. Slow. That ain't long. I'll be right back. Before you get finished."

He just stared. Calvin's face disappeared. One…two…three…there was a loud crash beside him.

He jumped up and ran toward the back. The kitchen was burning up. It was so bright. So bright. And hot! It hurt his face. Fire! He turned back. Now the front parlor was as bright as the kitchen. He looked around. Fire! He counted, wildly, blindly. The wall in front of the house seemed to move. It did move! It was heading for him. The fire was going to kill him!

The wall grew and grew. Then stopped. Calvin! It was Calvin.

"Get under, boy," Calvin ordered. Something was thrown over his head, something wet. And hot. Calvin took his hand and was leading him. It was very dark and very hot. He couldn't breathe. He tried to hurry, stumbled, stumbled again. And then, suddenly, suddenly he could breathe. At last he could breathe. And he saw the light of the street.

As he ran he could see other people on the sidewalk, in the street. There were shouts, excited shouts that somebody had called the fire department. And people were calling to him. They asked questions: Was anybody still inside? Was he okay?

"I'm okay," he called back. "I'm okay."

He saw the station wagon right in front, across the street. He dove for the open door.

"Is everybody okay?" he yelled.

The girls squealed from the back seat.

"Hey Towhee!" he yelled. "Phoebe, Phoebe! You girls okay?"

"They's fine, Mister Billy," Virginia May said.

"Virginia May!" he said. "Your house is burning up."

And it sure did. They all sat and watched from a safe distance. By the time the fire department got there both houses were burned to the ground. Only the car still burned. And when they put that fire out, there wasn't anything left but a smoldering shell of bare metal.

All this time, about twenty minutes, nobody said much. Towhee and Phoebe cried a little for their dolls until Virginia May hushed them.

Finally, Calvin said it was time for them to leave for Ashville. Ashville? And then he remembered. He looked at Zero's cage, and it all came back at once, but in a confusing rush.

He hugged Towhee and Phoebe and promised to send them a postcard. Then he stepped out of the car to say goodbye to Virginia May. She took him in her arms and hugged him hard. And he hugged just as hard back. He could smell the smoke on her clothes. Her arms were firm and her breasts dug into his chest.

"You've been awfully nice," he said into her shoulder.

"Well," she said, "it's easy to be nice to such a nice boy."

He couldn't think of what to say.

"And Billy?" she said.

"Uh huh?"

"It shore is good to have you back."

He pretended he didn't know what she was talking about.

"Well, I ain't left yet, Virginia May."

She looked him square in the eye.

"Yeah," he said, grinning. "Me too."

FOR THE FIRST twenty minutes or so they didn't talk. Calvin gave all his attention to the driving. And he spent that time trying to calm Zero down. She couldn't seem to get enough of his petting, climbing all over him, demanding all his attention.

Finally Calvin said, "I reckon I don't have your address, honey."

"Just Cleveland," he said. "That's all I know."

"Maybe you could send it to me? I might want to send you a postal card."

He didn't answer.

"Something bothering you, boy?"

"I can't figure you out."

"Why do you say that?"

"How could you leave this way? Your house was burnt down. Your car was burnt up. My goodness! It was awful! But you don't act like it was awful at all. Don't you care? If you don't care about your house, what about Virginia May's? How you could leave like this without—I mean, ain't you gonna do *anything?*"

"What you want me to do?"

"I don't know. But you got to do something."

"And why is that?"

"You just can't let them get away with it."

"Who's that you talking about, boy?"

"Whoever set the fires."

"What makes you think somebody started it?"

"Why, you heard! We all did. Everybody was saying how it won't no accidental fire. And Virginia May asked you if you smelled the kerosene."

"And I said I couldn't smell no kerosene. Could have been a spark from a stove."

"Shoot! I don't think you even want to find out who did it. Not me! If somebody burnt up my house—"

"—Ain't my house."

"Well, what about all your things? What about all of Virginia May's?"

He paused, then said triumphantly, "And what about your car? You ain't gonna pretend that you don't care about your car are you."

Calvin looked at him sharply, but he went ahead anyway.

"I would've at least called Papa Bacon."

This time Calvin didn't bother to even look at him. Billy tried to act like he didn't care. He turned to look out the window, but what he'd said made him feel bad, so bad that he didn't even see the lights of the small towns they drove through. Here he was yelling at Calvin. Like Calvin hadn't just saved him from being burnt to a crisp. Like Calvin wasn't the best friend he'd ever had.

After a while the silence got to be too much for him.

"What if Elizabeth ain't there in Cleveland to meet me?" he demanded.

"She'll be there."

"Well, what if she's not?"

Calvin looked at him. In the darkness he thought he could see the white flash of a smile.

"Course she's gonna meet you," Calvin said. "What you expect she's gonna do? Make you live in that there train station?"

"She might not be able to find me."

Calvin laughed softly.

"Then I expect you'll find her."

For a few miles more neither spoke.

"You feel better now?" Calvin asked.

"Yeah...."

"You gonna have a wonderful time up north."

"No sir!" he said. "I don't want to go nowhere."

"Lord, I sure wish it was me going to Cleveland," Calvin said. "I never got to Cleveland when I was railroading. Chicago, New York, Pittsburgh, Phil-I-Del-Fi-A, all of them, but never Cleveland. You are shore one lucky boy."

"I want to stay in Athena."

"No sir!" Calvin said in a way that surprised him. "This here's your chance, honey. You got to take it."

A sign said that Ashville was fifteen miles away. He watched Calvin's big hands on the steering wheel as the station wagon turned and dipped through hairpin curves, yet climbed steadily up the mountain. They drew closer and closer to Ashville. Soon, much too soon, they were speeding straight along the ridge above Tryon only minutes away from the station.

When they got to the station they were too busy to talk. They unpacked the car, captured a nervous Zero and got her settled in the baggage car and, finally, boarded the waiting sleeper car.

When he was finally settled in his berth Calvin said, "I'm putting your ticket here, honey, right on this here clip. That way the conductor won't have to wake you when he comes by."

He couldn't wait any longer.

"Calvin?"

His voice was husky, too weak for what he wanted to say.

"Calvin?" he repeated.

"What is it, honey?" Calvin said, sitting down on the side of the berth.

"Calvin…I heard. When you were talking to Papa Bacon? I heard what he said to you."

Calvin looked at him. His steady gaze was neutral. It didn't say go ahead. But it didn't say stop, either.

"Where will you go?" he said. "What will you do?

"Oh, don't you worry, honey. I won't have no trouble. I can always go back to railroading. Or, I might just join the Army—"

"The Army? Why, you're too old. They don't take nobody over thirty-five."

"That right? Well, maybe they got a special age for cooks. What the soldier boys need is some of Calvin's good cooking. That's a fact."

Afterward they talked about soldiering and the Army like it was real, like it was a sane possibility in a crazy world. A big black man and a thirteen-year-old boy dreaming about dreamy things, things that had no more chance of happening than a fat pig jumping over the moon....

He fell asleep then. When he woke the next morning Calvin was gone and the train was speeding through the gentler hills of Ohio. He stayed in his berth for a long time, watching out the window, watching the land change shape and color.

ACKNOWLEDGMENTS

The gestation period for this novel has been long and sometimes arduous. The campaign to publication couldn't have been won without the untiring and continuous support of my family, friends and colleagues. I'm deeply grateful, especially to my wife, Marcia, my daughter, Abbie Fosburgh, my son, Matthew, and his wife, Janet Rumble, for their unstinting loyalty to me and to the work we all produced. I'm especially indebted to those friends who read the manuscript and/or offered their support and constructive criticism in many ways, Sylvia Ellis, the late John Tuohy, his daughter, Patrice Vilic, William Tuohy, Marcy Rosenblat, Roberta Rubin, Garth Stein, Dick Muzzy and Liza Fosburgh. My special thanks to the novelist, Frank Baldwin, who lent generous and constructive support when it was most needed. Finally, my thanks to the members and staff of Washington Writers' Publishing House, particularly Laura Brylawski-Miller, Elizabeth Bruce and Elisavietta Ritchie, my editors, for their direction and exacting and scrupulous work to bring this novel to fruition.

—W. L.

ABOUT THE AUTHOR

This is WILLIAM LITTLEJOHN's first novel. He attended the University of Virginia where he earned BA and LLB degrees. After serving in the U.S. Marines he practiced law in Chicago and Michigan. He presently lives in Washington, DC.

LaVergne, TN USA
28 September 2009
159246LV00005B/32/P